PRAISE
YANKEE

"*Yankeeland* tells a fascinating story of dreams, dislocation, and—above all—humanity. It is the story of Brigid, a woman who had the courage to imagine a different, better life, but was frustrated by circumstances, betrayed by a society that does not value her, and mistreated by a patriarchal medical system that fails to hear her voice and does the bidding of a cold, callous society. *Yankeeland* is a tale of hopes raised and eroded, lives lived and suspended, stories told, untold, and retold. But *Yankeeland* brings hope. Brigid's life, with all of its complexity and tragedy, also has magic, beauty, and infinite possibility."

—Brendan Kelly, professor of psychiatry, Trinity College Dublin and author of *In Search of Madness*

"With rich detail and lyrical prose, Fewer transports the reader to a bygone era with a story that nonetheless echoes of the present. Brigid's journey of courage and resilience will break your heart, lift your hopes, and beg questions around society's persistent failings towards women that history would prefer we leave unasked. A layered, compelling read."

—Rachel Stone, author of *The Blue Iris*

"A lyrical and deep exploration of the immigrant experience. Families torn asunder when the dreams of the young conflict with the traditions and social expectations of their parents and families. *Yankeeland* captures both the amazing potential and the pain and frustration of trying to realize your dreams when reality hits hard in the new land. A solid addition to Irish-to-America literature."

—Dean Cycon, author of *A Quest for God and Spices* and *Finding Home (Hungary, 1945)*

"With a deft and delicate touch, floating on prose that rings as clearly as a morning church bell, Lacy Fewer traces bloodlines and heartlines that reach back generations, and, as she does so, shines a light on the commonalities that bind us. Her characters embody who we are through their aspirations and dreams, loss and resiliency, and that most precious of qualities, hope. This is a book of layers, part history, part exultation, and a quiet examination of the sorrows of the lost who cannot find help. As such, *Yankeeland* merits multiple readings. A brilliant first novel, and one that speaks of glories to come."

—Greg Fields, author of *The Bright Freight of Memory*

"A beautifully written and deeply evocative novel, this story weaves past and present seamlessly, immersing the reader in both the struggles and triumphs of its unforgettable protagonist. The prose is rich and lyrical, capturing the complexities of family, ambition, and the quiet strength of women who refuse to be erased. With masterful pacing and emotional depth, the author delivers a tale that lingers long after the final page."

—Dianne C. Braley, author of *The Silence in the Sound* and *The Summer Before*

"*Yankeeland*" is a stunning achievement, a work of great beauty, elegance, and boundless compassion. Born from countless discovered letters of the Kelly family, Lacy Fewer's remarkable debut novel is both sprawling and intimate, devastating and inspiring, exquisite and suspenseful—seeming contradictions that ignite and energize this deeply moving and shockingly original immigrant story of the early modern age, an epic that spans westward from a village in Ireland to Ellis Island to California. When Brigid Kelly sets sail for America, leaving behind her beloved family and heartbroken father, she believes in a promise that seems like destiny, and we believe in the dream, right along with her, with unceasing hope, through the book's powerful and revelatory final pages, when the loving bonds of family bring this artfully crafted saga full circle a century later."

—Jim Zervanos, author of *American Gyro*

"Lacy Fewer's lovingly researched novel of the Irish diaspora beautifully interweaves the adventure of a new life in America with heartfelt loss and tragedy. Detailed scenes transport the reader to a past age as we explore the sights and sounds of 'Yankeeland' at the beginning of the 20th century. Yet alongside material prosperity runs a darker truth. I felt a deep sympathy for Brigid, who as she enters womanhood eagerly forsakes her old life and her family ties, yet finds that married life in a new country becomes a struggle for her emotional and psychological survival."

—Maybelle Wallis, author of *Daughter of Strangers*

"*Yankeeland* is a powerful generational story that peeks into the family secrets of mental health and misogyny, so brilliantly told that putting the book down is impossible. Its vivid century-old characters—parents, siblings, cousins, and spouses—combine to ask a timely question: Are we doing enough today to address the urgent need for mental health care, and how much has really changed?"

—David Randal, author of *Kelsey's Crossing*

"Lacy Fewer's *Yankeeland* is a sweeping tale of hope, resilience, and transformation that weaves through decades and continents. Centered on Brigid Kelly's journey from a stifling Irish village to the promise-filled shores of America, the novel explores family dynamics, societal expectations, and personal ambition. Brigid's dreams clash with her father's traditions and her stepmother's rigid control, culminating in her determined escape to the New World with her husband, Ben. What unfolds is a compelling narrative of immigrants grappling with love, identity, and survival in a land where opportunities are as abundant as the challenges . . . I felt the weight of Brigid's choices—her sacrifices, her hopes for a better life. The novel's themes of familial duty versus personal aspiration struck a chord. Fewer's portrayal of immigrant life is both harsh and hopeful, never sugarcoating the realities but always highlighting the perseverance and ingenuity of her characters. The bittersweet yet triumphant ending left me reflecting on the cost of dreams and the resilience required to achieve them. I'd recommend *Yankeeland* to readers who enjoy historical fiction with strong, complex female protagonists. Fans of Colm Tóibín's *Brooklyn* or Christina Baker Kline's *Orphan Train* will find much to admire in this heartfelt tale. While it's not a breezy read, its rich storytelling and poignant themes make it a journey worth taking."

—Literary Titan

YANKEELAND

Yankeeland
by Lacy Fewer

© Copyright 2025 Lacy Fewer

ISBN 979-8-88824-605-4

All rights reserved. No part of this publication may be reproduced, stored in a retrieval system, or transmitted in any form or by any means—electronic, mechanical, photocopy, recording, or any other—except for brief quotations in printed reviews, without the prior written permission of the author.

This is a work of fiction. All the characters in this book are fictitious, and any resemblance to actual persons, living or dead, is purely coincidental. The names, incidents, dialogue, and opinions expressed are products of the author's imagination and are not to be construed as real.

Published by

◤köehlerbooks™

3705 Shore Drive
Virginia Beach, VA 23455
800-435-4811
www.koehlerbooks.com

YANKEELAND

LACY FEWER

VIRGINIA BEACH
CAPE CHARLES

To Ferghal, Jamie, Lauren, and Juliette—you are my world.
This is for you.

To Brigid and Kate—thank you for trusting me with your story.

PROLOGUE

Boston, September 1993

I'll never know why fate handpicked me that beautiful midweek East Coast morning. Sitting on the floor, two large black sacks sat by my side. I was told I could do as I wished with them, as they had brought nothing but sadness to the previous finder.

The bags, you see, held their story.

Closing my eyes, inhaling the smells of the past, I smiled as they enveloped me.

I had always carried a passion for a story; no doubt the lure was the escapism. A great lover of history, I held a particular fascination with my own. With each envelope their lives shed their shadows, their truth no longer needing to hide.

The "To whom it may concern" from the parish priest in Ireland attesting to their character. The agent's receipt for the first-class passage aboard the *Lusitania*, postcards from across Europe, the travels of a chaperone. Snapshots of somber, gray, distinguished, and disheveled-looking people. Picture cards of famous Hollywood stars, letters from attorneys, doctors' reports, state of California police testimonies. Bundle after bundle, so carefully preserved.

Time stood still as I sat on the basement floor watching the purposeful feet of the passersby as they rushed about their day through the small casement windows that ran along the top of the wall. The beams of the sun caught the dust of the past.

I had never been in a basement office. I had never been in a Brownstone. Warm, comforting mahogany furniture was placed thoughtfully throughout the main floor, heavy Irish lace curtains dressing the windows and tables. A Waterford crystal chandelier hung in pride of place above the dining table, a wedding gift from Ireland. A staircase that went up and then down again dominated the center of the home, an ornate lamp on the post of the banister. It all seemed like a grand hotel.

I took the obligatory photographs; it would not do to arrive home without pictures of this home few had visited before me.

Cosseted in the coziness of the basement, I sat on the floor, the contents of the bags spread across the checkered carpet. I was in my happy place. Lost in their story—my story. Piecing it all together with each envelope, discovering the people and the places. I was humbled and ecstatic that it was I who was seeing some of these letters for the first time since they had been penned.

I was undeterred by his mumbling. "All that stuff. Don't know why she ever kept it." I just thanked every lucky star that she had. But these papers led to so many questions: Who had been the chaperone to young Lady Doyne? Who was "fond cousin Molly"? Why had James disappeared?

I sensed an uncomfortable familiarity catching me unawares as I opened and read the letters written and sealed all those years ago, some of which were never posted, never sent to fond cousin Molly. What had happened?

The generations of pain overwhelmed me.

A pain that was familiar.

I grieved for a life lived of the unspoken word.

That is just how it was.

CHAPTER 1

Moling, County Wexford, Ireland
April 9, 1919
My Dear Brigid,

Thanks so much for your letter. I must apologize for not replying sooner, but one thing or another put me off. I do not think I have anything further to add to what I have told you already. I was sorry to be the bearer of so much bad news, but you were bound to hear it sometime.

Mrs. Kelly is settling in. I think she and Thomas get on well—they always did. Why don't you write to him? It must seem strange to Thomas that you don't. Even though I have them next door, I don't get to see a lot of them. How I might say I've no one belonging to me, but God's will be done, they are far better off.

I have got three kiddies. The two eldest are at school, so I've only Agatha at home. Will you find us some news of James when next you write? We hear so many different stories about him—one time he is dead, another time married, another in the army. I am sure Ben does everything to make you comfortable. God gave us both good husbands. I often think of the old days and all our foolishness and how I suppose we were no different from others.

This place, as you may guess, is lonely now. Even the Healy girls have left. They started a hotel in Dublin and are doing splendidly.

In spite of a good husband and three dear kiddies, I often feel very lonely thinking of all that are gone and how if I am at home of an evening, I haven't one of the old crowd to go to. I wonder, will we ever meet again in this world? But I suppose even if we do, we will be disappointed—things can never be the same, for people have changed. So, I suppose, have I.

I am afraid a trip to Yankeeland is out of the question for us, unless we get rich sooner than we expect. Why don't you people who have no encumbrance pay a visit to the old land? We would all be delighted to see you. My good man has gone for a motor run to Dublin today with a friend. So, I am left alone, and I do not at all like it, even though we have a mission on here at present—isn't that great excitement! Can you picture Moling at all? Just now looking out when writing this, the thought just struck me that if you could arrive in the village this minute you could imagine (except for all those that are gone) that it was only yesterday you had left the place. Sometimes I get very sick of it all. Like you when growing up, I always wished to get out of it, but here I have to remain for the rest of my days.

I do not think I have anything else to tell now, so shall conclude with love and best wishes from all and hope that you won't drop us out of your life altogether but still write occasionally at least.

Your fond cousin Molly

In July 1886, Brigid was the firstborn to businesspeople who ran the village shop, gentle, warm, and loving, just like her mother. The light of their lives, she always set a good example to the younger ones and was adored by everyone.

As her siblings were born, Brigid was never far from their cradle. First

James, then Kate, then Thomas. As Thomas entered this world, their beautiful mother left, victim of a postpartum hemorrhage. There was to be no talk of what had happened to their mother, no thought given to a need for explanation to her children. It was simply "God's will."

Their loss was particularly felt in the mornings with no fires lit, no table set, and only the constant ticking of the clock, their mother's pride and joy. It was all darkness but for the light from the store, where their father shuffled from shelf to shelf, lost to his world of the damned stock. All light had been sucked from their warm, loving home and replaced with individual struggles to exist.

Even at the tender age of six, Brigid, with her sense of responsibility and an innate protectiveness, knew it was up to her to keep their mother's memory alive, even if their father forbade it. He'd demanded they clear all traces of her from their home, never to be spoken of again. For Brigid, the day her mother had died all sense of belonging died with her. An ache remained, and a want to escape this life that had been shattered by grief.

Brigid grew sullen, moody, and withdrawn with the years. It was of no help that she had access to the pictures in the magazines, pictures of what the world outside her village had to offer. She loved nothing more than to sneak into the store and look at the magazines that were forbidden to her, taking a copy of *Lady of the House,* lingering over the "high-class" journal devoted to fashion, the beautifying of the home and person, and many other matters of interest to educated women. Brigid paid particular attention to the fashions and cosmetics, as she knew that her new life would require a bit of a transformation. Her father had a sense of her wanting to change her life, hushing it all away as just silly notions.

Molly knew everything, including Brigid's deepest of secrets. With only a few houses, their shop, a pub, and the church in the village, it was just as well they had each other. Molly lived in the big house; Brigid lived across the lane over the shop. Inseparable since birth, their mothers had been sisters.

Brigid and Molly's grandfather, knowing there was never any question that either of his daughters would take over his doctor's surgery, had bought the adjoining shop from the spinster Easton sisters, wanting to provide a future for his beloved girls. Brigid's mother was first to marry, taking over the shop with her new husband, Patrick. Molly's mother remained in the big house until she herself married, a doctor like her father. She took on the care of her parents and the running of the farm.

Brigid made sure to stay in bed until after she heard Molly's voice below, knowing her father had called her in from next door, asking her to help out with the papers before the morning rush after mass. Brigid was lost to her thoughts of how she hated life in this sleepy village that suffocated her and vowed to get as far away as she could—and soon.

"Brigid, would you get up out of that bed!" shouted Patrick from the store below.

Patrick, always teasing her and her big ideas, often reminded her of her responsibility to her family. He'd made it crystal clear that she would not be getting the place; it would be going to James as the eldest son. Not that she wanted it for all the tea in China.

Brigid's sister Kate was what they called "different."

One year of age when their mother had died, she was excused as having the "trauma" in her soul. As far as Brigid was concerned, she was an embarrassment, that's what she was. Kate had no get-up-and-go in her, causing nothing but upset with her strange ways. The five years between them could have been twenty. They had never been close, and Brigid hated how Kate was the one her father always worried about. He was always telling Brigid to be kind to Kate, making her take Kate out with Molly on their jaunts. That was never going to happen, as there was no way Kate could know of Brigid's dreams; it would never do to have her getting ideas. Molly and Brigid vowed to always share their hearts. Nothing could ever come between them, as they considered themselves to be the real sisters.

Thomas was quieter, while James was gentler. Thomas had his reason for being quiet—it wasn't easy for a six-year-old boy to focus solely on keeping his hands out of sight. He could see others wince at his crusted warts at mass as he shook their hand at the sign of peace, and he dreaded the weekly shaming. Father Dempsey would tell him at the top of his voice from the top of the altar, "Do not even think of using those hands in the Lord's house," as Thomas hid behind his father's back at the altar.

His condition had its pluses; he would never be forced to have a career as an altar boy, although he wasn't sure which was worse, mass or his father asking him to work behind the counter in the shop. Father Dempsey had confirmed his contamination, who would want him to serve them with those hands? They were a constant reminder of the badness in him, and he knew when customers pretended to be intently reading some item or other while keeping a watch of their place in the queue.

Morning, noon, and night all he could think about was how he could get through the day without using his hands. Then one morning Granny took him to see old Mr. Hartigan. He had a gift, she said. He was mad, said everyone else. Just like that, old Mr. Hartigan took his hands and held them like they were the holy chalice. The smelly old cloth he wrapped them in reeked so badly it brought a tear to Thomas's eye. Only God himself knew how many inflictions it had seen. As Mr. Hartigan held his hands, he closed his eyes, mumbling words that made no sense. Granny closed her eyes too. Thomas refused to close his eyes—he was not going to miss a minute of this madness.

"Off you go now, son. You won't be troubled anymore," said old Mr. Hartigan.

Granny told him to say thank you and to trust in the gift he had been given. The next morning, as the day dawned, so did the feeling that he no longer had the badness in him. Both of his hands were perfectly smooth, without a mark to tell they had ever been any different.

Patrick, with four young children and a business to be run, needed a woman by his side. He had done his best in the early years after Ellen had passed away, managing the home and the children, knowing at some point he would have to bring another woman into their home. It was expected of him—a man of his standing needed a woman by his side and those poor unfortunate children needed a mother. Patrick had done his best to deter the goodwill of the parish ladies, but Father Dempsey's little chats after mass every Sunday were wearing him down. Patrick had been acutely aware that the day Ellen was laid to rest there was not a person in the church who was not wondering who was going to be the next Mrs. Kelly, acknowledged in the nods and winks and the hushed tones by her graveside.

As soon as Father Dempsey knew Patrick was ready, the prospects were drawn up. Biddy O'Connor, leading the parish ladies, had set to work on who was in and who was out. The first task at hand, the required attributes: available, no encumbrance, preferably barren, basic levels of intelligence, strong of stature, and above all, proven housekeeping skills—cleanliness, after all, was next to godliness. After much deliberation and a lot of tea, a suitor was successfully recruited: Miss Agnes O'Brien from the parish of Kilgowna.

Agnes, a spinster living at home with her parents, was acutely aware of the stigma this held for a mature single lady. She made no bones about explaining her choice of path in life, happy to tell all and sundry she'd had other professions open to her in which the hours were shorter, the work more agreeable, and the pay higher than looking after a husband.

When approached about the idea of marrying Patrick, Agnes did not at first quite see the importance of this arrangement. However, it was decided that the four young children needed her far more than her elderly parents, and the town needed the business to operate efficiently. No consideration was given to the need for love—the love of Patrick and his new wife or the love the children would need from the new mother in their lives.

Brigid was eleven years of age the year Patrick and Agnes married. Agnes assumed her new role with precision planning. At the top of her list were those children. They'd had more than enough time to get over their loss and there was nothing quite like routine. A meeting was held to review the tasks and her expectations. She had her list, and they had theirs. No dillydallying. There would be no breakfast until her inspection was complete. She had given up her life to devote it to this family; the least they could do was to show her the respect she deserved. Agnes loved to lament the crosses she had to bear: raising those children, having to travel to Dublin to buy their clothes—nothing but the best for the Kellys, who needed to be kept in the style they were accustomed to. But the children themselves had never cared, nor had their father. It was all of her own doing.

As the boys became more and more involved with their father in running the shop and the farm, it was to be the girls who bore the brunt of Agnes's authoritarian ways, which transcended not only the home. The village school, a short stroll away along the back road, did not escape her attention. Mr. Brennan was the principal, alongside his wife, Winifred. They had no children of their own, accepting their calling in life to educate the children of Ireland, with priority given to their religious and moral instruction.

Prior to the introduction of the Free Education Act, the lighting of the fire and the cleaning of the outhouses had been left to the less well-off pupils. Now Mr. Brennan felt it was his duty to provide all children with an education, not only on their literary but also their moral obligations in life. A rotation list was done up for the chores: The boys looked after the fire and the girls cleaned the outhouses. There was to be no discrimination—the jobs were assigned between all the boys and girls irrespective of their social standing. That was, until Agnes got involved. Never before had the principal of the school been questioned.

"No daughter of mine, step or otherwise, will be cleaning toilets—their own or those of others," declared Agnes.

It was not up for discussion, not even with Patrick. He had tried to intervene and begged Agnes not to make a fuss for the sake of the children. Father Dempsey was called in and Agnes said the pope himself would not change her mind. It was an impossible situation. Mr. Brennan would not back down and Father Dempsey was raging. Four weeks passed with little or no sign of a resolution. Father Dempsey, under pressure from Patrick to resolve the issue for the sake of everyone's sanity, was left with no choice. Down came the commissioner for education from Dublin. His decision was final: Either Brigid and Kate resumed their cleaning duties, or they would have to consider alternative arrangements for their education.

And so it was that they were forced to travel by foot or bicycle the five miles every day to school in the parish of Kilgowna. Agnes's cousin was the principal and ran a far more "suitable" operation in his school. There the role of the children from the lower classes attending to the upkeep of the school was not questioned. It was inconceivable that the Kelly girls would carry out such tasks that were far beneath their station simply because they were female. Patrick knew they were the talk of the town and probably the county, but Agnes held firm. Molly was distraught. She would no longer have Brigid by her side, their morning routine taken from them. No more skipping up the back road to the schoolhouse, giggling about their secrets in the safety of the surrounding fields. Those days would be no more.

CHAPTER 2

The Doynes lived at Wells House, the only grand house that Brigid had ever known. It was said that the Doyne family was related to the British royal family and enjoyed all the trappings of the lifestyle that went with it.

A bright young girl, Brigid had the honor of cycling the three miles to Wells House with telegrams, one of the few jobs she made herself available for. She had strict instructions as to the dos and don'ts and was only ever to call at the pantry door and hand the messages directly to the footman. Everyone had their job, and house rules had to be followed. The responsibility was not lost on her.

She would rest her bike against the pillar at the main gate to give herself more time to stroll as slow as her feet would take her. Following the line of the avenue, she felt the fear of God with every step as the house stared her down. She'd wonder which ghost was peering out at her today before losing herself in the glitz and the glamour. The air was always different up there.

To catch a glimpse into their lives was worth every journey—hail, rain, or shine. Lady Harriet Doyne was an outdoorsy type, often appearing from a distance, her shiny dark head of hair flowing from beneath one of her many hats. It was hard to miss her. "She's a class act, that one," the locals would say. "One of them damn Yankees." She'd brought more money to that marriage than Ireland had ever seen.

Brigid made sure to idle her way along the avenue, pretending to hurry when Lady Doyne appeared commanding, "Steady yourself, girl," if she was in the mood for a chat. Lady Doyne had little else to do with her days, and often deigned to speak with the locals. Talking with Lady Doyne stirred fear in most as she found it impossible to hide how much they bored her.

Brigid was different.

"Milady, my, what a beautiful hat you have on you today. Is it one you brought with you from America?"

Lady Doyne saw a spark about Brigid that would take her far from the uncivilized village into which she'd been born. Not quite what one would call handsome, Brigid had that solid Irish frame: thick in the waist, broad in the shoulder, and chunky in the leg. However, it was relieved with a fine head of hair, the bluest of eyes, and an air of intellect just enough to be attractive and not enough to be of concern. Lady Doyne knew good stock when she saw it.

Brigid was transfixed as she studied the noblewoman's flawlessly translucent skin, her hazel-green oval eyes, and her tall, willowy figure, encased in a perfumed air. Strolling the avenue, Lady Harriet, as she liked to be called, was intrigued with Brigid, something Brigid could never understand but would not dare to question. Lady Harriet would ask about Bridgid's family, daily routines, school, whether she liked her father's new wife. So in awe was Brigid, she would tell her everything and then some.

Brigid would lose the run of herself and tell of her dream to go to Yankeeland and of all that she would do with her new life. The clothes, the style, and most of all, the freedom. It connected Lady Harriet to a past she longed for as she talked of her home in New York, the streets, and the people from countries Brigid had never heard of, who spoke languages she would never understand. The smells, the food, the shops, the merchandise that could be bought for those that had the money. Who held the best parties, who was the most fashionable, who had the most money, and most importantly, who was eligible.

"One usually knew who one was promised to long before any coming-out party. Of course, it was a given that one only ever stayed within one's circle," said Lady Harriet as she spoke of the boredom of seeing the same faces at the same house parties and house visits. They all joined the same clubs and holidayed in the same Adirondack resorts.

"Mother had it all arranged. Mr. Stanley Rothchester was to be the lucky man to take me up the aisle—that was, of course, until she came across Charles. Mother soon changed her tune," said Lady Harriet, smiling. "Poor Mr. Rothchester was forgotten, not to mind all those years of planning with Mrs. Rothchester. Mother's ultimate wish was for a title in the family, so really there was never going to be any other outcome. Father, of course, feared that my dowry was the aphrodisiac."

Lady Doyne had been born Harriet Lydia Weber, the name one of the most sought-after in New York social circles. Harriet had enjoyed all the trappings of her lifestyle, her mother made sure of that. It was her father who gave her an awareness for those less fortunate, never losing sight of his own childhood. He'd been born in the German quarters of New York after his parents had emigrated from Germany in search of a better life. Life was still hard in America, though. They'd never made it past the workhouses of Kleindeutchland and were destined for a life working in the textile factory while raising their five children. There they'd toil six days a week, with Sunday as the only day when the family came together. Rising early for mass, they'd pack a lunch for afterward, when they'd head to the Elysian Fields. On foot to Barclay Street, they'd catch the Fairy Queen ferry across the river to Hoboken. There they could meander in the shaded walks, enjoying the cool of the breeze, meeting with other Gothamites in search of relaxation.

Jacob Weber observed from an early age how other people lived their lives: the grand houses, the clothes they wore, the carriages they traveled in, and the food they ate. It gave him a sense of the pleasures that life had to offer those that had the money. Notoriety and fortune followed, but he could not buy himself his ultimate wish—a large family of his own.

Harriet was his pride and joy, and he made sure that everyone knew it would be only the very best that life had to offer when it came to his beloved daughter. Having no desire to take part in the rounds of society dances and balls, he left Harriet's social development in the capable hands of his wife. The frantic trend of the arrival of the English aristocracy was lost on him, and he only became aware of his wife's plan when it was too late. Harriet had fallen in love with Charles Mervyn Doyne of Wells House. The connection to the British royal family had sealed her fate. There was no finer a marriage proposal.

Jacob was distraught. He could not bear the thought of his beautiful daughter leaving his side. How would his dear Harriet navigate married life without access to all that New York had to offer a young lady as beautiful, talented, and educated as she? Of all the places in the civilized world, it was to be uncivilized Ireland where she was to begin her married life. The stately pile that his wife spoke of was just that, a pile, in much need of his dollars and his Harriet.

Brigid lost herself in the stories, aghast as to how anyone could give it all up for love. Was it possible that love alone could do this to a person? Brigid desperately wanted to know more and was not afraid to ask. "So that was it. You fell in love because your mother wanted you to and you gave up your life in New York City to come here with only the horses to keep you company. My goodness, milady, I cannot believe you would leave that life behind you for Wexford."

Lady Harriet smiled. "Brigid, oh Brigid darling, of course I adore the ground Charles walks on. I would travel anywhere to be with him. Don't worry, you will know all about it someday."

Brigid became familiar with Lady Harriet's routine, riding out early in the weekday mornings with the afternoons free to take at her leisure. She knew when to time her trips to be assured of the noblewoman's undivided attention. More often than not, Lady Harriet seemed pleased to see her, and at times Brigid felt that she had been waiting for her. It was those long, hot summer afternoons with Lady Harriet that left Brigid in no doubt as to where her future would be.

CHAPTER 3

Brigid and Molly were sent to Dublin to visit with their great-aunt, Sister Concepta. The nuns lived like peas in a pod, lined out at morning mass, silent in prayer. The girls giggled at their made-up stories about what the nuns were really thinking. Surely, they were all terribly sad to have left their families behind and maybe even a romance. Both Molly and Brigid were very certain that they had never received "the calling."

Sister Concepta delighted with her captive audience, lecturing them on how to be good Catholic girls and how they must always cross their legs and say their daily prayers, preferably at mass. Soon realizing they were not going to be following in her footsteps, she turned to talk of boys. It was the mother of all challenges for the girls, sitting without squirming, for what advice could the old nun have to give when it came to romance? The moral of the story, she emphasized, was to never ever allow a boy into their life until it was the man that would walk them down the aisle. No sidewards glances, no smiling, no encouragement whatsoever, as the boy could not be held accountable for his actions with a girl of disrepute. Shrieking with laughter on the journey home, Brigid and Molly vowed they would never tell a soul their innermost thoughts for fear of retribution.

As Brigid and Molly turned into young ladies, they never missed the dancing at the crossroad, where many a love story had begun. Starved of entertainment, these dances gave an opportunity for people to gather. Whichever musicians would arrive would determine the dancing—it might be a jig or a reel or both. Molly and Brigid had been allowed to join in as soon as they had turned thirteen. It was considered cultural education for young ladies. Cultural education was not exactly what they had in mind.

Agnes had warned them. "None of that aul giggling out of either of you when the boys come looking for you. They'll want to be doing all sorts of things with you and not just dancing. You'd better make sure to turn the other way and not let them next, nigh, or near you."

At the first dance, Brigid and Molly were bitterly disappointed when not one of the boys came within ten feet of either of them. All their preparation in front of the mirror had gone to waste. They chattered endlessly about who was the tallest, who had good teeth, who was the best dancer, and who might have had a bit of a smell off him. With time, the boys grew more forward. Being asked to dance was the ultimate prize for the mothers who looked on at the matches that were being made. Brigid had an air about her as she held her head high and mighty, her sights set on faraway fields. She had no interest in a local boy. Molly would chat away to them all, too kind to refuse a dance no matter who did the asking as Brigid happily sat alone, watching the festivities while dreaming of her future.

Few had the confidence to approach Brigid, for those that did were always refused. It did not take long for word to spread that Brigid Kelly was a "tough act." Ben McCarthy was intrigued by this beautiful young girl who was not like the others. He had watched Brigid over the years as she stood off to the side while the other girls pushed their way to the front for the set dancing with an air of desperation. Ben had asked lots of girls to dance but his sights always settled back on Brigid. There was something about her confident stance and wistful stare. He never commented when his friends gave out about her and called her names. He quietly kept his feelings to himself. Brigid was considered a prize catch and many a mother pushed their son her way. All were rebuffed, and it became a fixation for some as to how Brigid Kelly ever thought she would find herself a man that would match up to her standards.

Ben knew she had absolutely no idea who he was and quite possibly had never as much as looked his way. Ben waited and waited until one evening at the dancing he pushed through the crowd and walked right up to her.

"Would you like to have a dance?" Ben asked.

"Are you a farmer?" replied Brigid looking the other way.

The indifference that had horrified the others only attracted Ben more. He saw in Brigid a girl who knew her own mind, a girl who was filled with confidence and ambitions of her own. Ben never gave up and took every opportunity to engage Brigid in conversation, always prepared for her attempts to push him away. The others laughed at him saying, "God loves a trier," assuming he would never have any hope with Brigid Kelly. After all, it was no secret that he would not be getting the family farm. What in God's name did he think he would have to offer any girl, let alone Brigid Kelly? It was a fella with a big farm of land that would secure that one.

Over time Brigid slowly warmed to Ben as he sat quietly by her side. She admired his resilience and his persistence. At each dance he would come over and sit, uninvited. Molly would glance over at Brigid, who would look for their secret signal as she twirled about with her dance partner. She'd swoop in if Brigid needed to be saved. Brigid would nod back and smile to let Molly know she was okay. They giggled at how Ben had become quite the fixture by Brigid's side at the dances. It was as plain as day that he had a crush on her. He never batted an eyelid at the stares and comments from the others. Ben only had eyes for Brigid, listening intently as she opened up about her plans to leave Wexford and Ireland. Brigid was going and that was that; nothing was going to keep her from following her dream.

"You are fond of that Ben fella, aren't you, Brigid?" asked Molly.

"Would you go away outta that, Molly! I told you nothing would ever come between us. I am just passing my time with him. It's a bit of fun, that's all."

"I hope you don't go telling him about our plans for Yankeeland. It wouldn't be good to put ideas in his head."

"Molly, enough talk about me, what about you and John? You

are keeping him all to yourself. I see you talking to him in your kitchen until all hours."

"My mother has my heart scalded with looking after him. John this and John that. I told her she can take him to the dance."

John O'Sullivan was a trainee doctor who had come to work with Molly's father in his surgery. He was from Dublin and a little more sophisticated than the boys she had met at the dances. Their fathers had studied medicine together in Dublin many years before and had a strong bond of friendship. Molly had never met John or his father, as she was never taken to Dublin when her father went on his "business trips." Her mother had always said it was far from business they would be talking about on a golf course or in one of the fancy hotels in Dublin.

John had lodgings at their home for the duration of his stay and her father loved having him help out in the surgery. They talked long into the night of their patients and the latest advancements in the medical journals that her father stored in his bureau. One evening her mother suggested Molly take John to the dance along with Brigid, as it would be good for him to mix with more people of his own age, seeing as how her father had the poor young man worn out with all his talk of patients and their ailments. Molly was mortified. She would be the talk of the place; they would all be looking at her and would assume he was with her. He was a nice fella, but bringing him to the dance with her was another thing altogether. She asked Brigid to send a note to Ben and maybe the two of them could meet up and go together; it would stop the gossip and make it easier for her to enjoy herself and not be worrying about John all night.

There was little for Molly to worry about. John was the hit of the dance. The girls were queueing up to meet him, and she barely saw him the entire evening. Everyone was talking about the handsome fella down from Dublin—a doctor no less.

"Brigid, can we go? I don't feel that well and I have a bit of a headache. Is it all right if we leave now?"

"What's wrong with you, Molly? You've been looking forward

to the dance for ages. Are you sure you are feeling that bad that you want to go?"

Molly made a face at Brigid. "Yes, Brigid. I do feel *that* bad. Now let's go."

Molly raged as they walked home. "And who does he think he is, staying in my home and me minding him all the time, and he has the cheek to make eyes with every eejit that showed him any bit of attention. He will have them slobbering all over him, the fool. I won't stand for it, Brigid. He can explain himself to Mother when she asks me why he didn't walk me home."

Ben had walked back to the village with the two girls and was wondering what else the fella could have done. Molly had gone out of her way to offload him. She had made it quite clear that she did not want anyone getting any ideas about the two of them. It was very hard for a fella to understand what the right thing was to do when it came to the girls—they were the whole time changing their minds.

Brigid took Ben aside. "You had better go back and tell that John fella to get back here fast, or he will have some explaining to do for himself."

When Ben got back to the dance, John was having the time of his life. He told Ben not to be worrying about him and to go on ahead without him. He would stay till the end and make his own way back when the dancing was over.

When Ben got back to the girls he told them, "Eh, yeah. It was hard to hear him over the music. I'm not sure he could understand me, but I tried to tell him to come on away home with me. He just mouthed something back to me and I wasn't quite sure he understood. I didn't want the two of you to be waiting, so I said I would head on back. I'm sure John will follow me."

Molly threw herself into Brigid's arms, crying. "I'll be the laughing stock of the place! The big eejit hasn't got a bloody clue what he's after doing to me. If he's the last man on earth, I swear to God, I will never ever speak to him again."

Brigid listened as Molly whined about how he had no manners, off gallivanting with anyone that would have him. What kind of respect was that to show for her family, who had welcomed him into their home? Brigid didn't dare interrupt Molly's rant. She wanted to suggest that maybe Molly could have been a little more friendly to John and shown an iota of interest instead of going out of her way to avoid him.

Ben waited in the lane for Brigid. "You must be exhausted after all that commotion."

"She'll be grand. I've never seen her like this before, but I'll bet you anything she is fond of him and doesn't want to admit it. I tried telling her to calm down and not to wait up for him or else she might say something she would regret. Her mother came down to us, and all Molly said was that she had a headache and she had told John to stay on. That he'd met some nice lads, and they were talking about the hurling."

"That was some change in her tune all right. I guess we'll have to watch this space then," said Ben with a confused look.

"Oh, don't you worry your little head about any of it. I will talk to her again in the morning and get it all out of her. You wait and see," said Brigid, smiling.

The evening of the next dance, Molly strode confidently down the road linking arms with John. She had done her reflecting, and this time she was not going to leave him to the vultures that were waiting for him. Molly was going to make it very clear that he was a guest in their home and that he was in capable hands—her hands.

Molly's father had asked John if he would consider staying on a more permanent basis. The practice was growing, and he was finding it increasingly difficult to meet the needs of his patients. John was a fine young doctor with an impeccable bedside manner. Molly's father was impressed; Molly's mother was ecstatic for differing reasons.

Brigid was helping out in the shop, and Ben was getting by working with his brother on the farm. It was very difficult for any young man who had little prospect of ever being any more than a worker on another man's land. Ben was now the one who talked incessantly about a life of opportunity, a life where he could see a future for himself and a family someday. Molly was busy with John, and there was talk of a match being made. Molly and her parents had made a trip to Dublin to meet John's family, and they had stayed in a fancy hotel on St. Stephen's Green. It was all Molly could talk about—John this and John that. Brigid was happy for Molly and was very fond of John, but she was saddened that her traveling companion was now taken. Molly no longer talked of their plans to leave the place behind and see what the world had to offer. But Ben more than happily filled the void in Brigid's life, and whether she liked it or not, she, too, was falling in love.

Patrick had known of their match for a while and had kept it from Agnes, sensing she would have a thing or two to say about a suitor who had little in the way of material prospects to bring to a union. Patrick had made it clear to Agnes that she was not to meddle in Brigid's affairs. His daughter was an adult now and capable of making her own decisions with or without their input. Patrick knew there was little love lost between Agnes and Brigid, and he did not want any further cause for a splinter in the family.

It came as no surprise to Patrick when Ben asked for Brigid's hand in marriage. Ben made it clear that while he had little to offer in the way of material assets, Patrick could be assured of his love and support of Brigid all her days. Ben was a man of honor, and Patrick had a sense he was not going to settle into a life of being a farm laborer. If Brigid was happy, Patrick was happy. He would not stand in her way. Brigid was a formidable young girl and would not accept his proposal unless she was very sure of her decision.

On a Monday in early September 1908, at the age of twenty-two, Brigid married Ben McCarthy in a small ceremony with Molly by her side. Ben had his brother Sean, who was happy, as it would be good for Ben to start making his own way in the world. Patrick gave them his blessing. Kate had said she was busy that day and wished them well. The marriage was the least of Patrick's worries, as the newly married couple soon announced that they were going to start their married life in America. Patrick had known of Brigid's unhappiness in her surroundings and had expected Dublin, but never America. The only women who traveled were those left on the shelf with no man to take them off it, and Brigid was now a married woman. It must have been that American woman up at Wells House putting ideas in her head all these years. And there they were, thinking that she had taken a shine to Brigid, preparing to ask her to be her lady's maid!

Patrick had relied on Agnes for his advice with the children, which was not always in their favor. A few years earlier it had been Agnes who found Brigid's stash of Penny Dreadfuls on the top shelf of the hot press, under the good linen for the visitors that never came. Corrupting images, Paris fashions, how to do her hair and paint her face, whatever for? "Heavens above. What would the Catholic Truth Society make of this? Preaching from the very pulpit across the very road, the society had warned about these magazines' contents being unwholesome stuff, compact of sickly sentimentalities or worse. In every case deriving its inspiration from sources especially repellent to the Catholic mind," Agnes cried. "There can be no doubt in anyone's mind that the present age is a dangerous one for our young owing to the disseminations of Godless literature."

Agnes had been in a rage and nothing would do but for Brigid to be sent to the convent. "Only Our Lord above and Sister Monica Mary can fix her now."

It had taken all of Patrick's might to save her from that one. So Patrick knew there would not be any words of encouragement from Agnes; she would be only delighted to see the back of Brigid as she left for America, as if all her prayers had been answered. Patrick was alone in his loss, for Brigid was the living image of her mother, with her inquiring mind and passion for life. A life cut short. How could he deny Brigid this opportunity, for whoever knew what the road ahead would bring any of them?

Brigid's father paid for their second-class passage on the condition that Brigid's brother James travel with them, a chaperone of sorts. Patrick gave them each forty dollars apiece to start their new life. They boarded the SS *Adriatic* from Queenstown on a Wednesday in late September. Their passage afforded them far more luxury than Ben had ever experienced in his life. He reminded himself that he was going to make something of himself and ensure Brigid a continued life of comfort. The SS *Adriatic* was a newer ship, the first of its kind with a swimming tank and a Turkish bath. It was filled to capacity with mostly steerage passengers and less than one-third in first and second class. Brigid was anxious about the journey ahead and became overwhelmed when anyone mentioned the length of the journey. Seven days was all she had to get through. If they could occupy themselves during their time onboard, it would hopefully pass without cause for any concern.

The journey was made easier since they traveled in the latest comforts and style of the day. Brigid chatted away easily to the first-class passengers.

She approached one older couple on the first night of the journey. "Hello. This is my brother James, and my name is Brigid."

"Arthur and Mildred Beauchamp," the man answered in a clipped British accent. "And where is it you come from?"

"We are from Ireland."

"Oh. I'm surprised to see you in the dining hall."

"Well, my word. Where else would we be?" Brigid answered, her eyebrows raised.

"Oh no, dear. Of course it is wonderful to have you join us. I just wanted to make sure you had not gotten yourselves lost on the ship. It can happen, my dear. What did you say your cabin number was?"

"I did not say what my cabin number was, and I shan't either. Good day, Mr. Beauchamp." Brigid and James turned from the couple. Under her breath Brigid whispered to James, "And good riddance! How dare they. As soon as they heard we were Irish, they assumed we were penniless. I know exactly what Mr. Beauchamp was thinking. And Mrs. Beauchamp physically recoiling as if we were diseased! My Lord, I will *not* be shy about giving them a piece of my mind. They had better keep out of my way!"

"No better woman. Good for you, Brigid. Leave it to you to sort them out," said James, smiling at his sister.

Ben was nowhere to be seen. He had been on edge from the moment the steward had shown them to their cabin and had offered to stay behind and unpack their suitcases and lay out their clothes. Brigid had told him not to be worrying about any of it, as she and James were going to make the most of the trip and head off exploring. Brigid begged Ben to come with her in the electric lift but no, he said he was tired and worried that he might feel seasick, so it was best if he rested himself. Ben was out of his depth, and it was lost on James and Brigid, not through ignorance but simply through a lack of experience for the lives of those who came from a less-fortunate background. Brigid did not let it stop her; she was determined to make the most of the experience. She laughed while swinging herself around in the imposing mahogany armchairs that swiveled on cast iron legs bolted to the floor. And she heartily enjoyed the food and the choice of menus as they sat at the dining table, each with its own electric lamp dressed with pretty pink lampshades that cast a rosy glow over the passengers, and listened to the musicians that provided pleasant background melodies. The seven days ahead suddenly did not seem long enough for them to enjoy all the ship had to offer.

Brigid, Ben, and James had heard the stories that filtered back to the families in Ireland from their recently immigrated loved ones. The first letter home was always the same, telling of the horrors of the journey, the cramped conditions, the foul smells, and of those that had not made it, succumbing to disease or accidents along the way. They paid no heed to any of it, not quite dismissive of the plight of the steerage passengers but indifferent to its relevance.

For now, all they had to do was sit back, relax, and enjoy the latest comforts of the day as they traveled in near splendor.

James told Brigid she had better go back to Ben; he might be wondering where she was, and it would be better for her to spend her time with her new husband. Brigid had not quite thought of it like that and thanked James for his advice before running off to chat with two young ladies she had seen earlier traveling alone.

James was happy to wander about on his own. He had no need of engaging with the other passengers and was happier to observe. He would keep an eye on Brigid, as there was no knowing who she could fall afoul of if anyone else dared to snidely comment about their presence in the upper decks.

Ben stayed in his cabin for the first few days, taking little in the way of nourishment to avoid adding to his already upset stomach. He had a feeling he was the only passenger on their deck who was using the washrooms for that purpose as every time he went in there to be sick some gentleman would comment "First time, young man?" Ben would just raise his hand and wave, too afraid to open his mouth lest he vomit all over the gentleman's oxford shoes!

No matter where Ben went, he felt out of place. If he opened his mouth, the passengers would recoil and ask if he was Irish, whispering to each other and walking away. If he was sick in the bathrooms, they would comment about how he was not a seasoned traveler. If he went to dinner with Brigid, his suit was out of place in the formal dining room. Every waking moment Ben had a heightened sense of his place. Watching James and Brigid easily navigate all that was on display did not help to ease his worries and only added to his unease.

Brigid had dreamed of the moment when the wonders of the New World would come into view. She knew all the tales of standing out on the deck—it'd be like nothing she could ever imagine; the hairs would stand up on the back of her head. It was to be the highlight of their journey, and Brigid made sure that all three of them were prepared for the moment. The deck was crowded, as everyone had the same idea, and the three of them huddled close together. They silently stared, sighing with relief to have arrived, in union with the other passengers, many of whom shared a heart heavy for the betrayal of those back home.

Brigid, Ben, and James did not need to concern themselves with the ordeal of Ellis Island. The ship first stopped at the checkpoint off the coast of Staten Island to allow the doctors to board and check for disease, clearing the way for the immigration officers. First- and second-class passengers were briefly interviewed and allowed to disembark at one of the west-side piers along the Hudson. No papers were needed. All that was required was to verbally provide their details upon boarding the ship. The rest of the passengers were herded into small steamboats and shipped to the island to go through the grueling process of medical checks and interviews, observed with suspicion from the moment they set foot on the island to the moment they were cleared and allowed entry.

Bridget made sure to keep their letters of recommendation on her at all times. They afforded them some comfort that they would be met with acceptance and assured suitable introductions. Monsignor Glennon had been only too happy to supply them with a reference as practicing Catholics from good Irish stock. The Kellys, after all, were essential contributors to the parish purse. There was little for Brigid, Ben, and James to worry about.

They had the address of a friend of a friend, a Mrs. Brennan, who had emigrated some forty years prior, writing home only at Christmas. They knew little of her life, only that she had left to work in service, which had not allowed for marriage or family, and that she now ran a boarding house that thrived from the arriving émigrés. She had made it clear that they would be paying guests.

Lady Harriet had provided introductions for the group on fancy paper with Wells House embossed on the top. Brigid had no intention of calling upon these people. The letters were an honor in themselves, but Brigid sensed a life in service would be the expectation. Emigrating to make a living was not Brigid's motivation. It was not about money; it was excitement, anticipation, opportunities, and living her dream in a new world, far removed from the one she had been born into.

Patrick had given them a few bob to make a start, taking some comfort from James being by his sister's side—blood, after all, being thicker than water.

James was fond of Ben. He was a good man and cared for Brigid. Kindness and respect were all he could ask from any man. It was not his place to be his sister's chaperone, as Ben more than adequately filled that role. James knew their father had made the decision for him to accompany the newlywed couple in haste without time for thought or reflection. He respected his father's decision, even though he did not agree nor feel comfortable with the responsibility that had been placed upon him.

James could never see a life for himself in the crowded New York City, with more poverty than he had known possible. His native countrymen, whom he had naively assumed would want to build a life of prosperity, had satisfied themselves eking out an existence in their "wonderful new world" of Five Points in Manhattan. A life far worse than any of the slum tenements he had heard of in Dublin, alcohol was the only constant. The other immigrants drank together as the best of friends and fought as the worst of enemies. It was a way of life, as the children ran wild all hours of the day and night, the women trailing them so frail it was hard to discern who was the parent and who was the child.

James was not a drinker, so the Irish did not trust him and the rest looked on with suspicion. Those first days were the most miserable of his life. They would never speak of the horrors they had seen at Mrs. Brennan's boarding house, which was no more than a filthy tenement.

She had warned them, "Don't be telling any stories back home. I have forty years of connections in this land."

Ben had the name of a fellow Irishman, George Hanan, who had previously been appointed mayor of the new city of Niagara Falls. Monsignor Glennon had known George's father and told them he was a great man for helping his fellow countrymen and of how Niagara Falls had become an important town for industrialization, with any number of opportunities. Ben needed to get them out of New York City quickly and quietly, for some would say Brigid and James had been born with a silver spoon in their mouth. He made his inquiries; it would take some ten hours at a cost of between ten dollars for a standard fare and upward of twenty dollars for first class. James told Ben not to worry about providing a first-class fare, as they were more than happy to travel in standard. They needed to manage their money carefully.

James was curious about the talk of the West, especially San Francisco—the Paris of the Pacific. Father Dempsey had told him of Thomas O'Shaughnessy, a Limerick man who had left Ireland in 1885 to further his engineering career opportunities. He had done well for himself and was involved in a number of major building projects following the earthquake of 1906. O'Shaughnessy had written to the Bishop of Limerick looking for Irish laborers to travel to San Francisco. The Bishop had put out a call in the Catholic circular that went to every parochial house across Ireland, wanting to support O'Shaughnessy, who had never forgotten his Irish roots and was very good to the folks back home. Father Dempsey had read about it and told James before he left that he might seek his fortunes in the American West. San Francisco was awash with Chinese and Japanese, and the cultural barriers were proving to be too much, so O'Shaughnessy was eager to bring on any hardworking fellow countrymen he could find.

James spoke with Ben about the opportunities in San Francisco and of the work that was being done to rebuild the city. But Ben felt that it would be a risk for all of them to make that long journey so early into their arrival, not to mention the cost of three fares. James's loyalty to his father's request weighed heavily on him, but he grew increasingly uncomfortable with the role of chaperone. Traveling to San Francisco would provide an ease to this burden, but that was not something he could verbalize to Ben. Brigid was not consulted, as this was a decision the men would make.

When Ben did not put any obstacles in his way, James decided to head West to see for himself if the reports were true, telling himself that as soon as he had seen the opportunities with his own eyes he would write to Ben and encourage him and Brigid to follow him. James figured that what his father didn't know wouldn't hurt him.

CHAPTER 4

Arriving at a bustling Grand Central terminal for their train journey to Niagara Falls, Brigid marveled at the grand arches while Ben listened to the noise of the steam engines as the conductors calling out the destinations competed with the newspaper vendors. Men in suits and hats and women in their finest dresses milled about as the porters carrying their luggage ran after them. Ben had reserved two standard coach tickets with the New York Central Railroad, assured of adequate comfort in cushioned seats and access to a dining car.

Settling into their carriage, having made suitable introductions to their fellow travel companions, they watched the Manhattan skyline and the busy streets below lined with horse-drawn carriages and noisy street vendors slip out of their view. Ben was not sorry to leave the city behind them and was relieved when he saw the wide sparkling Hudson River and the fiery fall foliage, pointing out to Brigid the small boats and the larger steamboats as they traveled the waterway. Ben was intrigued by the views as Brigid nestled in to rest by his side in awe of the cliffs and the mountains, listening to the other passengers as they pointed out the military academy, an imposing, stately building perched on a hill.

Approaching Albany, Ben had his first sense of the industrial importance of the area as he observed factories, warehouses, smokestacks, and trains filled with goods. Then on to Syracuse by the canals, rolling hills, and farmhouses as Rochester appeared, with its vineyards and apple orchards providing a feast of color in the autumnal landscape.

Brigid was awakened from her sleep by the conductor walking through the train alerting the passengers that they would soon reach their final destination. Ben was deep in conversation with a companion about the extent of the industrialization of Buffalo, pointing to the bustling harbor as it came into view, the towering grain elevators, steel mills, and factories. All of the passengers stood to watch as the train neared the powerful Niagara River flowing toward the falls with its white-water rapids.

The station in Niagara Falls was filled with tourists and vendors selling postcards and souvenirs. The falls roared as crowds gathered at the viewing platforms, eager to be rewarded with the powerful and mesmerizing view.

❦

James set off a day later, also from Grand Central Terminal, happy that he had worn his best shirt and tie in an effort not to stand out among the more seasoned, smartly dressed travelers. As he settled himself into a general coach car with rows of cushioned seats, two young chaps came rushing onboard just as the train pulled out of the station, laughing and clapping each other on the backs that they had made it. James smiled as the two young men threw a small bag overhead and took out a pack of cards.

"What's your story, kid?" the dark-haired fella asked James, punching his friend in the arm and giving him a wink. "Off to meet the girl of your dreams, are you?"

"Eh, no not exactly. I'm headed West. I've just arrived and am looking for work," replied James.

"Right so. We'll keep you company then. We're headed the same way—heard there is any amount of work there for young fellas like us, and plenty of good-looking gals. Gonna find ourselves a sweetheart to look after us, if you know what I mean!"

James had an idea what they were referring to. Ben had warned him to stay away from the rooming houses and hotels filled with gambling and drinking, as he had sensed it would not only be the landscape that James would become acquainted with on the journey.

Settling themselves in, they agreed to take it in turns to sleep and look out for each other. As they played cards, there was little interest shown in the passing landscape. James wanted to ask them questions about the towns they passed, to see if they had ever been to these places, but did not want to seem too eager. The young men had spoken of how they had grown up together on the streets of New York and were tired of scraping a wage, stuck living at home. They wanted to move to a place with opportunities for hardworking young men who were looking for a better start in life. The boys talked about the jobs they would look for, finding lodgings, and how they would soon build their own homes and start families. James listened to them and deflected their questions when they asked about his story, telling them that he had recently arrived from Ireland and had the same dreams as them. They would not understand why he had left a family business behind him in Ireland or why his father had made him travel with his sister, who had a husband. It was easier to say nothing. The boys were busy talking over each other anyway, and James left them at it.

"Whoa, look at that!" exclaimed James as they passed over the Great Lakes, boats and freighters in the distance. The men were sleeping and no matter how hard he tried to engage them, they had no interest. The other companions in the car were eagerly taking in the scenes, and James listened in on their conversations, desperately trying to learn as much as he could. He spent hours watching as the train sailed over the flat plains of the Midwest, comforted by the golden fields of harvested wheat and grazing cattle under the wide-open sky. The endless horizon and the scale and remoteness of the land fascinated James. Soon after, the mountains came into view and the train snaked its way through the Rockies, passing snow-dusted peaks, rushing rivers, and dense pine forests. James was exhilarated as the train slowed, navigating the steep terrain through dark tunnels and over high trestle bridges.

"Tommy, Tommy would ya look at that!" the dark-haired fella said to his companion. "My oh my. Salt Lake Desert, now isn't that some beauty. If I never saw another field in all my days, it would be worth it just to say I saw this."

James could not understand the sudden interest in this stark, desolate landscape and was relieved to see the forested Sierra Nevada mountains and alpine lakes, a return to the landscapes he was more familiar with. But nothing could have prepared him for the exhilaration of seeing the lush farmlands and vineyards of California's central valley filled with workers harvesting the crops.

Exhausted and relieved, they exited the train in Oakland, searching for the ferry to take them across the bay. Pushing their way through the businessmen in suits, the families, and the day tourists on board, they found a spot along the railing to take in the view. Wide-eyed as they passed Alcatraz Island, sniffing the air as they tried to make out the smell of the eucalyptus in the warm autumn air before making their way toward the exits as the tall clock tower on the ferry building came into view.

James had made his decision early in the journey that he would part ways with the two young men when they arrived at their destination. They were looking for a different sort of lifestyle, and he did not want to hold them back. The men were far too excited whistling and calling after the young ladies that passed their way to be upset with him. They just clapped him on the back as they rushed after two young ladies who had glanced back at them.

James headed straight to the nearest church, where he was given the address of the Young Men's Christian Association on Golden Gate Avenue. Monsignor Glennon had once told James's father that this was the only suitable environment for a young man in any city, concerned for young men's spiritual morality, aware the amusement available in many cities was monopolized by money and not morality.

James was handed the sixteen-page pamphlet outlining the development of the religious and moral aspects of a young man's life, with a secondary attention to the social and physical. They would assist with finding suitable employment, guarding him from temptation by introducing him into Christian and refined society. The YMCA boasted 140 rooms, bathrooms with hot and cold running water, and a telephone for which James knew he would have no use. Gymnasiums, a swimming tank with shower baths, a barber shop, a restaurant, and an educational department all further ensured an environment suitable for spiritual growth.

Loving his time at the YMCA, James wanted to stay, but the reminders were regular: It was only a temporary solution. He would need to secure lodgings on a more permanent basis. The contacts he made gave him the start he needed, and he sought out Mr. and Mrs. O'Toole. They took in lodgers and lived in a quiet, rural area outside the city on Caselli Avenue, a fine two-story building over a basement, which became his new home.

A busy boarding house in its day, with a constant flow of Irish immigrants, Mrs. O'Toole ran it like it was Nobby Clarke's grand folly at the top of the street. There was no finer a home away from home for any immigrant. Many a heavy heart had left as soon as love came along, for the O'Tooles only ever boarded men. Few remained long, as there was no shortage of love in the city. Mrs. O'Toole often reminded them of her words of wisdom—"never marry for love alone"—before they got too carried away with their newfound freedom, spoiled for choice with beautiful young companions. By the time James arrived there were only two other lodgers, both with families back home in much need of their hard-earned dollars, so they had little time or interest for anything else. It was a nice enough house, but the O'Tooles were not getting any younger and the place was in need of a little care.

Picking up a January 1909 edition of the *San Francisco Chronicle*, James knew he had made the right decision.

> *It will be the busiest year in the history of the city. No city in the United States is growing as San Francisco is growing. The shaking*

> up we have had has sharpened the wits of our businessmen, suddenly jarred into the necessity of exerting themselves. For never in San Francisco was house building so active as now save during the first rush of rehabilitation in the latter part of 1906. There is home building everywhere and no cessation in the construction of flats and apartment houses. This movement is going on before our eyes. It is evidence of the confidence that exists in the minds of all of us and is inspiring us to earnest endeavor. It is enterprise and confidence which builds a city.

All he had to do now was encourage Brigid and Ben to follow.

James sought out Thomas O'Shaughnessy and spent a few days on the sites, but he quickly realized the life of a laborer was not for him. The men were coarse, and James had no interest in being in their company. There was plenty of opportunity, and James settled on work as a freight handler at the Southern Pacific Company. The wages would cover his board, and he could save the rest to bring home with him when he returned to Ireland. He thought of all the improvements he would make to the place when he returned.

The O'Tooles showed James the respect of a son, with wholesome meals as good as he had ever tasted, chats about his day, encouragement in finding friendships, and advice about the associations to join that would be good for a young Irish man. James's focus was his work and saving his money. Having to leave Moling so suddenly had broken his heart, with little time for thought and no time for disagreement. Happy and settled there all his young life, he had a real passion for his family business; he had never known any other way and never needed to. The place would be his someday, God willing, and he would pour his blood, sweat, and tears into it all from a place of loyalty, an honor to carry the generations. How had he not known of Brigid's plans to come to America? She might have borne the brunt of Agnes's harsh ways of mothering and taken the hits for the others, but she'd never shied away from challenging it. He was secretly proud of her for that. He'd never realized how truly miserable she must have been to want to flee so far.

Mrs. O'Toole was always asking James about home. "Are you mad in the head? Leaving the place behind you . . . sure what would you be thinking, working here for another man when you have a place of your own?"

He knew she did not mean any harm and that she was just saying what everyone else was thinking. He was unable to think, never mind talk, of the morning his father had called him into the parlor. It would never settle in him. He had assumed it was about the business, that maybe Father was going to slow down, and it was time for James to take over. Not for a moment did he ever imagine it would be an instruction to give up his life for his sister. If she so badly wanted out, why could she not have followed Kate to learn her trade at the bakery in Wexford? Kate was sure of her path, happy to support their father's wish to supply their own home-baked goods at the store, just as their mother had in the early days. It was a great comfort to their father to know that she would support the family business in this way. So why, in the name of God, did Brigid have to choose a country they knew nothing of, when she had no need to flee a life of poverty, like most that had to make that journey. There was never any doubt as to marriage proposals for the daughter of Patrick Kelly, even before she had met Ben. She'd always known that she would be assured of a continued life of plenty with any number of interested parties.

Patrick said he had done all he could to try and stop her, but she was not for turning and there would be no more talk of it. Brigid had married Ben McCarthy in the knowledge that they would be starting their life together in America. The fight had gone out of Patrick, and his only request was that James travel with them to give him some sense of peace. His son and heir, sensible and trustworthy by her side in this New World he knew nothing of. Knowing James would not question him had broken Patrick's heart. Thomas was only a boy, not yet eighteen and would be living at home for some years yet to finish his schooling and help out with the business and the farm. Kate had been happy with his advice to live in the town of Wexford and make something of herself. Baking was all she had ever shown any interest in and if it gave her a sense of peace, he was happy to leave her at it. Patrick knew in his heart that James was the only one of his children who had what was needed to take on the running of the business—Kate and Thomas would never be any match for James.

James knew he and his siblings had been luckier than most. Even though they had lost their mother, they had never needed to concern themselves with a roof over their head or food on their table. Without questioning his father, James had accepted his fate. He would stay until he knew Brigid had settled into her life before returning to resume his role by his father's side. San Francisco was providing him some excitement of his own, as well as helping him find a permanent place for his sister to settle.

CHAPTER 5

Ben and Brigid made do with lodgings arranged by Ben's new employer, which required sharing with another recently arrived immigrant family, a temporary arrangement until they found their way. For now, Ben's concern was settling into his work at the aluminum factory and learning the trade. The work was manual, and he was unsure of his strength for the long days on the factory floor, having only ever worked outside in the fields with the fresh air. Ben knew to align himself with the supervisors, making sure he was center stage in their mind's eye for all the right reasons. With the influx of migrant workers being mostly Italian, Ben had an advantage as the others struggled to understand their orders.

Brigid and James had agreed that Brigid would write the letters to home and that all correspondence would go through her in Niagara Falls. There was no need for them to be worrying their father just yet about the change in their arrangements. There would be plenty of time once they were both settled and sure of their plans to explain. Brigid sent word to home telling only of the basics: their lodgings, Ben's work, and their prayers that the good lord would bless them. Thoughtful and reflective, she wrote just enough to satisfy Father and ensure Agnes knew they were doing just fine. She remembered to tell Father to pass on their thanks to the monsignor, as his kind words had opened many a door. Mr. Hanan had been impressed—a referral from a monsignor no less—insisting Brigid join the parish committee. He assured her that she would fit right in and ordained her a Child of Mary, more out of tradition than devotion.

Brigid felt the weight of the suffocating hypocrisy, a factor which had encouraged her decision to leave the repressed environment of Ireland in the first place. The other parish women called themselves Christians as they secretly calculated a person's acreage and weekly dues, remarked on how many days they went to mass, speculated on whether they said the Rosary once or twice daily, and gossiped about how many children the wives bore their husbands and how good they were at keeping house. Heaven forbid if one missed their criteria—that would result in certain banishment from their insular world.

But Brigid tried to remind herself that it was perfectly normal to feel a little overwhelmed. It would take time to find herself a routine and a suitable set of interests. She had not factored in the prospect of sharing a home with strangers who did not speak the same language, and their noisy children made for earlier starts than she would have liked. Frustrated by the unfamiliar endless choice of food, she stuck to the basics. Ben would inquire about her plans for the day, sensing her forced enthusiasm was not necessarily a reality. But Brigid would never voice her worries, for she knew that this was all her own doing. It would just take time.

Her letters home were written with precision, telling of the magnificence of the famous falls.

Too nervous to explore on her own, Brigid would wait till Sunday and, with Ben by her side, they would venture together on the streetcars, traveling at a marvelous pace. Ben had become quite the expert, using them for work as he did. Sunday might be a day of rest, but not for participants in the "train parties", who Ben and Brigid would avoid, as Brigid found the crowds overwhelming. It was on these weekly outings that Brigid would take in the sights to relay to Molly—the streets, the shop fronts with their pretty canopies overhead, and the hotels, too many for her to keep count. They had little experience of hotels, having only ever visited the one in Wexford town on very special occasions.

Ben suggested a routine for Brigid, as she was finding her days in

Niagara lonesome. Brigid liked to visit the shops daily, but she was flustered by the food in tins and not wanting to appear foolish by having to seek out recipes, she'd return home with the same old same old. She found solace in the city market for its reliable source of fresh produce that she could easily navigate. Strolling through the carts lined up in the field, the horses grazing nearby, she would close her eyes and think in that moment that it was market day in Wexford, and she was by her father's side, sorry now for how she had complained. The mundane familiarity she had most wanted to leave was what she now missed the most.

Ben managed the money, giving her a strict budget of $5.76 for the weekly shop, allowing only for necessities, as the rest was set aside for savings with little ever leftover for discretionary spending. Brigid had never known a budget and struggled having to add up the cost of the items, determining which were necessities and which were, as Ben called them, luxuries. Knowing that it would not always be like this, in those moments Agnes's words came back to haunt her—"When the bills come in, the love goes out the window."

One day, like many others, she told Ben, "Don't fret, dear. It's just a few initialed handkerchiefs, a mere forty-nine cents for six, and an untrimmed day hat. I simply cannot venture another day with the ladies without a hat, an investment for sure. And these catalogs from Macy's of New York, should we consider your own dress requirements, offering the finest of suits for only seven dollars."

"And what is wrong with Silberberg's here in town? You know exactly what you are purchasing: 'Cotton for cotton, wool for wool, no misrepresentation at the Silberberg store.' I have no need for any fancy catalog to send me a new suit or, heaven forbid, undergarments," replied Ben, shutting down the conversation.

Ben was concerned that they would never move forward with such frivolous spending. It seemed that no day was complete without some purchase or other that was always deemed a necessity, and he wondered if this was the way of all women. Was this really how they occupied their days?

CHAPTER 6

James awoke with enthusiasm at the dawning of each new day, as the fervor in the city was tangible and infectious. Never a man of obvious emotion, especially since excitement had not factored in his life before, he soon discovered this new feeling to be a constant. Always a steady pair of hands, rarely lost to his thoughts, he was now wandering the city as if in another world. A world he had never wanted nor considered was bringing him so much more than he could have ever known. Those early days were all about the experience.

"Where will you be headed today, James? You have great get-up-and-go about you. What poor unfortunate will be the better of having met you today?" Mrs. O'Toole would say at breakfast.

James was usually thinking about where he might explore that day, allowing plenty of time for meandering the city streets. He loved meeting people from other communities. Some spoke his language, but there were many who did not. For those that did, he made the time for chats and for the rest his smile and a wave was enough to elicit a warm response. The circumstances to which these people found themselves was not lost on James. He knew of poverty, albeit at a distance, but he had never quite seen anything like the barefoot, ragged children and the worn-out, distraught mothers behind them. Quake shacks dotted about the place, but many others seemed to have no fixed abode. He struggled with these two worlds: his own, with all the opportunities it had to offer him, and that of those that did not know where their next morsel of food would come from.

"Sure, aren't we all God's creatures? They are no different from any of us—just fell down on their luck," James would reply to Mrs. O'Toole's questioning, considerate as always.

The O'Tooles considered themselves the lucky ones that it was their home where James had found his way. Hard workers who had built a good life for themselves, they recognized a kindred spirit in James. They'd talk long into the night of the sights James came across on his day, lingering awhile on those less fortunate. They came from differing backgrounds and points of view, but shared a mutual respect for humanity. The O'Tooles and their families had escaped a life of poverty in Ireland, one of the many who had made the journey for survival. Raised in the same community on the East Coast, they'd fallen in love, marrying as soon as was allowed, then moved West, full of plans for their future. Only ever knowing a life of hard labor, they'd saved for a home of their own, the ultimate mark of success which few before them had known. Those who came from where they had were always the tenant and never the landlord. The O'Tooles wanted more out of life.

Mrs. O'Toole had a quiet acceptance at not being able to procreate; it was God's will. Instead of children of their own, they filled their home with young immigrant men in search of a roof over their head and a hot meal on their table. These young men received far more than their weekly rent could have ever subsidized, receiving the care of the O'Tooles as a parent would cherish a son.

Mrs. O'Toole had found her calling—the spiritual welfare of these boys who needed to be guided and protected from debauchery. God forbid those innocent young men would end up on Irish Hill—not on her watch would any of her boys get mixed up in that den of iniquity. Filthy, noisy, polluted, filled with nothing but prostitution, gambling, and barroom brawls. "You go up on Irish Hill after work, and you won't see the light of day till morn," she'd warn them. She knew the drill, having grown up with the people who ran these boarding houses, saloons, and so-called hotels. All were drawn to the darker side of the greed to make money out of another man's misery.

Her father had been their best customer. He rarely had the time or the clarity of mind for work and when he did, what little money he earned spiraled him back into the same cycle of drinking. Her mother quietly accepted her lot. Her children always asked her, "Why would you marry such an eejit? Why did you ever have children, and him barely able to mind himself?"

Her mother, weary with it all, would tell how it hadn't always been that way, that her father had once had dreams too. But what hope did he have, coming from a long line of drinkers? She'd taken her marriage vows seriously and the duty of bearing him children. Only once had she alluded to the fact that it was far from in love that each child had been conceived. Alcohol was his priority, and driven by rage, fury, and abuse, they had all been at the receiving end of his tirades. Then the melancholy would set in, and he would spend days, weeks, months in the bed, grumbling and barking orders at their mother, calling her a "good-for-nothing whore." It was just how it was and always had been and sure they were no different to most.

At times Mrs. O'Toole would get to talking and there would be no stopping her. Telling of how she'd navigated play time with her friends in a constant state of high alert, anxiously awaiting her father to appear staggering around the corner, she'd make up a game of hide and seek until she knew the coast was clear. Some days he came home happy and would sing and dance with their mother, twirling her around the kitchen telling of his great love for her, trying to kiss her. She would pull away and tell him to "Stop acting the eejit."

She loved him. "In sickness and in health" was her response when the children challenged her for putting up with him. That, and how he would never look at another woman, made up for staying in a loveless, abusive marriage.

"Sure, who else would have him?" they would say. "There isn't a woman in the land that would put up with his shite." They all left, one after the other, falling into the same cycle of life in which they'd been reared. But not Mrs. O'Toole. She swore to herself that even if he was the last man on earth, she would never marry a drinker or a fool.

She wanted a man that would be her version of what a father should be—kind and gentle, guiding his family, providing food on their table and a roof over their head.

Mr. O'Toole's childhood was no different; he just did not talk about it. As they became young adults they'd found solace in each other's troubles, vowing to never bring any child into this world to have to experience what they had in their young lives. They talked only of how it could be, of how they would make it their duty and honor to raise children in a home that they owned, a home that did not embody all that was Irish Hill. But the Lord worked in mysterious ways. Never having children to call their own, they created a home for these young immigrant men with all the qualities they had dreamed of.

James listened to their talk of the olden days and how hard it was for the Irish who had left behind the only life they had known to continue to simply exist in this world, no ability to consider a future. There were the few who had the foresight to create a different life, one which took absolute belief and a resilience for whatever challenges came their way. Those were the Irish who had risen through the ranks to make a name for themselves, not always a good name, mind you, at times lured by the corruption that often comes with acquiring wealth. "You can't buy class," Mrs. O'Toole would say. New money often brought with it a kind of vulgarity.

James knew he'd been born into a life of privilege. His challenge was having to leave the home he loved to honor and respect his father's wishes, realizing that nothing could compare to the challenges of the people of this city, most especially the children who, through no fault of their own, succumbed to a life of destitution.

Childhood hardship for him had been the 5 a.m. starts for the cattle–rain, hail, or shine. He managed the store and ran the farm seven days a week, with little time for rest. Having to deal with Agnes's scheming manipulation of their lives without any consideration to their wants, not to mind wishes. But he realized how his hardships paled in comparison to the life the immigrant children in America faced.

James thought of Brigid almost every day and worried that she had not settled in Niagara, as her letters spoke only of Ben and his routine. He had tried to find the words to describe what he saw and how it made him feel, but he knew they would need to see it for themselves before Ben could understand the opportunity. San Francisco was a "Wonder City," with all the discoveries of the modern age laid out before his eyes. It was not his place to ask Brigid how she was coping, nor would he interfere in Ben's plan for their future. But as long as he felt this unease, he could not return home to Ireland—how could he confidently assure his father of his daughter's happiness? That was what he told himself as he continued to settle so happily into this new, albeit temporary, life.

CHAPTER 7

March 21, 1909
Dearest Molly,

I sit here by the water's edge to write you this letter. There is simply nothing quite like it in all the land. You sit there till you see nothing else than that which you have come to see. It is almost as if you were at one with the tumbling river, among the waters as though you belong to them. The cool liquid green rushes down without hesitation before flowing away to the distant eternal ocean. Oh Molly, how I wish you could see this sight—it's like nothing we ever saw in those magazines. So consumed were we with the fashions and the bright lights when there was a natural world of such splendor. To be in the presence of such beauty. They come in their hundreds to see this sight and stay for the day to wander by the water's edge.

Ben is doing splendidly, some eight weeks now at the factory and already on first name terms with the supervisors. Aluminum this, aluminum that—why, I will soon be an expert myself on all things aluminum.

Ben travels by electric streetcar to work. I only use it of a Sunday when Ben is with me. How I would love for you to travel with me on it, observing the fashions and wondering at other's lives and what brought them here, mostly sightseers to witness the water. Their style is just as it was in the magazines. Ben assures me that as soon as he is settled and confident of a steady income, he will take me to one of the ladies stores to choose a new wardrobe for the winter season. We are told the cold is colder than we have ever known—there is even talk of the water in the falls freezing over.

I busy myself with the home and a daily outing to mass, who would have thought! I have met some nice ladies there, if rather grand, who occupy themselves with charitable duties. Not at all like the mass goers back home, for these ladies do seem to actually care.

You might find it strange to know that we are living in a house with others. This is how it is done over here. They stay home all day cooking foods that I am not familiar with, spices on almost everything! I stick to what I know, as it would not do for either of us to be sick. We need to remain in good health for the excitements that are sure to come our way.

Please tell Father we are very happy here, and as for Agnes, you can let her know that our life is as prosperous as we had hoped. I think of you almost every day and knowing that you are thinking of us is a great comfort.

Your fond cousin Brigid.

Brigid found it exhausting keeping a tone of enchantment that was not quite congruent with how she felt. She told herself that this too shall pass and before long she would be going about her days with the very same fervor and excitement of the other ladies, integral to society and most of all to Ben. He had the patience of a saint when it came to allaying her fears, dearest Ben, trying so hard to help fill her days, unaware that trying to educate her on the workings of the aluminum factory was not quite what excited her. It was knowing they may take a trip to one of the grand hotels where she would be a match for any of the ladies or attend the parties and balls which she longed for them to be invited to that kept her spirits up.

In preparation for these outings, Brigid sought the advice of her new friend, Mrs. Loretta Hosford, wife of the esteemed Professor Ernest

Hosford, who by all accounts had mastered the art of introduction and kindly offered her services to Brigid.

Lady Harriet had given Brigid a parting gift of a book *Manners for Women* by a Mrs. Hopkins, which Brigid had earnestly studied.

> *Chapter 1: The Girl in Society—Learning to Laugh.*
>
> *There are many reasons why the careful culture of the laugh should be attended to and the theater is the very best place to study the matter when an amusing piece is being played. Look around at your neighbors in the stalls and see how many of them know how to indulge themselves in the expression of their mirth. For every one whose laughter is melodious, there will be found a dozen who merely grin and half a dozen whose sole relief is in physical contortion, bending forward, folding themselves almost double. Cachinnations in every key resound on all sides, varying from the shrill and attenuated "He! He!" to the double chuckle 'Ho! Ho!' fired off like postmen's knocks, at tremendous speed so as to be ready, decks cleared for the next joke. Cackling suggestive of the farmyard, and snorts not unreminiscent of pig-style variety. As to the grins, very few of them can be, in the remotest sense of the word, described as pleasing. Pretty teeth may redeem some of them from absolute ignominy, but, as a rule the exhibition of whole meadows of pale pink gum is inconsonant with one's ideas of beauty.*

Brigid wondered how Mrs. Hopkins would survive the American ladies with their loud and rambunctious ways, as not a day passed when Brigid did not hear many such laughs. The objective, to master a ripple of silvery notes so as to make the person who evokes it feel pleased with oneself, all felt quite ridiculous as Brigid sat in their cozy two-roomed lodgings—it was not exactly London High Society. Brigid assumed that Lady Harriet felt the need to impart this information to her in the knowledge that she could never have known such etiquette.

Loretta was not to be deterred, delighting in her captive audience.

"How very exciting, Brigid. So wonderful to have a new lady join us at church. I do so enjoy my role in understanding the relative position of our congregation and the art of bringing everyone pleasantly together. As you are new to both myself and indeed this town, it is important that I understand your experience and maybe assist a little and share my expertise. Do let's begin. So, to introductions, when to, how to, and when not to. They are, of course, necessary at a dinner party, or in the case of a house guest and should always be made at a dance. Introductions are distinctly desirable on 'at home' days. A popular hostess, such as I, is always one who introduces a good deal. Everyone wants to know Mr. Somebody, but Mr. Somebody will not thank you for bringing along Mr. Nobody. Supposing Mr. Nobody says to you, 'Will you introduce me to Mr. Somebody?' If the reply is in the negative, you must manage to evaporate in the crowd and avoid Mr. Nobody."

Brigid was confused and hoped that they would never be considered Mr. Nobodys and subject to such embarrassment as would warrant all of this fuss.

"Now Brigid, I see you are distracted, and one might think how to introduce ought to be simple, and it very well might be if people would only recollect one rule—always present the inferior to the superior, introduce the commoner to the person of rank, the unmarried to the married, and above all things, the gentleman to the lady. It is an unpardonable error to say 'May I introduce Miss Dash to Mr. Blank,' or as some girls say 'When I was introduced to him!' I do not know why people are so apt to become incoherent when they introduce, but I fancy the uncertainty to which name to place first may have something to do with it. If the introduction is not to be a fiasco, one must ensure there is no element of nervousness into what ought to be done in the most easy and natural way in the world," said Loretta with a tone of delight.

Brigid's enthusiasm was waning. She was tired, and her head was starting to ache. Loretta was in her element. With no sign of stopping, she prattled on.

"Now to cards, the etiquette of the visiting card. You might think it should be simple, but it is often misunderstood. The card must be a thin white piece of pasteboard, absolutely plain, without border or ornament of any kind. Your name occupies the center and is always in copperplate italic characters. In making a call, the visitor—that's you, Brigid for you surely will not be receiving people to your current lodgings—will not send in the card if your acquaintance is at home, but only leave it on departure or if your friend is out. Most importantly, as a married woman you should at all times leave two of your husband's cards, with one of your own. Of the two, one is meant for the lady called upon and the other for her husband. If the lady called upon is unmarried or a widow, then be sure to leave only one of Ben's cards," said Loretta.

After two hours of Loretta's incessant instructions, Brigid was exhausted.

"As to dress, a lot of our women dress irrationally, and I admit it fully and completely. Our menfolk lecture about it and even Father O'Brien himself has been known to comment. I can assure them for every point they bring against it I could tell them four or five more. I am sure you will agree that it would not do for Ben to consider you dowdy and not want to escort you to your pet restaurant or to the theater or dare I say to church. They really are so sensitive to public opinion. Dearest Ernest always compliments my attire, almost every day. Why Brigid, you will see before you now how I myself go about such matters, and I trust it is pleasing even to your uneducated eye. To conclude, and while I in no small way wish to offend, I feel it is incumbent upon me to get straight to the point: There is intense vulgarity in those loud colors and glaring styles that you love to wear. They may have been popular in your home country. However, and quite simply, they will not do for our sophisticated society, and I implore you to dispose of them. Now, I really must be off, as I do have a number of other engagements—such is the demand of my presence." With that, Loretta's work was done for that day.

Good riddance and not a moment too soon. That was beyond exhausting and too much for Brigid's "uneducated palate." Calling her dress vulgar, her style glaring—Brigid had never heard the likes of it in all her days. Brigid decided she would be sticking only to Mrs. Hopkins for her advice from now on.

Brigid was excited, as she had bought a new cover for their bed from one of the curious Native women who sat by the water's edge. She liked to stand silently by their stalls, for they did not speak her language, watching as these women, with heads bent, created the most wonderful items for the tourists who sought out their wares. Knowing Ben would be anxious at her spending, she justified the purchase. Surely, he would not deny her this one item? She simply could not go another day looking at their spartan rooms so desperately in need of a little comfort. All this talk of "conspicuous consumption" had filled his head with needless worry that she would become a leisured lady spending his money.

They would be moving soon to be closer to Ben's place of work, where only English would be spoken. This would be easier for Brigid, as maybe then she would make some friends to go about with on a fine day. It had started to get cold, and Brigid's clothes were not suitable. She had one good coat, which was perfectly fine on a cold day in Ireland, but it felt like she had no coat at all when the wind howled and the icy froth of the water blew in.

James's letters to Brigid were sparse, telling only of the wonders of the West and asking them to consider moving their life there. Ben had no wish for his encouragement—they were doing just fine in Niagara. It had been difficult having to mislead their father and she hoped it would not be a worry for too much longer, as James would surely be returning home soon. Brigid would write and tell him to make sure to allow adequate time to visit with them in Niagara, for those at home would surely want to know all about the place, anxiously awaiting his news.

Ben was daunted by the prospect of a big city like San Francisco, with all the modernizations of the day. He was not one for flamboyance, a "steady pair of hands," as his father would say. The toll he put on his shoulders was immense, and Brigid knew that he worried about their future and how he would continue to provide for them and, in time, their family. Not just to have a roof over their head or food on the table. No, Ben was keenly aware that Brigid had come from a family of means and berated himself that she deserved a life at least equal to that which she'd been born into. It had not been lost on him, the mumblings that she had married beneath herself and that he had made a match above his station.

No matter how hard Brigid tried to allay his fears, it was there, deep-rooted, manifesting in his absolute determination to prove them all wrong. He was not for changing. Brigid loved him and knew he cared for her like no other, knowing only tenderness. There was no other man in the land for whom she would give her affection. He had always believed in her, and they would be together for all of eternity. Ben understood and embraced the wildness in her that had been drawn to the uncertainty of America.

CHAPTER 8

October 25, 1909
Dearest James,

Thank you for your concern for our welfare and your continued desire for us to travel West. Please be assured that Ben is building a more than agreeable life for us here. We are quite settled and have moved into new lodgings. Our life is moving along splendidly.

Father would be happy to know that we are building a good life and that I am helping those less fortunate through my charitable work at the church. For now, we no longer wish to hear of the West country, as we are happy and settled.

Please do let us know if you have made plans to return home. I have some items I would like for you to take with you which I know will be of great interest to those in Moling.

Your loving sister, Brigid.

Well, that was the end of that. A little perturbed by Brigid's tone in her reply, it had never been James's intention to overstep the mark. All he had ever wanted was for them to know of a life that could offer them far more than any other city in the land. How could James consider going home when he knew that Brigid may need his support should they change their mind? It would be selfish of him to return, for when he did, it would be with a heart full of experience and none of regret.

James never took for granted waking to the shining sun in the bluest of skies, Mrs. O'Toole singing away, preparing and providing a solid breakfast for her men. He took pleasure in being the first to the table to observe her in preparation of her day. "The devil is in the detail," she'd say, as she set the table with freshly baked bread and freshly squeezed orange juice in the smallest of glasses—a mouthful was all that was required to give the zest of energy. It was heartening to see such effort and love in menial tasks; taking pride in one's table was not quite what James had known. To Agnes, the table was merely a means to provide sustenance, and eating in silence was important to aid with digestion. If that was true, then how these young men could digest their food with the quick-fire round of questions from Mrs. O'Toole as she barely drew a breath was beyond James—there was never any doubt about who the boss was under this roof. Mrs. O'Toole had her favorites who would be relieved of her questioning, sitting back to take in the enjoyment as the others navigated explaining where exactly they spent their free time without alluding to their trips to "Irish Hill."

House rules meant that the *Catholic Monitor* was the only source of news allowed to cross the threshold. Monday evening dinner brought a review of the latest edition. Mrs. O'Toole concerned herself with all that was wrong in the world while Mr. O'Toole would regale with the latest round of "Answers for Askers," wondering at how these people had the inclination to write such questions, not to mention the poor unfortunates who had to read them.

> *Question: Is it a vocation in life for a girl to keep house for a priest?*
>
> *Answer: Vocation! No. Vocation is either to the religious life or to life in the world. When one's vocation is settled for life in the world, it can hardly call its various professions, trades, and occupations a vocation. We do not speak of a girl's vocation to the telephone exchange, or to the stage, or to hat-making. Keeping house for a priest is neither more nor less than a job—a job hedged by many necessary qualifications.*

James knew Brigid would enjoy this one, which had caused the greatest of surprise that it ever made it to print:

> *Question: Rich Priests and Poor People—How is it that Bishops live in such luxury and leave thousands behind them when they die?*
>
> *Answer: The answer to the latter half of the question is of course quite clear—because they can't take their thousands with them.*
>
> *Bishops are spiritual princes of the church and must live in a manner becoming of their state, and as a matter of fact nearly all of their wealth comes to them from personal inheritance, or from the generosity of faithful Catholics who never complain of luxury or ask "How is it that bishops live in such luxury?" They leave that croaking to those who give very little. They have nothing more than enough to eat and wear and defray their official expenses, and many of them have a very poor living at that, the most simple, saintly, and abstemious of men.*

Mr. O'Toole was good at picking the ones he knew would cause a stir and a clip around the ear from Mrs. O'Toole, who would soon put a stop to the shenanigans.

⁂

As James strolled past Nobby Clarke's folly at the top of the road—the turrets, the balconies, the stained glass, and the ornate double front doors a feast for the eyes in all its glory–he was never quite sure if it was the building or the history that intrigued him most. Alfred E. Clarke, a fellow Irishman, had traveled in search of his fortune in the gold rush of 1850. The tales differ depending on whom you listened to, those who knew him or those who only knew of him. James liked to believe that he was a good man who'd fought for justice, and there was little doubt as to Clarke's resilience and desire. Having not found his fortune in gold, he found work as a patrolman with the police force in the city, where it is believed he got his nickname. During an altercation, a seaman bit his hand so badly he was called "Nobby" thereafter, being the Irish way to make humor out of another man's misery. Becoming a clerk to the chief of police, Clarke began a side business lending money to patrolmen, and the real money started to roll in—not for long though, as he was found out and removed from his position. He went on to study law and, passing his bar exams, returned to the police department in 1870 as the chief legal adviser. Nobby had found his calling—he loved the lure of the courts, and the stories were legendary of his near daily appearances. He had a fondness for filing cases against the police commission, who he said were persons with "evil eyes, depraved minds, and abandoned hearts."

Mrs. O'Toole knew him and spoke of how he and his wife were founding members of the Calvary Presbyterian Church, and for a time he had served as its deacon. He had also set up a widows and orphans aid when he was in the police department and took an active role in many other opportunities where he saw others had been overlooked or ill used by the system.

James was impressed at how this great house would be there for many years to come to forever keep this Irishman's memory alive. No one had understood why he had built his masterpiece in such a remote location, knowing his wife would never leave her sophisticated life in Nob Hill to move to the "uncivilized" countryside. Not everyone was happy to see it, or Nobby, coming to the area, and plenty of eyewitness accounts circulated about his fist fights with his neighbor, Mr. Joost, right there on Caselli Avenue. Two great men with everything a man could want in life, and they just could not get past their egos and downright pure thickness. Caught up in hatred, they lost sight of all else, and it was to be Nobby's downfall, for he lost sight of his business.

All that remained was this fine house to show for his courage, nerve, and high spirits when Nobby Clarke had landed all those years ago in search of his fortune. They say he either died a gnarled, contentious person of uncouth physique or a genial man with a tufted beard and broad shoulders. James was sure the truth lay somewhere in between. Quite possibly it was the dream that had killed him; it had certainly cost him his fortune. He did all he could to save the house, but it was all in vain and it was lost to him forever. A medical college bought it, as no one family could possibly afford to reside in it. Mrs. O'Toole would not allow any talk of the funny business that they called "eclectic medicine" that had been practiced there and was delighted when she saw that it was being remodeled into apartments.

"More money than sense, they have, trying to right themselves of all their evils. Eclectic medicine—a bunch of aul weeds if you ask me," said Mrs. O'Toole.

Mrs. O'Toole regularly tried to convince James to take up one of the nice office jobs advertised in the *Monitor*. Working behind a desk was not for him. He would only be in San Francisco for a short while and wanted to make the most of the experience by meeting with new people, hearing their stories, and learning about their ways of life, all the while telling himself it was research for Ben and Brigid.

James had no desire to live with the hordes of Irish who were crowding the downtown area, happy with the O'Tooles in the relative peace and quiet of the countryside, which seemed to him a link to home. The three-and-a-half-mile walk each way from Caselli Avenue was the highlight of his day. He changed his route as he meandered the streets, learning and discovering with every step. The landscape was ever-changing, the pace frantic, the hustle and bustle of the city palpable.

Waiting for him on his nightstand as he arrived home from his work would be cutouts from the paper of articles entitled "Grand Gaelic Ball will be held Thursday evening at the Auditorium on Page and Fillmore Streets. General Admission 50 cents" and the like. Placed there with the best of intentions by Mrs. O'Toole, he knew she wanted him to meet people of his own age, but how could he make her understand it was not for him. He was perfectly happy with the two of them for his company. He had no interest in the wild ways of the Irish he worked with, or their talk of the saloons and the women that frequented them. James never took part in those conversations and knew they talked about him, questioning how he could call himself a real man with no want to have the most "basic" of man's needs met. He did not care for their rough language and brutish talk of women. Happily, he kept to himself, enjoying the customers and their journeys to the places he would never see.

One notice, however, did capture his interest:

> *On Sunday April 25th, the members of the Society of St. Vincent De Paul will assemble at the Holy Cross Church (Eddy and Scott Streets) at 3 o'clock. The second general meeting of the Society for the year will be held at Holy Cross Hall, adjoining the church. This is the first visit of the Vincentians to Holy Cross Parish. A large attendance of members will not only be an encouragement to the local conference, but in all probability will be also an incentive to many of the parishioners to become members.*

This was the name James had heard over and over from the poor unfortunates he met on the streets, the kindly people they spoke of who gave them food and clothing. Their mission was to simply "assist those who need the help most." James had been raised by his father to always remember "there but for the grace of God go I," and to never forget anyone could find themselves in a time of need through no fault of their own. James had a sense this would be a better use of his time.

CHAPTER 9

Patrick read aloud a letter from Brigid over their Sunday dinner, knowing at some level her sister and brother must be curious. Thomas had never inquired, and Kate was always preoccupied with something or other.

> *May 10, 1910*
> *Dearest Father,*
>
> *I do hope that this letter finds you in good health. I think of you all often and pray that the good Lord above is watching over you. You need not worry, Father, for Ben is taking very good care of me and is working hard to build a good life for us. Ben has been promoted to supervisor at the factory, and his increase in wages has allowed us to move sooner than we had expected. We now have the upstairs of a wooden two-story house which is very modern, sharing the bathroom with the young couple who own the house and live downstairs. It is usual over here for people to have tenants live with them and help pay for the build of their homes and the upkeep of what they call the plot.*
>
> *Most exciting of all is that at the end of the road, only two houses away, is the most spectacular view of the river. The sheer drop is much like a cliff edge, and I never venture too close, Father, so you need not worry. We are living at the edge of the town and there are green fields all around us. The house is made of wood and has a red tile roof, with windows on three*

sides to allow for the cool breeze in the heat of the summer. I busy myself with keeping our home and meeting with the ladies of the church, all of whom have been helpful and kind. The food is different over here in the store (their name for a shop). They sell a lot of food in tins, but I prefer to stick to fresh vegetables and meat direct from the farmers. We have a weekly market, and but for the people speaking with different accents and the sun shining a lot hotter, I could think I am at home with you on market day. I meet the nicest of people who are eager to talk when they know that I speak English and am from Ireland. There are not quite as many of us in these parts, and we appear to be somewhat of a curiosity. Heavens knows why, but it is quite fun.

There is so much of interest to see. Just this last week I visited the Niagara Falls Museum with the ladies from St. Mary's to discover the curiosities that are kept there. A calf born with two heads and three legs coming out of its back, on view in the "deformity exhibition," I found to be very unsettling. The people here do seem to enjoy a curiosity. Apparently there is money to be made in such things. It is not encouraged or indeed discussed by most.

James is doing well, and I will leave him to tell of his own news. Please do give my love to all and to those that ask after us. We are doing splendidly as we continue to build our life here. I will be sure to keep you all in my prayers and will write again soon.

Your loving daughter, Brigid

Patrick thought about James. He had only written the one letter telling of his safe arrival and no more. To break the silence Patrick spoke to the table, "Ben has been true to his word, working hard and taking good care of our Brigid. By all accounts they are settling in well to their new life."

No response came.

"It will soon be time for James to return home," said Patrick.

Agnes tutted and Thomas lowered his head. Kate, who was home for the day, sat motionless in her all-too-frequent state of melancholy. Patrick left it at that and said no more. It would be best to have James home, as there was too much work for himself and Thomas, and he knew that James had left with a heavy heart and must be eager to return. His lack of news said it all. Thomas was a hard worker, but he just did not have the same way with the customers as James. It was time now for James to return.

Thomas was raging as he listened to his father read Brigid's letter. Isn't it well for them—living the high life and him working morning, noon, and night. And to think that it was all for James as the eldest son. Thomas would not benefit in the fruits of his own hard labor. Did his father really think that he would sit there and listen to him talk of James needing to return to his rightful place? He was no fool. He knew they looked at him with pity, as just the "boy about the place," keeping it afloat for the brother.

"How is the main man himself? Won't he soon be coming back here with great ideas, and we will all be the better for it," said Biddy O'Connor at every opportunity.

She just loved to rub Thomas's nose in it, loved watching him turn away thinking it was in despair when it was to stop himself from telling her what he really thought of her and her incessant gossip. He had no one to confide in and wished that Kate could think to ask how he was. If only she could see what it must be like waiting for the son and heir to return. It was okay for her, off enjoying herself in town, no doubt soon to be married off to a suitably prosperous farmer with a family of her own. Although, with Agnes interfering it might be a while yet. Kate was showing little interest in the men that had been lined up for her. God only knew what she was getting up to in the town. Kate didn't like to talk much—she never had.

Lady Harriet was curious as to how that nice young girl Brigid was getting along. She missed their talks, as life was mostly rather dull at Wells House. They had their Saturday to Monday guests and those from further afield that always overstayed were usually a bore. Listening to their chatter about London and Europe, Lady Harriet had little knowledge as to who these people were and could never quite get in on the spirit of it. They thrived on the misfortune of others and liked to call it the "art of conversation." She called it as it was—gossip.

Charles had his gentlemen's club in Dublin and in St. James in London. Keenly aware of Harriet and her sensitivities to the locals, he'd encouraged her to pop over to Moling when she was next out riding. "You seem rather taken by this young Kelly girl, whose family are the finest of people known by all at Wells House for their honest dealings. Perhaps you should pay the family a visit, dear."

Dearest Charles, always considerate and worrying that she would find life in Wells House too dull, inquired as to news of her day, entertained by her impatience with society. He never bored of her stories and loved Harriet for what he called "her spirit," that and taking no nonsense. A kind man, considerate and tolerant, he was quite unlike the pompous lords in his circle, born into this way of life and never knowing of any other until she had come along and shown him how to live with a greater respect for others outside of his gilded world. He even stood up to his sisters when they clicked their tongues at Harriet's fraternizing with the locals. She never bowed to their rules. She found she discovered far more about the Irish ways of life by speaking with and taking time to understand all those she came into contact with, rich or poor. She saw everyone as her teacher.

Lady Harriet rode out the next morning with the stable boy leading the way. Arriving at the prettiest of villages, the Kelly shopfront came into view. The sound of the bell on the shop door announced her arrival. The shop was empty, and Lady Harriet was surprised that there was no one to welcome a customer as she rattled the bell on the door for attention.

"All right, all right. I am coming! What in the name of God is your hurry?" shouted Agnes from the storeroom, her displeasure at having a customer apparent.

Lady Harriet smiled; it was not difficult to make out who this brusque woman must be. "My good lady, I am here to inquire after Mrs. Brigid McCarthy. To whom am I speaking?"

There was no reply from a stuttering Agnes.

"Forgive me if I have startled you, I do not wish to interrupt your day. I wish only for word of Mrs. McCarthy."

"Yes, yes, of course, milady," Agnes sputtered. "Why, you must come into the parlor and take the weight off your feet. Let me get you some refreshments."

"No, no, no need for all that. I am perfectly fine as I am."

"I insist, I won't have it said that you did not take the tea." Agnes was not about to pass up an opportunity.

"I appreciate your kind offer. I have no desire to linger, as I am merely passing. I wish only for news of Brigid," said Lady Harriet, walking toward the door.

"Oh yes, yes, our dearest Brigid. She is doing fine, just fine. Settled herself in very well. Such a sweet girl—never forgets to write to her dear father."

"And where has she settled in well?"

"A village outside of the city of New York, a Niagara Falls. Would you know of the place?"

"Why yes, I have visited many times. How interesting, and do you know what takes her there?"

"Ben has secured a job there—a supervisor no less," said Agnes, cocking her head with pride.

"Interesting. Do please tell Brigid that I was asking after her and hoping she might find time to write," said Lady Harriet, turning on her heel.

"Of course, of course, milady. Why, I will write to her myself this very day. So very kind of you to think of her and to visit our village. What an honor it is for us to be graced with your presence."

"The pleasure has been all mine, Mrs. Kelly, I can assure you. Brigid is a fine young lady. You must be very proud of her."

"Why, thank you, milady. I made it my life's vocation to rear those poor children after the untimely passing of their dear departed mother."

"You did a fine job, Mrs. Kelly. A fine job."

Agnes was beaming, where was Biddy O'Connor when you wanted her? Who would believe that Lady Harriet Doyne herself had graced them with her presence.

"Let me hold the door for you, milady. And do take some fruit for your horse—an apple maybe," said Agnes, rushing out the door behind her.

Lady Harriet wondered why the woman kept shouting her name repeatedly. Was she trying to disturb the entire village?

That was indeed Agnes's plan.

CHAPTER 10

"Molly, Molly, where is your mother? Oh, my goodness, where in God's name is she? I need to sit down. Pull over a chair, for my legs can't carry me," said Agnes, collapsing into the kitchen chair.

"Agnes, Agnes, what is it? You are white as a ghost," said Molly, worried that Agnes was taking a turn.

"Oh, dearest Lord in heaven above. She was like a vision before my very eyes." Agnes was now lying back in the chair with her arm across her forehead.

"Who, Agnes? Who was, what are you talking about?"

"The Lady Doyne herself. She walked right into the shop this very morning, not ten minutes ago. Put the heart across me, never have I been so close to a lady in all my days. The smell of her, all perfumed, and the beauty of her face. Asking after Brigid, she was. Imagine, of all people, and she came to see our Brigid. I let her know in no uncertain terms that it was all my doing. Yes, it was me who made her into who she is. If it was not for me, she would have ended up in a home," said Agnes, all shock gone, now sitting up and shaking her finger.

Molly had to turn away and do all in her power not to speak out at such untruths, as her mother would never forgive her for being rude to Agnes. Everyone knew she was a miserable, interfering old witch, but no one ever said as much. Patrick was held in high regard, and it was for him they kept the peace with Agnes.

Molly's mother made Agnes a cup of tea with lots of sugar in it to calm her down. They would never hear the end of it. Goodness, Molly thought, Brigid wouldn't believe it either. She won't believe that Lady

Doyne took the time to visit and ask after her. Molly thought about how she had delivered those telegrams after Brigid left and hadn't received so much as a nod of the head from the great lady. No, Lady Doyne had no interest in chatting with Molly or sharing her stories. She'd had the same dreams as Brigid, but she'd given up on them and Brigid never had. But she accepted her lot, knowing she'd been blessed with a good man by her side, a doctor just like her father, and the kindest of men who took good care of them all. Molly had not a minute spare in the day, what with looking after her mother and father and now a baby. There was little time for reminiscing.

Molly told herself that if Brigid was still there, it would never be the same anyway. The frivolous hours they had spent together, those days would be no more. Molly missed Brigid fiercely. She missed her sense of fun and her confidence and knew there was never any doubt that Brigid would leave the village in search of glitz and glamour, living the life of both their dreams. God willing, someday they would both have daughters who would share the friendship they had treasured in their youth.

Kate couldn't make up for the loss of Brigid—or rather, she didn't want to. She had always been quiet in herself, lost to her thoughts. It was impossible to know what went on in her head. Brigid had always been the star in the Kelly house, and it had been easy for Kate to disappear. Molly had hoped when Brigid first left that maybe Kate would have an opportunity to come out of her shadow. She tried to get closer to Kate, inviting her to the dances, out for walks, a trip to town, but every effort was rebuffed. She never held it against her; Kate had always preferred to be alone. Molly guessed she was not going to change her ways now.

Molly had heard Uncle Patrick chatting with her mother and asking her advice as to what they would ever do with poor Kate and how she would not have any talk of returning home to Moling even though she'd long outgrown her time at the bakery. Patrick retreated every time it came up for discussion. Agnes would berate Kate, telling her to not be outstaying her welcome in Wexford and that it was time for her to be settling down. Kate showed no interest in Agnes's advice or her father's wishes. She became more elusive about her life in Wexford and started limiting her visits home.

Agnes complained, of course, telling anyone that would listen that it was time for Kate to settle down. Poor Kate was like a slave to Agnes. Maybe she was better off out of it. Molly's thoughts soon turned to the excitement of James's imminent return. Patrick's decision had been final. Brigid and Ben were settled and making a life for themselves, so there was no longer any need for James to stay in America. James's place was at home and these last few years had taken their toll on all of them. Well, that's what they said, but Molly had a sense there was more to it. She had overheard hushed conversations, something about talk coming from Wexford that Kate was causing a fuss. That and the immediacy of James's return. Patrick had paid for a first-class passage, some twenty-seven pounds, a small fortune.

Patrick was like a new man now that the decision had been made and the fare paid for. He would have his James back by his and Thomas's side. Thomas could do with the help, as he had never shown quite the same interest in the place. If Patrick did not know any better, he would think it was because Thomas knew the place would not be his. Patrick did not like to think of such things, but Agnes was all the time putting these thoughts into his head, and he had begun to think maybe there was some truth in it. Patrick would always be the shopkeeper as long as he was able, with his sons by his side. All three of them could share the farm duties and, God willing, Kate would settle down and return to make a home of her own.

Agnes had given up long ago in her quest to find Kate a suitable match. Paudie O'Leary had come once for dinner after Sunday mass and Kate had not as much as looked at him. There she sat, head bowed with no sign of it lifting and poor Paudie doing his best. Agnes could not contain her rage. "She is twenty years of age now, at her prime, and if she doesn't start to show some interest, she'll be left on the shelf.

She had better settle herself and start a family of her own. She was a very lucky young lady that she has a queue of potential suitors only too happy to marry into the Kelly family." That was what Agnes told everyone and what Patrick had told himself.

Thomas was forlorn, it would only be a matter of time before the prodigal son returned, and on a first-class passage, no less. Father must have put the money aside, as surely he had kept that outlay from Agnes. She would never approve of such extravagance. And there was Thomas, taking a meager wage, abiding by the belief that the profits had to be kept in the business for that rainy day that never came. He had no one to blame but himself. James had not asked to leave; none of this was of his own doing. It was hard not to despair of the situation in which he found himself, with nothing but love for this place. Every inch of it carried a sense of their mother, who'd given her life for him to enter this world. Surely, he could be content with his position. He may never have a home to bring in a wife or raise a family, but he would always have a roof over his head and work he could busy himself with. James was a good man and would see right was done by him. Kate would marry and it would be one less worry for their father. Agnes was showing no sign of retiring, and as long as she was alive, she would always be the mistress of the home.

Agnes had been preoccupied with the visit from Lady Doyne. No doubt her letter to Brigid would recall every moment of the visit, which would not be a challenge for her, as she had spoken of little else. She had been the first to mass the next morning after the "royal" visit, standing at the door of the church. Not a parishioner passed without hearing how Lady Doyne had graced the Kelly shop with her presence. All and sundry that came by the shop were regaled with exactly where Lady Doyne had stood, how she'd spoken, what she'd worn, how she'd held herself and her praise for Brigid, yes, Brigid, with whom she was so taken that she'd ridden all the way over to ask after her. It had been a cause for great excitement and much delight except for Biddy O'Connor, who had been too busy to stay and chat.

Brigid was to receive letters from half the village with varying accounts of the visit. It was, of course, Agnes's letter which had a singular view.

> *August 18, 1910*
> *Brigid,*
>
> *We had a visit from Lady Doyne of Wells House, who you may recall was rather taken with you. I made my feelings clear to you at the time, and of course you should have heeded my advice. You should never have left this village. Be in no doubt that had you stayed you would be a lady's maid now, mixing in circles fitting of a Kelly daughter. Lady Doyne as good as said so. She had great plans for you, Brigid, saw the potential in you, could see all the fruits of your fine rearing at my behest. All those years I put into showing you how to flourish as a young lady and now the mortification of it all. Not a word could I utter in your defense—the height of ignorance, you up and leaving, not to mention marrying a man of no means. Lady Doyne, of course, was too polite to say it out straight, but I know what she was thinking. The shame of it. You are the talk of the place. The Lady had to come over to see for herself what kind of people we were to rear such a girl. You have made your bed, and now you may lie in it. I have spared your father the knowledge of this letter, so there will be no need to be bothering him with your whinging. There is no more to be said on the matter. You may live out your days in the knowledge of the shame in which you have brought upon your family.*
>
> *Mrs. Agnes Kelly*

Not so much as a "Dear Brigid." The very first letter Agnes had penned since Brigid's departure, and it was to berate her and take pleasure in doing so. There it was. Brigid had always guessed as much—Lady Harriet had frowned upon her match. All that talk of the importance of a good man and how it accounted for everything, how one could be assured of a life of ease if the demeanor was in order. The endless chatter about love and how horrified Lady Harriet had been when Brigid had told her of Agnes's advice, "When the bills come in, the love goes out the window." Lady Harriet had referred to how she could not quite understand a man that would marry without having a suitable source of income, which Brigid had taken as irrelevant, as Lady Harriet was from far greater means than Brigid could have ever known. Why else would Lord Doyne have sought her out for marriage?

Brigid was devastated by this news, feeling foolish for ever thinking she was anything more than an experiment, a source of entertainment. She was relieved that she had never called upon any of Lady Harriet's introductions to New York society, as she was sure to have been taken pity upon, more fodder for their amusement. Molly had been far too gentle not to allude to any of this in her letter, with only kindness in her words and pride for the excitement of the visit.

Frustrated after Agnes's letter, Brigid thought good riddance to the small-mindedness of her old life. She may have been fooled by Lady Harriet, but she had no regrets. Every moment spent at Wells House had inspired her to believe in her dream that there was a new life awaiting her, a life that she could truly live with experiences beyond her wildest of dreams.

Thinking of her father, it pained her to know that he hung his head in shame, a shame that she had brought upon him. She'd had to leave, and Ben was her way out of that life—kind, good-hearted Ben, a man who had only ever known love and adoration for all that she was. He must not ever see these vile words that so cruelly belittled and ridiculed him. From that very first moment when Brigid had confided in him, he never once made her feel foolish. He, too, had a dream, a dream he had not thought possible, a dream he would never have lived if not for her. Brigid took solace that she was free of their cruel way of life, free to truly embrace a life lived to its fullest with far more opportunity for a young lady than the village life into which she had been born.

CHAPTER 11

The O'Tooles asked James to accompany them to see Mrs. Tetrazzini sing for the people of the city on Christmas Eve. They had seen her at the Tivoli before the quake had destroyed the place, and the papers were filled with the news of her visit. It had not been an easy visit to arrange, but Mrs. Tetrazzini had always spoken of her great love for San Francisco and had gone to great lengths to make it happen.

"I will sing in San Francisco if I have to sing there in the streets, for I know the streets of San Francisco are free," the soprano said herself.

James had never been to a live performance, other than the stations of the cross. Not quite sure what to expect, he made sure to show his enthusiasm for the occasion. When the day arrived, they left Caselli Avenue with plenty of time to walk to the city, and as they neared Market Street, thousands were all headed for the makeshift stage that had been set up at Lotta's Fountain, James was mesmerized by the amount of people converging on one place. As the evening closed in and the stars lit up the sky, there was a roar from the crowd, and all heads turned to a window in the Chronicle building. There they could see the outline of a lady who sparkled and waved her handkerchief to the crowds below. The deafening sounds of chatter disappeared to stillness as Mrs. Tetrazzini was introduced on stage.

"My good people of the City of San Francisco, hear me now. You are about to witness how God himself has placed in Mrs. Tetrazzini's golden throat the gushing wells of glorious music and, you will now know something of songs the angels sing," said the master of ceremonies as Mrs. Tetrazzini entered the stage.

Appearing like an apparition sheathed in white, sparkling and glistening at every turn, clasping her hands upon her breast. "Look, my great family! I see everybody my brother, everybody my sister," exclaimed Mrs. Tetrazzini in her melodic Italian tone.

Stretching her gloved hands, she gushed, "My heart, it is so big. Oh, I am so happy."

Mrs. O'Toole had tears in her eyes as Mr. O'Toole smiled and told her to settle herself and not be getting carried away when not a note had been sung. The woman glorious and the throng worshipful, there they stood, listening to every crystal-clear note, every distinct word. Absolute silence, save for her voice, spread over the city like the silence of the night. Streetcars stopped. Horses, wagons, and the few automobiles all stood still. Not a sound came from the usual clanging of the cable car bell, not as much as a murmur from the two hundred and fifty thousand people present. As this great lady sang the last lines of "Auld Lang Syne," all of the city sang with her, and as she finished, the crowd went into a frenzy of clapping with joyful tears streaming and hats and caps flying in all directions. Even Mr. O'Toole's cheeks were wet.

They walked home in silence with joy in their hearts that Christmas Eve, lost to their dreams sprung from the emotion of the great lady's haunting tone. Bathed in peace and serenity, James lay down his head and closed his eyes, wearing the smile of an enriched heart and mind on the eve of the Lord's birthday.

Christmas morning brought the distant ringing of the church bells throughout the city. Mrs. O'Toole started her day without stirring the house. How lovely it was to be part of this home and to share another Christmas in their warmth. A letter and a small parcel sat on the table for James. Mrs. O'Toole said they'd arrived a few weeks back, and she had put them away as a surprise for him to have something to open on the day itself. It was surely not from home, as they were never a family for present giving, a needless luxury in Agnes's eyes. They had a roof over their head and food on their table, what more could they want?

It was a day of quiet reflection and prayer in remembrance of our Lord and in celebration of his birth.

Father always had a stocking for them with some fruit, and he would place a bar of chocolate under their pillows as they slept. He'd give them a knowing look and smile as they came down for breakfast as his way of an acknowledgment. They were no different from others, for few knew of the luxury of gift-giving.

That was before James had come to experience Christmas with the O'Tooles. A gift for everyone lay beneath the tree, wrapped in paper of different colors, decorative boxes, and colored bows. The tree stood in pride of place in the "good" room—only ever allowed in on a Sunday or on special occasions. The lace curtains on the window were opened throughout the month of December for all to see the beauty of the decorated tree. Mrs. O'Toole sure did love Christmas, with preparations in full swing for months in advance. Puddings hanging in the pantry, cakes in the tins ready to be iced, the house cleaned within an inch of itself, not a nook or a cranny escaped. Mr. O'Toole would give out about her fussing, but they all knew he loved Christmas just as much as she did.

"I have the fry on for you now, James. You go and open your parcel by the tree, and I will call you when the food is on the table," said Mrs. O'Toole.

As he opened the parcel, he could see it was from Brigid, with a letter from home enclosed. Brigid had continued to manage his post from home to save any confusion with the addresses. Opening the parcel, he found a pair of socks and a tie. He was disappointed with himself that he had not thought to send Brigid and Ben a gift, but he wouldn't know what to be buying them anyway. Enclosed was a short note wishing him a good Christmas and that she was excited to be seeing him soon. Soon! He was at his wit's end trying to tell them to come out West. Had Ben saved enough for the fare? Maybe, just maybe, they were starting to come around to his way of thinking. Opening the letter from home, he smiled as he saw his father's elegant handwriting.

November 12, 1910
Dear Son,

You are needed to return home. The agent has advised that there are limited travel arrangements available. Enclosed you will find a contract for your return passage departing New York February 14th aboard the Lusitania, Cunard Line. It is a 1st class passage to Liverpool, as this was the earliest available option. God willing, we will await your safe arrival.

Your Father

James read the letter over and over, each time bringing with it a different emotion. Looking through the Christmas tree onto the now familiar street as the sun danced through the holes in the lace, James's mind stood frozen. Had Brigid known of Father's plan? Had she told Father of their arrangement? Or was father unwell, or had perhaps Thomas had an accident? Was it the shop or a failed crop? He had only a matter of weeks to prepare to return to a life all too easily forgotten. James was desperate to contain the torrent of emotions and waves of depression that coursed through him. His mind shook inside his head as if it were about to explode. His heart was heavy as he physically felt the loss before his mind had time to contemplate it.

"Is it a ghost you've seen, James? What at all is the matter with you? Are you still caught up in the magic of Mrs. Tetrazzini? My oh my what a joy she is. We could hardly close our eyes last night not wanting the magic to disappear, only to awake with her sweet tones still ringing in our ears. I hear the others stirring now. We might wait for them to come down before we eat. Won't that be nice, James? All together having our Christmas breakfast. We can share our stories of last night. Don't say a word to Paschal—he doesn't approve of us fraternizing with strangers on the eve of the Lord's birthday, or will we tell him of all that he missed? Surely the Lord would not deny any soul such joy and pleasure celebrating his birthday. Aren't we blessed to have all this on our doorstep, James? Would they ever believe you at home—an Italian Soprano singing for the people of the city in the open air. You must put pen to paper this very eve before the memories escape you. James, are you listening to me at all? What is it outside that window that has you transfixed?" said Mrs. O'Toole as she put down her tea towel and rested a hand on James's shoulder.

"I'm sorry. I was lost in my thoughts. I am listening to you, all right. Yes, it sure was a memory to behold for all of my days. We had better start eating the breakfast, or all your hard work will go to waste. We don't want the food getting cold now, do we?" said James, trying to disguise his frantic thoughts.

"How right you are, James. Let's hurry the others along and enjoy the start of a day of feasting," said Mrs. O'Toole, thinking to herself that maybe he was tired after the late night they'd had in the city.

James hid behind Mrs. O'Toole's constant chattering, needing to process his news before sharing it. It would mean little to the O'Tooles anyway, as they were used to the coming and going of immigrant workers and the transiency of that life. Not that any of it mattered—his father's decision was final. It was his duty to return to support his father and their family in carrying on the Kelly business, passed down through the generations. James had been taught from an early age the honor that had been bestowed upon him. He had never had a moment's hesitation as to where his future lay.

Or maybe it was that he had never known any different.

CHAPTER 12

Brigid was happy and a little relieved that James would be returning home. It gave her a sense of excitement to be truly alone and a sense of comfort to have her father's acceptance. No more sleepless nights, worrying that he would find out about their deception. It would be closure for James too, allowing him to return to his own life.

The O'Tooles were devastated, the news having caught them by surprise. James had become the son they never had. Kind-natured James, tolerant of almost anyone, how could they not have fallen for him and been assured of his presence in their home? He had never caused them a moment's worry, living every day for what it was and no more.

James did not know how he was going to pretend to be happy when he saw Brigid. His heart was heavy, and he did not think he would ever feel a lightness of spirit again as he packed his case with little to show for his two years in this material world. A very different man to the boy who had arrived, he now had a head full of experience and a knowing of another way of living the life of a young man.

Brigid was unable to contain her excitement as she waited for James to arrive. Ben told her to settle herself and not be bothering James with all her questions, all of which fell on deaf ears.

"Oh James, I can hardly believe you are standing here before me!" Brigid said. "I have thought of little else since Father wrote of your return. How I wished I could have seen your face as you read Father's letter. You were surely jumping for joy. I do hope it did not upset the O'Tooles too much to see your happiness. Oh James, you must not worry about me. I have no such wish as you to return home—I am very sure this is where I am to stay for all my days. James, are you listening to me? Oh, I am sorry, Ben warned me not to overwhelm you with my prattling on," she said, taking a breath.

"Can't you see the man is tired? Let him recover himself," Ben chided her as he showed James to his room. "He will need his rest to continue his journey."

James slumped onto the bed, having told them he wanted to freshen up before dinner. He had no need to be assured of Brigid's happiness, or of her having become an integral member of the community, of their outings to the fine hotels, of Ben's progression at the factory, their charitable works, the draw of the curiosities of this place. He didn't want to hear any of this talk, as to his mind there was no finer a place than the city that he had departed. There would never be any other town or city that would hold his heart as did San Francisco.

James would never voice these thoughts, not to the O'Tooles, not to Brigid, and certainly never to his father. That was his way, the only way he knew how to navigate the life for which he had so much to be grateful. Damn any semblance of discord, there was no place for anything other than eternal gratitude for this life where he was honored to carry the Kelly family name.

Brigid later fussed about the kitchen, trying to make everything perfect for James, wanting him to leave with the very best of impressions for those back home. It mattered little to James. Knowing Brigid was happy was enough; outside of that it was for Ben to concern himself with as her husband. James felt sorry that he had only allowed one day to visit. He could see how much it meant to Brigid, wishing he had given more thought to her in all of this. Forcing a smile onto his face, he linked Brigid's arm as they headed out for the famous falls.

Brigid fell into bed exhausted that night. She was thrilled James's visit had been a success. It was obvious that he loved her new home as much as she and Ben did, and he could see the many attractions of the place.

Brigid chatted with Ben after James had gone to his room. "I could sense a longing in him, a longing for home. Moling always held his heart. It was just as well Father wrote to him—and not a moment too soon. He can't wait to be home. He does not have quite the same sparkle in his eye, God love him. It must have been hard out West on his own. Wasn't he so good to do as Father said in the first place and travel with us with not a word of complaint? He will have his rewards. Father is sure to hand him the reins, and maybe in time he will look back fondly on his time here. Time, after all, is a great healer."

◈

James was embarrassed by the fuss made of him upon boarding the ship as the porters shouted, "Make way, make way!" as he was escorted from shore. Not wanting the focus nor the attention, he had no wish to feel superior to any man in the isolation of this gilded life, navigating the top hats and diamonds en route to his cabin. The steward directed James to the elevator, but he indicated he wanted to take the stairs. They passed along the bright corridors of doors, until the steward rested his hand upon a gold handle that opened the door to a sumptuous interior. The cabin was neat in size with two brass cot beds, one on either side. Neither bed had been disturbed, therefore James assumed he was first to arrive. The steward informed James that he would be on hand to attend to his every need, from arranging his laundry to assisting with dressing for dinner. James replied that there would be no such requests from him, and he did not expect he would have any need of a steward's services for the duration of his trip. Encouraging the steward to take his leave, James sat down in the love seat for two, taking in his surroundings. He was confused by such grandeur in a place of rest. The walls were white, edged in gilt, and luxurious silk throws, crisp bed linens, and feather pillows adorned each bed. Four electric lights illuminated the room, including a small, circular glass dome on the ceiling and candelabra light fittings above each bed. There were separate light switches for each guest and one above the wash area. A dressing table and mirror sat adjacent to a single wardrobe. The door to the cabin, the wash area, and porthole were all curtained off in heavy floral damask for privacy and needless decoration. And a deep patterned carpet lay thick beneath his feet. If this was the least costly of the saloon cabins, he dared to think of the luxury afforded to others. Not knowing what else to do, he sat stiffly on the love seat to await the arrival of his traveling companion. Anxiously, he listened to the loud raucous voices booming along the corridor, shouts of "jolly" this and "tally-ho" that heightening his sense of discomfort.

James nodded off but was soon awakened with a loud, brisk knock on the door. "Mr. Marsden awaits your acquaintance," the steward announced.

James opened the door to see an older, well-dressed gentleman standing before him.

"Hello, my dear sir, and to whom am I to spend these next five days?" said Mr. Marsden.

"Mr. James Kelly, sir," replied James, holding out his hand.

"I see, an Irishman. Interesting. Never before have I had the pleasure of sharing with a man of your standing. And your occupation, my good man?" asked Mr. Marsden, looking down his nose.

"I am a business owner . . . of sorts. And you, Mr. Marsden, are you traveling for pleasure?" said James with an open smiling face.

"Pleasure, I suppose. I am with my traveling companion, Sir Theodore Bloomfield of Kent," Mr. Marsden proudly declared.

James wondered why two "companions" were not sharing a cabin.

"Sir, do you have a preference as to which bed you would like for the journey?" said James, being polite.

"Yes of course, why the one nearest to the watering closet," said Mr. Marsden in a tone that told James he should have known.

James had no such requests. Turning his back, he pulled his suitcase onto his bed and began to remove the few items he had from his suitcase to hang them in the wardrobe. Mr. Marsden jumped up exclaiming, "Young man! Young man, I have strict dress requirements throughout my day and will require the sole use of the wardrobe. Be a good boy now and leave your items in your case. It should fit nicely under your bed. I am sure you understand."

"Of course, Mr. Marsden. Why, I will hang my jacket on this hook by the bed and my case fits beneath," said James, a little less enthusiastically.

"Now James, as to the duration of our stay, I rise promptly at seven and retire at ten. I shall require sole use of the wash facilities at these times and preferably in private. The electric light is to be left on at all times, as I do not like to be in darkness. Nor do I appreciate guests in the cabin at any time, day or night. There are ample areas for such fraternizing," said Mr. Marsden, satisfied that he'd had his say.

James could see a long five days before him with the demands of the gentrified class. There was a lot to be said for being normal.

Once they had all the rules out of the way, Mr. Marsden and James got along splendidly. Mr. Marsden spoke of his time with Sir Bloomfield's family, whom he'd been with since he was a boy. His father and grandfather before him had been companions through the generations. James had inquired what the role of a companion entailed, to which Mr. Marsden replied, "A companion of sorts. I help keep Sir Bloomfield out of trouble, quite the experience really. We are constantly on the move: Europe, America, wherever takes Sir Bloomfield's fancy."

James had a sense neither Mr. Marsden nor Sir Bloomfield had worked a day in their life. "Old money," Marsden had said, passed down through the generations—however, not quite as much as there had once been. There was some talk of Sir Bloomfield having to curtail his expenditure, which would surely put a stop to his gallop. Mr. Marsden spoke little of himself, and James did not inquire. James was happy to talk of their shop and farm, but he talked mostly of Brigid and their travels to the New World.

Mr. Marsden questioned James and the sensibility of his return. "My good young man, surely there is tremendous opportunity in

America for a man as fit and able as you present. I understand your place is at the helm of your family business. However, take it from me, once you have got a taste for the New World, it will be hard to settle yourself. No offense now, James, but the cold, drab, gray of Ireland is no match for the sun-drenched shores of the Western Coast," said Mr. Marsden with widely traveled wisdom.

James assured Mr. Marsden that his place was with his father in Moling, and their conversation came to an end. Taking Mr. Marsden's earlier advice of proper utilization of his time onboard, James set off to explore his surroundings. Deck E, Room 42 was all that he had to remember, and to avoid the ladies' washrooms. Mr. Marsden had warned him, many a gentleman had mistaken the ladies' facility and was not the better of it, the shock of a lady crouched mid-deed, screeching and wailing as if it was the devil himself before her, and all because he had opened the wrong door.

James was content to be in his own company, making pleasantries with those he passed or sat beside at meals. He never lingered, happy to eat and excuse himself. He was not a smoker, therefore did not have the same interest as the other gentlemen who were happy to lounge in the smoking room. He preferred to sit with a pot of tea in the Veranda Café, with its trellis of ivy adorning the walls. Giving him some semblance of peace as he looked out to the great ocean before him, it was easy for him to be anonymous.

Mr. Marsden kept a very different schedule and acquaintance, being familiar with the etiquette of travel and acquainted in some way or other with many of the saloon passengers. It was not difficult for James to pass his time. There was always some activity to be seen or heard. He enjoyed the melodies from the orchestra filtering the stairwell, the pianist by day and the entire orchestral entourage by night entertaining the jubilant diners. The menus were opulent and plentiful, far too extravagant and rich for James's palate, so he feigned sea sickness when questioned by the worried waiting staff who could not understand why anyone would eat so sparingly.

James sat at the same table each night just inside the door of the upper dining saloon, a smaller area from which he could come and go without fuss. There were few traveling alone in first class, unlike the lower classes where most ate alone. James had taken time to speak with the passengers in steerage on his last trip across the ocean, listening to the stories of how they were taking the fate of their future into their own hands, so eager to share their dreams, full of wonder and hope. This was a different journey for James, no longer filled with the expectation of what lay ahead, knowing all that he had left behind, all that he had never before dreamed of nor wished for, but that which life had so joyfully placed before him. It was all now lost to him for the remainder of his days.

CHAPTER 13

As James made his way back across the Atlantic, Patrick traveled to Wexford town to see what all the fuss was about. Dr. Murphy traveled with him, saying it would do him good to go for the spin. The doctor had his own thoughts as to what might be ailing Kate and knew that if he was correct, Patrick would need his assistance.

They set off early, as the journey would take them some eight hours there and back. Arriving at noon, they called straight to the bakery. The shop door was closed, and they could see Mr. O'Dowd peeping through the blinds waving to them. Flustered, he opened the locked door and hurried them through to the back kitchen.

"Mr. Kelly, come in, come in. I am very sorry we had to trouble you like this, but you will just have to take Kate away with you—we cannot have her stay a moment longer. She has caused nothing but disturbance, and it is beyond my remit to be able to manage this situation. We have done all we can for this young lady, and she has shown nothing but contempt. Why, this very morning she flew into a rage at my good lady wife. Kate has been troublesome for some weeks now, silent, and dull, far more than usual. She has been the best apprentice the place has ever seen, but whatever has come over her this last while . . . I don't understand. She has been staying in her room, constantly moving about, making a racket, getting up at all hours of the morning, hardly ever taking sleep. We have tried all manner of ways to help her, as it simply cannot go on. She will have to go and not a moment too soon. A good rest at home may be all that she needs before she is quite well again," said Mr.

O'Dowd, barely taking a breath and leaving Patrick in no doubt that he wanted Kate gone.

Dr. Murphy stood by Pierce's side, his greatest fear now a reality for this poor unfortunate young girl with her life ahead of her. Patrick was mortified and asked to see Mrs. O'Dowd to apologize. Kate had been raised in a good home, and he could not understand why she was behaving like this. Shocked by what he had heard, he needed to see Kate for himself and find out what in God's name she was thinking.

Kate had locked the door to her room.

"Kate, it is your father. Now open this door immediately and let me in. Stop your carrying on and open this door now." Patrick was met with silence.

"I will not stand for this behavior from any daughter of mine, open this door, *now*!"

Kate's instinct somewhere inside of her knew that her father was there to help, so she opened the locked door as her father pushed through. Patrick gasped when he saw his daughter standing before him. His beautiful Kate was disheveled, her unwashed hair hanging limply about her face, and an air of total destitution about her.

"I do not want to speak to anyone, I want to go home," she said quietly.

"Kate, please, you have to explain yourself. What is going on here? The O'Dowds say you've been causing a commotion."

Kate turned to her father, screaming in his face, "Get me out of here now! Get me away from these people. I cannot bear it—they have been horrible to me."

"Kate, stop it! Keep your voice down. There is no need for that talk out of you. The O'Dowds have always looked out for you."

"You don't know anything. They have been cruel. They have betrayed me."

Dr. Murphy came to the door assuring Patrick that it would be best to listen to Kate, best for everyone if she returned home—and not a moment too soon. Patrick thanked the O'Dowds for their understanding and apologized profusely for the upset and disturbance. By way of an explanation, he mentioned that Kate struggled with the loss of her mother at a young age.

Kate showed no desire to pack a case, so they loaded up a few items, not wanting to stay a moment longer. Kate sat in the cart silent, shivering from having forgotten her coat. How could she not have remembered an item as simple as her coat in the near dead of winter? Patrick did not want to have to go back to the O'Dowds, as he was embarrassed by his own daughter. And to make it worse, he had Dr. Murphy by his side to witness his shame.

"Don't be worrying, Patrick. It could happen to anyone. The poor girl is beside herself with tiredness. There are plenty of blankets here to keep her warm, and it won't be long now before she is back in the comfort of her own bed," said Dr. Murphy, trying to smooth over the tension.

They journeyed in silence as Patrick considered just how he was going to navigate this one with Agnes. She had always shown disdain for the girls, and with Brigid gone from the home, Kate was now the sole focus of her attention. Finding a husband would have to take second place to helping her recover her health. Patrick was relieved when he saw Kate close her eyes and rest. Dr. Murphy, observing the agitated flicker of her eyelids, knew she was far from resting.

Speaking privately with Patrick, Dr. Murphy asked that he be kept informed of Kate's progress over the coming days and that he would check in on her after she'd had a good rest.

Agnes took over as soon as they arrived home, all businesslike. "Into the bath with you now. You're in need of a good scrubbing, we will cut off all that hair and wrap your head in wet sheets—it's the only thing for your brain fever. It will bring down that flushed look about you. You'll be right as rain."

Agnes told herself that the poor girl was like a slave to the O'Dowds. They must have inflamed her brain, getting her up at all hours, working her long into the night, cooking and cleaning like a servant. Who did they think they were? Agnes convinced herself and everyone else that mistreatment was the source of Kate's malady.

Kate sat transfixed as she saw her wet hair fall to the ground, the distortion of her features satisfying her tortured soul.

"Off to bed with you now," said Agnes.

There Kate lay, melancholy, for some ten days, taking only the tea and toast brought to her. Patrick asked Agnes for Kate to be allowed to rest for as long as was needed, on doctor's orders.

But the original compassion Agnes had shown Kate had worn thin. She had grown tired of the tension in the house, and she was losing patience with what she saw as Kate's indolence. It was time for Agnes to take matters into her own hands. Climbing the stairs like a woman on a mission, she flung open the bedroom door. Kate was sitting by the window as Agnes walked over, pulling open the curtains before stripping the sheets and covers off the bed. She told Kate in a fury, "Up with you now. No more lying about feeling sorry for yourself. There is plenty of work to be done about the place."

Kate did not move as Agnes rabbited on and on about Biddy O'Connor and how she was sick of her calling in inquiring after "poor Kate" and her health. "She no more cares about you than the man in the moon. Looking for gossip she is—she thrives on others' misfortune. Now up, you. Get like a good girl and let's get a move on," said Agnes, oblivious to Kate's motionless body.

Kate could see Agnes's mouth moving but could not hear her words. "Get out of my room," Kate hissed.

"What's that you say? Get out of your room? Now, young lady, you won't be lolling about here daydreaming any longer, not on my watch."

Kate walked to the dresser. Picking up her hairbrush, she flung it at Agnes. "Get out, goddamn you, get the hell out of my room. I cannot bear to look at your face! You are not my mother. I hate you. we all hate you."

"Dear Lord above, she is possessed! Holy Mother and Mary St.

Jospeh, she's gone mad in her head," shouted Agnes, running from the room.

Patrick intercepted Agnes as she ran from the room. "Calm yourself! What is it? What is the matter with you?"

Patrick should have known. Of course it was Kate. She was the sole focus of Agnes's attention. She just could not leave her be. All Agnes had to do was to let Kate come around when she was ready. The doctor himself had given that advice, and Patrick put his trust in him.

"Yes, Agnes, yes. I hear you, and if you don't lower your voice, the whole village will hear you. I will speak with her," sighed Patrick.

As Patrick approached Kate's bedroom, he could hear singing. Maybe Agnes had brought about an improvement after all. Opening the door to the bedroom, he saw Kate dancing wildly in her undergarments, oblivious to his presence, twirling about the room, singing at the top of her voice while holding on tightly to a crucifix.

"Kate, Kate! What are you at? Dress yourself at once, and give me that crucifix," commanded Patrick.

Ignoring her father, Kate sang louder and louder as Patrick pleaded with her to stop. Thomas, hearing the fuss from the yard below, had come to the door of the bedroom. Kate turned on them both, screaming, "Get out, out, out, out! All of you, get out! Get away from me. Don't touch me. Don't come near me! Leave me alone! You are all trying to hurt me," before collapsing to the floor crying and wailing. Patrick dropped to his knees, putting his arms around her, telling her he loved her. Kate, struck out, hitting his face and scratching his arms. Then it all stopped as Kate jumped up and walked to the corner of the room, whispering to herself.

Patrick tried to stop her. "Kate, there is no one there. Stop it, you are making a show of yourself."

"Mother, they are at me again. Stop them! Tell them to get away from me. Save me, Mother! Help me! They are trying to harm me," wailed Kate into the air.

Patrick told Thomas to run next door for the doctor.

"She will rest now. I have given her a little something to help her sleep. It is just rest she needs—she will settle herself with rest," Dr. Murphy assured Patrick.

Patrick did not relay all the details to Dr. Murphy. He did not need to, as the doctor had seen enough. Kate had screamed at him when he went to help her, throwing anything she could get her hands on, shouting profanities, telling them all to leave her alone. Patrick wondered at how she even knew of such words. What had they been teaching her in that town?

Kate settled somewhat over the next few days, but Patrick was far from settled. Agnes was constantly at him, telling him that Kate needed to be locked away. They could not be having this sort of carrying on in their home with them trying to run a business. Patrick thought only of the promise he had given to their mother—that he would always take care of the children. Blood is thicker than water, and he would not have it any other way.

CHAPTER 14

The sun was deceptive the morning James arrived home to Moling bitterly cold and tired from his journey, yet with an alertness to see the place he would always call home. His journey from Liverpool, where the docks were overwhelmed with travelers and hoodlums, had been more of a challenge than crossing the Atlantic, and James needed to have his wits about him. He took the next boat available to Dublin, traveling with the City of Dublin Steam Packet Company. The seas were wild, and there was no escaping the passengers experiencing varying degrees of sea sickness on the ten-hour journey. He had not wanted to inform his family of his arrival and cause them upset trying to meet the boat and coordinate his arrival. He took a tram to Dublin, then boarded the Great Southern and Western Railway to Wexford, where he took a horse-drawn cab at the station to take him on his final leg of his journey. The cab driver, sensing there was something different about this young traveler, asked incessant questions, doing his very best to elicit a suitable response. A man of few words, James did not make it easy for the frustrated cab driver. James jumped off the cab with his case just before the turn into the village, wanting to walk the back road past the schoolhouse, which looked as derelict as ever, but for the smoke hissing from the chimney with the fire he himself had lit many a cold morning.

It was, of course, Biddy O'Connor who was the first to see him. No doubt she had kept vigil to have the honor.

"James! James, is that you? Is that James Kelly I see before me? Would you look at the color of you, all brown, and your hair so fair, and what's that you are wearing? An overcoat and leather shoes—my goodness, you're like the prodigal son himself. I'll walk up with you. I have to go into the shop anyway. You'll want to be seeing Kate—sure that is probably why you are home."

James's heart sank.

Agnes rushed out the door of the shop when she saw James outside with Biddy O'Connor. "That'll do now, Mrs. O'Connor. You are very good to walk James to the door, but we will have to close up early for the occasion. Surely your provisions can wait—weren't you only in an hour ago?" It was at times such as this that Agnes came into her own.

James sat at the table in the parlor, his father beside him with his head in his hands as Thomas stood by the door.

Agnes fussed about. "You'll have tea now, James, won't you? I have the dinner on."

Patrick asked Agnes to leave them be. Straightening her housecoat and mumbling her way out of the room, she thought to herself how she was only too happy to leave them be, as she was sick and tired of all this fuss over Kate. If she'd had her way, that girl would have been locked up long ago.

"Father, where is Kate? What is wrong with her?" asked James.

"I don't know where to start, son. I just don't know. There were stories coming back from Wexford town that she was not herself. The O'Dowds had also sent word that something was amiss, and the doctor and I traveled to see for ourselves. And sure, she was not in a good way at all. We took her home, and she has been in her room since. She has barely eaten, and we never know if she is sleeping or not. She won't talk to any of us. Asks only for you, James. You are the only one she speaks of, poor child. She never recovered from the loss of her mother. She has always needed more support than any of the rest of you ever did. If you don't have family, you have nothing," said Patrick.

James did not say a word. He allowed his father the time to talk without interruption. Thomas had followed Agnes out of the room, mentioning something about the cattle.

James asked his father if it would be a good idea for him to go up to Kate's room and talk to her. His father said it could do no harm; she might just listen to him.

"Kate, Kate," James said softly as he knocked on her door. "It's me, James. I'm home."

Kate threw open her bedroom door, jumping into his arms, holding onto him so tightly he could barely remove himself from her grip.

"Shush now. I'm home. I'm here for you now. What is all this I am hearing about you?" said James in a soothing tone.

"It's all lies, James. Lies, lies, lies. They have kept me locked up in this room. They don't care for me. They have been cruel to me, James. I can't tell you how hard it has been. I only have Mother to talk to, and now you, James. You are the only people I can trust. You will take care of me, James, won't you? You could take me back to Yankeeland. Take me away from here. I am dying here, James. They are suffocating me. They want me gone, out of the place," Kate begged.

"Shush now. Shush, Kate. You know that we all love you. It was Father that called me home, for you," James replied, trying to calm her down.

"He only cares about that witch. How could he care about us if he brought her into our home," hissed Kate.

"Kate, stop that talk out of you. Agnes will hear, and Father will not be pleased," he whispered, making sure the door was closed.

"Stop it, stop it now. Stop talking to me! You are just the same as the rest of them. You are against me now too. What have they told you, James? What lies have they told?" Falling to the floor, Kate wailed and shouted at James. "Get out! Get away from me! Leave me alone. I don't want any of you near me."

"Calm yourself, Kate. I am here to help. I am not against you— none of us are against you. Father is at his wit's end worrying about you," pleaded James.

"Stop it! Don't talk to me anymore! You are being cruel. You are just like the rest of them—get out NOW," Kate screamed hysterically as she ran to the window. Pulling it open, she threw her head back and screeched at the top of her voice, "Help! Help me! Save me!"

James ran from the room, meeting Patrick at the bottom of the stairs. "Oh James, what are we to do?" Patrick implored.

James called next door and spoke with the doctor, knowing the advice he had been given would break his father's heart. The doctor was very clear. "There is nothing for it now, James. We will just have to take Kate to Enniscorthy. We don't have the expertise nor the medicines to care for her here. It is a fine place James, like a village in itself. Lord Doyne has arranged for Dr. Drapes himself to be on hand, and we can be assured of his confidence in the matter."

James only ever knew of it as the "madhouse." Mr. Brennan up at the schoolhouse would threaten them with it, telling them they would end up like the lunatics in Enniscorthy if they did not do their lessons.

Kate was admitted to the Enniscorthy District Lunatic Asylum for the Insane Poor of Mind on the eighteenth day of March 1911.

Dr. Drapes, a distinguished doctor and a man ahead of his time, was widely traveled and educated in the area of mental fatigue and lectured all over the land and as far as the British Isles. After mentioning the many papers he had written on the subject, he introduced himself to the room before addressing Patrick. "Mr. Kelly, you can be assured of my assistance to you and your family. Lord Doyne speaks very highly of your service to the community and to his estate. Now, I must ask as to any possible cause for this disturbance in your daughter's life."

Patrick was unable to look the man in the eye as he struggled for words. Dr. Murphy spoke for him. "Kate has been dull, silent, and indolent some nine weeks now, with little sign of change in temperament. She sleeps erratically, if at all, and has taken little in the way of nourishment. At times she has shown uncharacteristic violence, striking out at others and throwing objects. More recently she has begun to believe that her deceased mother is present and speaks with her on occasion. As the weeks have progressed, she has gone from laughing to singing to crying without cause. She is confused and regularly mistakes those present for dead relatives. Mr. Kelly here runs a business, and it has become increasingly difficult for him to care for his daughter at home, as she has shown little sign of improvement and is, in fact, deteriorating."

James interjected. "Kate had been learning her trade at a bakery in the town where she has been for a number of years without complaint before Father received word to bring her home. When he arrived at the bakery, Father was shocked to witness the situation in which he found Kate. She was agitated, speaking of her mistreatment at the hands of her employers. We believe she may have been overworked and suffering from exhaustion."

Dr. Drapes sat back in his chair. "I see. And are there any other factors in her life which I need to be made aware of?"

Patrick told of how they had lost their mother at a very young age and that Kate had always felt the loss more keenly. Dr. Drapes asked if any other family member suffered in this way. Looking at each other quizzically, Patrick immediately spoke up. "Absolutely not. We have no lunacy in our family—not now, not ever. This is the first time we have ever witnessed such a complete disturbance of life. It has been a terrible shock to us all."

Dr. Murphy, as the family doctor and trusted friend, offered to complete the required admittance forms, knowing it would be too much for Patrick and that James had already witnessed enough for any young man. Taking care of the formalities, Dr. Drapes and Dr. Murphy opened the leather-bound admittance volume before them:

Species of Insanity: Recent mania.

Bodily Condition on Admission—Clean or Filthy: Clean.

Expression of Countenance: Intelligent.

Habits: Dull, silent, indolent.

Temperate or otherwise: Always temperate.

Facts indicating insanity: excitable; noisy; violent; sometimes crying, laughing, or singing without cause or reason; use of improper language.

Dr. Drapes paused at the family history section, probing as to any family member who may have experienced symptoms, dead or alive or any knowledge of feebleminded persons in the family. Dr. Drapes was clear. "It is of great importance to explore this when trying to determine if Kate is afflicted with predisposing heredity."

Dr. Murphy gave his assurance. "You have my word. Should any information come to hand that may be of assistance in bringing Kate back to full health, I will advise with immediacy."

"As the family doctor, you need to understand that it will always be important for Kate to get her sleep. It is God's gift to us, and there is little that a good night's sleep cannot solve," warned Dr. Drapes.

The image of Kate being restrained at the door of the asylum would haunt James for all his days. Wrapped in a jacket to stop her arms from flailing and causing harm, as they took her away, she screamed, cried, and called his name, begging him to come back. The nurse had told him to hurry on away, as Kate did not know what day it was, never mind where she was, and that they would take care of her from here.

James was devastated as he tried to process what had happened. Dear God in heaven above, what had she done to deserve this? What had any of them done? Had they not had enough sorrow for one life? It had taken all his might not to turn back and take Kate in his arms, taking her home with him. Would she ever forgive him? Would she ever know of the torment in their hearts and minds at having to take her there? They had no choice. She was not going to get better at home. She was safe and in the right place. Patrick repeated those words over and over in his mind as they sat in silence on the journey home. She would be safe and cared for and would soon recover and be back to her life.

As they left the grounds of the asylum, passing through the gate lodge, the gatekeeper was full of the joys of spring, leaning into the cart as if for a chat. Not one of them were interested nor able to as much as look his way as they left the imposing red brick building behind them with its high walls with broken glass, steel, and nails reinforced into the top. James spared a thought for all those who had traveled this journey before him, thinking *there but for the grace of God go I*.

Thomas had busied himself in the shed as Kate had been removed, screaming, from her room. He could not bear to see his sister forced into the back of the cart and had covered his ears and closed his eyes as he hummed to himself to block out the sounds. He wished he could be there for Father as James had been, wished he had the courage to put aside his own fears and, most of all, be there for Kate. He'd watched as they held Kate between them, wrapped in blankets, and Patrick took the reins, the sound of the hooves taking them to a place that no father should ever have to take a child.

Thomas had stayed outside in the fields for as long as the day had allowed, knowing his father did not want to trouble him—that was his way. Agnes had closed the shop for fear that anyone would see. But if they had not seen, they had surely heard. That would be the end of it. She would allow no talk and no mention of Kate. James was home now, and they would all settle back into their old ways. Life would go on much the same as it had always done.

CHAPTER 15

Brigid was settling into a pleasant routine in Niagara Falls. She felt a newfound sense of maturity, alone now in this land but for Ben. It was this feeling of aloneness that led Brigid to realize that maybe now it was time for her to start a family of her own. The weight of the expectation had infuriated her, and, on reflection, maybe it was her stubbornness at giving in to the societal demands that had stopped her from wanting a family before now. She had half-heartedly referred to it in her correspondence to home, for she knew it was what was expected of her and what they would want to hear. It was not until now that she felt a sense that something was missing in her life.

Brigid had fully embraced her new life in this civilized society; it was everything she had ever dreamed of. Molly's effusive letters filled with her passion for motherhood were not lost on Brigid, and it had made her sad to think of how her own mother had not lived to see her children reach adulthood. Brigid could see no reason why children would change her life overmuch; why, all of the ladies at the church seemed to manage. Brigid had always achieved anything she put her mind to and becoming a mother would be no different. She had fought the want within herself for too long now, and the desire for motherhood soon became all-consuming.

They had survived the bitterest of winters, marveling at the freezing of the falls, the mighty cataract stilled by winter's grip. The place had become a winter wonderland, and with it a new idiocy called the Ice Bridge became an attraction. To think that the vendors built their stalls in these dangerous places to attract the poor unfortunates who were lured into a sense of safety. A sharp rogue built a shanty of boards right in the center of the massive ice bridge at the falls, freely selling liquor, and others soon followed. Thinking themselves clever, they built their shacks on the line between the two countries, thus evading the laws of both. Tourism they called it. The locals called these nefarious hucksters "humbugs."

One poor young couple who had been regular visitors to the area really should have known better. The talk was that there was a small tremor felt underfoot, and with it a loud groaning sound from the base of the falls. The Ice Bridge began heaving up and down and breaking apart. The poor souls caught up in the catastrophe ran to either shoreline for safety, except for Eldridge and Clara Stanton, who became stranded as the ice came apart. They were last seen holding each other tightly, surely aware of their fate as they plummeted down the river toward their death. And yet others still came afterward, thrill seekers who flocked by train to sled in the very place that held the ache of such sorrow.

> *April 25, 1911*
> *Dearest Molly,*
>
> *Thank you for your most recent letter. It is such a comfort to know the news of home and to hear that Father and family are quite well. I fear that I would be lost forever if I was to rely on James or Thomas to keep me informed, or Father for that matter. Is life really too busy for them to have the time to sit and write? James must be awful happy to be back home, by Father's side, settling into his old life so easily.*
>
> *I write only to you, for who else will understand the sense of excitement. Ben talks of the two sides of this town which we call home, the one in which Ben has no wish for us to become acquainted, that of the "humbugs" (some of whom I find intriguing) and the one in which he is keen for me to embrace, the ladies of the church. I never thought I would see the day*

when I would be grateful for the church. The people here, of course, are far more civilized than at home; we are enjoying living a life of sophistication.

This past week we visited the "Home of Shredded Wheat," a village in itself, set in ten acres by the reservation. The finest of homes were demolished to replace them with this "Palace of Light." Eight hundred and forty-four windows! Henry Drushel Perky is a very clever man, winning over the disgruntled residents, having the grounds of the factory complex beautifully finished with paths, a winding drive, playgrounds, tennis courts, and even plots for employees to have their very own gardens—all in the spirit of promoting a better working life and for the use of the city residents. There is a separate factory where the Shredded Wheat is made, a so-called administration building, the foyer of which resembles that of a grand five-star hotel with the finest furniture, rugs, and a great crystal chandelier. All of this is provided for the comfort of visitors and staff. Not only is there a writing and reading room, but a one-thousand-seat auditorium and a rooftop patio.

Oh Molly, it is incredible and open to tourists six days of the week to see for themselves how this man has made every effort to provide for the comfort and welfare of his workers. Agnes could surely learn a thing or two about how to treat her staff! There are strict rules for regular breaks during the day, and staff are encouraged to use the extensive library and take part in the classes offered in shorthand, typing, math, etiquette, dancing, choral singing, and various clubs—all of which is carried out during their working day at absolutely no cost! Marble bathing facilities with all toiletries provided, along with separate dining rooms for the ladies, who dine at no cost, and the men who pay a mere ten cents.

I busy myself with looking after Ben, who is much taken with his responsibilities now that he is a supervisor. His day *is long and his wages reflect his increased status. We continue to make good on our desire to build a life here, and I pray that we will be blessed with children of our own as soon as we are settled into a permanent home. You do not have to consider such matters, as I suppose neither would I, had I stayed at home. The good Lord will bless us in his own time.*

Please give my love to Father and the boys, and do tell of all news of home when next you write. I miss our times together, Molly, and forever hold you in my heart.

Your fond cousin Brigid.

Brigid longed to share with Molly her acquaintance with Annie Edson Taylor, but she had a sense that this was one secret Molly may not understand. Brigid was intrigued with the woman, who sat day after day at her stand on the main street, calling herself the "Heroine of Horseshoe Falls" as she called out to all those who passed to come and purchase her souvenirs. It was impossible not to stop and learn of this daredevil, who spoke of how the idea had come to her like a flash of light to go over Niagara Falls in a barrel. "If it was with my dying breath, I would caution anyone against attempting the feat. I would sooner walk up to the mouth of a cannon, knowing it was going to blow me to pieces, than make another trip over the falls," she'd tell anyone who would stop to listen.

Ben had no time for what he termed utter "madness" after he had found Mrs. Taylor's ten-cent souvenir booklet. It was of little surprise to Brigid, as she was keenly aware that he had an unrealistic expectation for all women to be docile, delicate, and fragile.

In Ben's view, Mrs. Taylor did not add an iota to the betterment of the world and if she should have any effect on people, it would surely only be to elicit their contempt. People are wont to deplore the occurrence of such events because of the light value it places on life. "The existence of people of Mrs. Taylor's ilk reveals the fact that bravery, when saturated with egoism, is as deplorable as cowardice.

I consider the matter closed. I do not wish to hear tell of her name under this roof again," he'd warned Brigid.

Brigid was not discouraged from wanting to be in Mrs. Taylor's company. In fact, she pitied the woman's misfortune—she'd been widowed at a young age, lost her son shortly after his birth, and now tried so bravely to make a life for herself. Brigid admired her great fearlessness and passion to progress her life, not unlike Brigid herself, who had vowed all those years growing up in Moling to follow her own dream. Why, she and Mrs. Taylor were kindred spirits.

Mrs. Taylor soon took Brigid into her confidence, sharing her special gifts, including clairvoyance and electric and magnetic healing, which she provided only for those dearest to her . . . for a nominal fee. Brigid had no need to bother Ben with these costs, for she had access to funds of her own. Father had insisted that it was important to always have one's independence, so she'd secreted away some of what Father had sent her with. Brigid felt rather special to have such an exotic friend and found it all the more thrilling having to conceal the friendship, as she had no wish to worry Ben when there really was no need. Mrs. Taylor was quite the companion.

> *July 10, 1911*
> *Dearest Brigid,*
> *How lovely it was to receive your most recent letter. I feel like I am almost there with you, imagining for just one moment that I am. How wonderful would that be? What fun we would have exploring the wonders of the New World. I have not much news to tell, just the usual goings on for, things never seem to change. Agnes is still ruling the roost, keeping everyone in check. I see your father almost every other day, coming and going. As for the boys, well, they seem to be busy further afield. What with Thomas delivering his post and James overseeing everything, they have time for little else. I have no news of Kate, as she does not visit often.*

We had quite the commotion with poor unfortunate Tomsey Byrne who is still on the whiskey despite his best intentions. He went and got himself into awful trouble at the Easter Vigil mass presided over by none other than Canon Hannon himself. Father Dempsey was going on and on about the visit for months, Canon Hannon this, Canon Hannon that. We were to be graced with his holy presence for Easter here in Moling. Such a frenzy like you have never seen, with the cleaning of the church to within an inch of itself, and then the baking and baking and more baking, trying to outdo each other with their produce. Of course, it was Biddy O'Connor's cake that the Canon was given to eat, and it wouldn't do but for her to present it to him herself. She said she wanted him to see that it was made with the very best of Catholic hands. Agnes said to me she hoped he got the flux after it.

There we all were, sat in the church for the Vigil, dressed in our Sunday best, not a child in bed, the whole parish out for the occasion. Tomsey, kicked out of Sutherlands and told to get across the road since they were locking up for the occasion, showed up drunk as a lord, falling about the back of the church with all sorts of noises emanating from him.

Canon Hanon, booming from the pulpit about the evils of the demon drink and how it was the ruination of all good men, bellowed from the top of his voice, "Alcohol is the Devil himself, and he is here among us this very night."

With an immediacy like never before, Tomsey shouted back, "Surround the bastard and we'll catch him."

Oh Lord above, the commotion! Canon Hannon stopped the mass while Tomsey was removed by the Sutherland boys, who had got him into that state in the first place, pouring the drink into him as long as he had the money to pay for it. Well, my word, I don't think Father Dempsey will be getting a bigger parish anytime soon.

The Eastons send their love, as does Paudie Keenan. He still holds a torch for you. The poor unfortunate has not had a smile on his face since the day you left. He was sure of his place in the Kelly fold and then you up and left on him. Oh Brigid, it really is just too funny to think of what might have been.

I must go now and tend to Mother and the kiddies. Give my regards to Ben.

Your fond cousin Molly.

Molly sealed the envelope and asked for the Lord's forgiveness for not being truthful. How in God's name could she tell her about Kate? "Brain fever," her father said, brought on by overwork at the bakery. She didn't dare to ask more, as she knew how her father would never discuss the ailments of his patients, family or not. Agnes had not said a word to Mother or to anyone for that matter, and it was not like her to have her lips sealed. The whole place knew Kate had not been herself, and the talk was about the O'Dowds in the bakery in Wexford running her into the ground.

Molly did not know what she would have to tell Brigid anyway, and there was nothing worse than half a story. Mother had said, "If you have nothing good to say, say nothing at all, and if Patrick or the boys want to write of it, then it is their place. It is not for you to interfere." Molly told herself it was just as well, as what could Brigid do about it anyway with the great ocean between them? And Brigid never had much patience for Kate anyhow. She was always saying how Kate had been spoiled by their father, with no list of jobs to do, never called before dawn like the rest of them to help with the cattle—the inequity had incensed her. As for Agnes, she would only ever have a go at Kate if she had already been through the others and was still in a rage. Letting off a little steam was how Patrick had described it. Molly thought that maybe Kate would want to return home and settle down into married life, that surely she had mastered her craft and could allow Patrick his wish to have her sell baked goods in the shop and give herself some independence.

Molly's mother had not been pleased with Agnes and her talk of Kate, saying, "Who would have her now, with the carrying on of her?" If Patrick had heard he would surely stand up to her once and for all. Molly's mother had put Agnes in her place and made it very clear that it would be best not to talk of Kate in that way; it was not of her own doing. She feared Agnes would do more harm for Kate than good if she continued to feed the already warm grapevine.

Molly was worried about James too, as he had not been himself since his return. She had no doubt it was all the worry over Kate. They had always been close. It was strange that he did not like to talk of his time away or of all that he had seen. Maybe it was not as wonderful as everyone thought it was. Maybe there was nothing to be missing at all, and they were the lucky ones for having stayed behind.

CHAPTER 16

James could not lift his spirits. He had none of the love for the work as before, and he berated himself as to what he had to be down in the mouth about—who would listen to him anyway? He wondered if he would ever recover from the shock of Kate and not being able to help her, having to leave her behind in the care of others in whom they had no choice but to put their trust. James took some comfort in the letters he had written to Kate almost daily, hoping it provided her with some semblance of comfort. The not knowing was the hardest. The asylum had promised to keep the family informed, telling them to be patient, for Kate had gotten herself into a terrible state, and her system would take time to right itself. It would be for the best to leave her be and let the staff there do their job.

James no longer awoke with anticipation for his day. He had no enthusiasm for the shop, the customers, the farm, or the village life into which he had been born and into which he was to stay for the rest of his days. He was unable to see himself with a wife and children and all that was expected of him as the future head of the Kelly family. James knew his father wanted to be assured of a successor, and that he was carrying the expectation of the generations. Why in heaven above had his father ever asked him to travel to America with Brigid in the first place? Why was his life disrupted? Why had he not asked Thomas? James prayed to God to erase all thoughts of his time in San Francisco from his mind, as it surely would do him no good to lament for a time that was now lost to him.

Patrick was at ease, able to lay his head at night safe in the knowledge that James was home. The decision as to why he'd ever asked him to leave was something he would always question—a decision made in great haste. But what was done was done, for the past can hold no power.

Agnes was none too pleased with the talk of Kate returning home. Patrick had been adamant that Kate would always have a roof over her head as long as there was breath in his body. He would not stand for any talk of what had gone on before, and put his foot down at Agnes's suggestion that Kate eventually return to the O'Dowds, to the source of her infliction. It would be no trouble for her to secure a new position in any number of establishments in the town where she could continue to perfect her trade and not be overworked or taken for granted. Patrick would never understand her wish to live an independent life and not the traditional one he had planned for her, with a husband and a family of her own. That being said, she would be assured of his support to go about as before, before ever she was struck down with such fever. He was satisfied that in time she would see sense; she was only young yet. James was a different matter. He was awfully quiet in himself, taking a long time to adjust. Patrick explained it away, telling himself that the travel and the differing environments had surely taken their toll, vowing never again would he put such an expectation on his son; the running of the business was enough, and what a fine head he had for it. Thomas held his own, but he was no match for James.

Biddy O'Connor loved to get a rise out of Agnes. "You must be delighted to have James home, and sure isn't he a grand lad altogether. He'll be looking to settle down any day now, and won't there be any number of young ladies only waiting for him to ask them. He'll surely be busy with it all, anyway. What with Kate's little upset and Thomas showing no interest, you will surely want one of them to be settling down. I am always here for you, Agnes, if you ever feel the need to blow off a little steam. I am more than familiar with the settling down of the children, what with four of my own happily married and three grandchildren for us to enjoy. Ah yes, I am reaping the reward for the hard work I put into the rearing of those children, but sure it was all worth it. All good and healthy, mind you, not a complaint among them. It was the good solid food I fed them, that and the power of our Lord's prayer. Not a day was missed with the rosary, not one day. I ran a strict house, and wasn't it all worth it when you see how well they have all done for themselves. It is the mother's influence in the home that makes all the difference, don't you agree, Agnes?"

That evening at dinner, Agnes relayed what Biddy O'Connor had said. James tried his best not to listen as Agnes went on and on about settling down, silently willing her to mind her own business.

Patrick told Agnes to be sure to tell Biddy O'Connor that no one in his household would be needing her advice anytime soon. Patrick could sense James's frustration; he was in no hurry, and it might be for the best to hold off on bringing a wife into this house for fear the women would not quite see eye to eye.

Thomas sat back, happy to let James take the heat, as he had been the sole focus of Biddy O'Connor and all the rest of them while James and Brigid were off gallivanting. "Who's that I saw you talking to at the back of the church after mass?" "Was that a young lady I saw you out walking with?" "You were late home late last night?" A fella could do nothing in this place without an inquisition. And Thomas knew they all laughed at him behind his back, snickering while whispering "He's only the boy about the place. He'll never amount to much." Agnes did not even try to hide it—she only ever worried about James settling down, with not a thought spared for Thomas. And now that James had returned, Thomas was no longer consulted on any decisions, never asked his opinion, all part and parcel of the existence of the second son.

Kate's thinking was tormented. Not knowing what had happened to her and not knowing if life would ever be the same terrified her. She had always been a worrier and now she was physically exhausted, with her emotions wildly swinging to and fro. The dim flicker in her spirit was fading fast. Why? What had invaded her? It tortured her in wakefulness, terrorizing her dreams.

Kate was unable to recall the defining moment or how long she had been out of sorts, but she was crystal clear that she had been very sick when she first arrived. Dr. Drapes had cared for her, kept her safe from herself and from others. The flashbacks had no rhythm, by day or by night. How could she have the strength or the will to want to hurt anyone, not to mind herself? They had put her in a room with walls padded for her safety. Visions appeared to her in moments when she did not know whether they were real or imagined.

Now Kate only knew for sure that she could not stay a moment longer. She could no longer bear to look at the beds all laid out in a row. She felt suffocated from the smells of the soiled sheets. She tried to close her eyes as the doctors blinded her with their lights, covering her ears from the incessant noise from the other patients who wailed and screamed in hysterics over the shuffling of the nurse's feet. They said she desperately needed sleep, yet they prodded and poked her to see if she was sleeping, taking notes in their book, the keeper of all their stories.

The days were no different. The food was basic, mostly inedible, and there were no baked goods. Good girls, they'd all take their seat at the table, some eating, most not. Kate never knew what would happen from one minute to the next, who would strike out, who would become enraged, who would sit by her side uninvited. She was not there to make friends, as she was not there by choice. She had been taken there against her will, and oh how she had begged them to let her leave.

The nurses said they needed to see an improvement in her spirit, so they put her to work in the laundry, where she performed the backbreaking manual labor they called rehabilitation. Kate was on her best behavior, showing them that all was quite well again. Every day she asked herself why her family had not yet answered her letters—not Father, not James, not Thomas, not one of them came for her. She had written letter after letter, carefully sealed, having checked the address over and over to be sure of its safe arrival. Kate had begged them to come and take her out of there, take her home. She promised to be a good girl, promised she would do as they asked. She had pleaded with James to come and visit her, sit with her awhile, let her know that he cared, let her know that he would be there for her. The deafening silence destroyed her. Nothing. She was utterly alone.

There was no one to speak with her, no one to answer her questions, no one to help ease her pain or to tell her how long she had been there and how much longer she would have to stay. The nurses smiled when she wanted answers, smiled and told her to shush now and rest, or to get some air as they forced her outside, making her stand as she refused to sit. Pacing, patients shouted at her to stop, be still. But she had to move, had to keep going or else her brain would explode. Then all would be calm as time stood still, darkness moved to light, the shadows gone.

It was the nothing that frightened her the most. She felt nothing inside or out, her mind no longer frenzied, no longer fevered, no longer her own. Why could they not just leave her be? Let her sit, lie in bed, let her mind be bare. She could no longer think, too afraid to use the mind that had betrayed her. They constantly prodded and poked her, demanding to know what she ate, what she drank. They pushed the foul veronal sodium on her, sometimes a small amount and other times larger quantities that they noted in their infernal book. Kate hated them for making her drink it. She knew they hid it in her milk; she could taste it. But she complied—anything to get her closer to being able to leave the godforsaken place.

And then it was over.

The man at the gate, who lived in the lodge, checked his list, checked the cart, making sure she was allowed to leave. He had nothing to say, so he smiled. Could he see that she was broken? What did he know? What had he heard? What had he seen? Him, the one who'd met the eyes of all those that passed through the gates. Kate wondered if she was really leaving or if they would bring her back and lock her up again, never to leave. She prayed that God would let her leave this place and never again darken its door as long as she lived.

Kate settled into life as before, but not as before—Father had insisted she take a new position. There would be no going back to the O'Dowd's bakery; she could not face them anyway. For Kate everything was confused. Had she imagined them overworking her, or was it all her own doing with the need to occupy her mind that had turned against her? Her mind became her enemy during those days. Speeding itself up seemed the only way to make it through the days and nights, so she worked nonstop. If she kept on working, she would be all right, her mind and body occupied. It was then that Mrs. O'Dowd had annoyed her, pestering her to take time off. The woman watched her, always questioning Kate. Had she slept, had she eaten, had she washed herself? Kate could not take it any longer; they were suffocating her. And then they had called for Father. The O'Dowds had betrayed her. Why had they not just let her be, let her recover? Then there would never have been a need for all that had followed. It was their fault. They had caused it to happen. They had enraged her, left her with no choice, forced her into a corner. But the doctor had said she was quite well now—just a case of overwork and exhaustion. He told her to put it out of her mind and to simply regain her spirit, learn her trade, and return home.

Kate took some comfort from being back in Wexford town securing a position with a new bakery. The new surroundings were sure to help her recover, and this time she had a companion, Mary. It was Mary's first time to be away from home, and she wanted to know everything. But she was more interested in the dances and the fellas than she was in her work. Kate assured her that she knew only of work and had made time for little else, that such frivolities were not what she had come here for.

It hit Kate hardest in the mornings—the realization that it had not been a dream. The advance of day brought a torture and a torment that physically took over. Consumed with fear, she prayed and pleaded, begging that the new day would bring about an ease, bring about a fading from her mind's eye. Was it visible, did she look like she had been in the "madhouse?" Could they see her scars? Her mind was always at odds with her body, her heart always pounding as she lay down to rest, beating as if out of her chest, her brain hurting inside of her head. The pain was physical. She was all right now; they had told her she was. But she didn't feel all right.

Certified sane.

That should have given her some peace. But the heart does not easily let go of pain.

CHAPTER 17

Brigid's decision was final—she had deliberated far too long, and Mrs. Taylor had afforded her great patience. Brigid had overcome her distress and with no other option available to her, she was forced to withhold from Ben her trip to Lily Dale. She informed Ben that she was going on a church retreat. They discussed it at great length and agreed that this would be a good opportunity for Brigid to bond with the ladies of the church and support her charitable skills. Ben had not yet made the acquaintance of the ladies, but he was of the opinion that the association could only serve to enhance their life. Brigid had shown a great love of these interactions, talking often of the kind ladies who were all united in a desire to do good.

Brigid felt a twinge of guilt at the deception, but was soon caught up in the excitement of a journey she knew Ben never would have permitted had she asked. The negotiation of the great adventure was eased somewhat by Mrs. Taylor having made the trip on many occasions. The two ladies took the train from Niagara Falls to Buffalo and transferred to Cassadaga. From there they took a horse-drawn trolley filled with mostly women who were all headed to Lily Dale. Brigid was impressed, commenting to Mrs. Taylor how this free-thinking and liberal way had quite the following. On arrival they checked into the Maplewood Hotel, considered the premium accommodation, only made possible with Mrs. Taylor's connections and Brigid's father's money. The other guests sat on the veranda, taking rest and making conversation as Brigid stood and looked about. She had a sense that she would be forever changed, peaceful and serene, having found a part of her that she had not known was missing. It was all the more special having Mrs. Taylor as a friend. What an enriched life these people led, upholding their spiritualist philosophies in a place to discover oneself and join with others on the path.

From the moment Annie had spoken to Brigid of Lily Dale, a meeting place for spiritualists and freethinkers, all Brigid could think of was how she might have the opportunity to connect with her dearly departed mother. Not ever in her wildest of dreams would she have ever known of such phenomena; never would she have had this path put before her if not for Mrs. Annie Edson Taylor. A person of great knowledge and depth, Mrs. Taylor had come into her life like a great blessing.

The first evening they all made their way to see and hear Miss Susan B. Anthony, a prominent social reformer and women's rights activist, as she addressed the crowds at the Lily Dale Assembly. "I declare that woman must not depend upon the protection of man, but must be taught to protect herself, and there I take my stand, Independence is happiness. Organize, Agitate, Educate, must be our war cry. No man is good enough to govern any woman without her consent."

They had come from near and far, some three thousand had assembled under the yellow of the suffrage movement festooned everywhere the eye could see. At night the Chinese lanterns twinkled on the plazas, as gorgeous as any Fourth of July celebration. All in honor of Woman's Day and her coming freedom. If not for the Skidmore family, this great lady may never have been presented to the people and they never would have heard her ideas about the concept of liberty for all. Brigid thought it very clever of Miss Anthony to dress in black, allowing for her words to be heard without any material distraction of her presence.

Following the address from Miss Anthony, they made their way to the Forst Temple, as it would be a good idea to be early and sure of a seat at the main event, the Thought Exchange Meeting.

The first speaker took to the stage. "There are no dead. We live and love you. Though invisible, we are still with you." The crowd sat enthralled with the dramatic opening, instilled with confidence in the speaker's mission to help those before him.

Mr. Slater was up next and told of the Science of the Soul, inspiring the crowd with his reading of sealed questions before their very eyes. Then came Mrs. Whitcomb, who talked of psychic remedies that could cure all ails. "My systems of treating disease are unlike those of other practitioners. Using psychometric examination of the patient's invisible spiritual aura by the faculty of clairvoyance, I am enabled unerringly to determine the cause of the particular manifestation we term "disease"—I seldom fail in my effort to restore harmony to the system. I treat thousands of people every year, attending to them personally or through the mail. My waiting rooms in Buffalo receive over one hundred patients per day. Physicians send their incurables to me. My mission is to heal the sick and restore them to vitality."

Brigid could not find the words to describe the feelings of comfort brought forth in her and was first in line to book a private session with Mrs. Whitcomb for the next available appointment. The anticipation and the wonder of it all had her giddy with excitement.

With far too many thoughts permeating her brain, Brigid had slept fitfully that first night, and the next morning Annie said she, too, had a dose of the fidgets and commented that it may have been the spirits coming to awaken one from their slumber of life as they knew it. Brigid knew it was simply a dose of the collywobbles ahead of her meeting with Mrs. Whitcomb and the worry of how she would prepare herself.

Annie suggested they walk to the Inspiration Stump, where Brigid could sit quietly and ask for guidance ahead of her allocated time with Mrs. Whitcomb, whispering that it was only for the use of the clairvoyants, but that she had a special dispensation due to her own special powers. Arriving at the Octagon House, Brigid bumped into a young lady who rushed past in great distress, visibly overcome and barely able to carry herself. Brigid's instinct was to assist the young lady, but she hesitated for fear of intrusion. Brigid was shaken as she greeted Mrs. Whitcomb, who asked her what had her looking so shaken.

Brigid replied, "Why, the lady who has just left!"

Mrs. Whitcomb smiled, advising, "It is not grief as we know it, but merely an outpouring of pent-up emotions so cruelly disallowed by society. Now, let me explain how I receive my gift. Your messages will come through me. It is not me who imparts these words but my great spirit guide. Whom did you wish me to connect with today? Are there any messages in particular that you would like to receive?"

Not knowing what to say, Brigid advised that she was visiting with her good friend Mrs. Annie Edson Taylor and that she had felt an immediate connection to the place, far too nervous to voice her greatest wish to hear from her mother. Surely Mrs. Whitcomb could hear her heart beating in her chest, so fearful was she that it might actually happen. Father Dempsey's words rang in her ears, damning her from the altar for this act of sacrilege and blasphemy—godless, unholy, and sinful.

Displeased with Brigid's response, Mrs. Whitcomb huffed and closed her eyes.

When suddenly, a man's voice, a great deep baritone rang out. Brigid looked around, sure that she would see another party had joined.

The voice spoke to her. "You have been brought here to spread the word. You have been chosen to assist those that question, using your education for the betterment of society."

Brigid looked about the room to see if anyone else had entered, rigid with fear as she thought, *Surely not. It simply cannot be expected of me to assist in this great advancement of our time.* She, who'd had to withhold her whereabouts from her own husband. *Please, no. Not me.*

Mrs. Whitcomb opened her eyes, taking some time to adjust, asking if she had received a message and if it was satisfactory. Not wanting to appear rude, Brigid hesitated and then simply replied, "Yes." To fill the silence, she ventured that it was most likely a case of crossed wires, for surely the message was not for her.

Immediately Mrs. Whitcomb proclaimed, "That is absolutely not possible. You will only ever receive the messages that have been written in spirit for you and you alone. It most definitely *was* for you."

Brigid needed clarity. "I have been told that I am to assist in this great work, to help others to see this path. Surely this cannot have any relevance to me."

Mrs. Whitcomb sat up straight, clapping her hands as if Brigid had just made the greatest revelation of all time, and pronounced, "It is only the chosen few who receive this great affirmation of their calling! You, too, have a gift. Why, I can help you with it. I run meetings for just that and would welcome you into our community . . . for a small fee, of course."

All that Brigid had wanted to know was if her mother could hear her. This was something entirely different. But maybe she did have a gift after all. Granny definitely had something; she always knew everyone's business before they knew it themselves. Then the fear set in, not knowing what she was meddling with and at what risk, considering if now was the right time to ask the Lord for assistance. It might be best to keep him out of it for now.

Brigid left with a bottle of Psychic Female Remedy No. 10, specific for all diseases peculiar to women. It was sure to provide a definite cure for her inflammation of the womb and affliction of the ovaries, and would help with overall strengthening and invigorating. Taken regularly as prescribed, for two to three months at best, and in severe cases a long time, it was sure to effect a cure.

Brigid had never bothered Ben with her complaints, but she was quite sure he must wonder, as did just about everyone else, why they had not yet been blessed with a child. Most declared it was for the best since they were only starting out and were far from settled. Brigid thought differently; she knew there was something not quite right with her and was overwhelmed with Mrs. Whitcomb's assurance that she could help, that in fact she had treated many ladies who had gone on to have very large families, some returning to ask if there was a remedy to reverse the process.

The experience had taken quite the toll on Brigid; her head and body ached, which Mrs. Taylor assured her was quite normal. At breakfast the next morning they sat with Mr. Johnson, a kindly gentleman of some years and a respected judge of great standing. He spoke very openly of how he had been withdrawn from society, laboring under a great depression of spirits, occupying all of his leisure in reading on the subject of death and man's existence thereafter. "I was all this time an unbeliever, and how I tried the patience of believers with my skepticism and refused to yield unless upon most irrefragable testimony. At length the evidence came and with it such force that no sane man could withhold his faith." Mrs. Johnson sat quietly by his side, head bowed, holding onto her husband's hand.

Mr. Meade, a physician and agricultural chemist from New York, burst forth with his skeptical comments, not before noting his membership of various learned societies. Mr. Meade loudly declared how he had commenced his investigation into Spiritualism in order to rescue, as he said, "his friends who were running to imbecility."

Quite the debate ensued, with Annie and Brigid caught in the middle of the crossfire. Soon there was talk of Mrs. Mary Todd Lincoln, who had been regularly visited at the White House by spirit ministers, whom she claimed had helped her overcome her grief over the loss of her child. The group agreed that surely Mr. Lincoln himself had sought their counsel in matters of this great country.

Mr. Meade was incensed. "My good man, surely you know that he merely humored his dear lady wife, referring to it as he did with great humor as the 'upper country.'" Mr. Meade was frustrated by the believers, and before long they turned on him for his irreverent behavior. Taking his hat and cane, Mr. Meade brusquely took his leave.

At the closing ceremony held later that morning, Brigid and Mrs. Taylor were reminded of the words of Mrs. Skidmore, "Remember this is—and always will be—a spiritual camp. Hold fast to this truth and say to those who would have it be something else . . . the world is wide . . . so go your way. We would have no new gods placed upon the altar. Spiritualism is enthroned in this camp and outside issues must be kept to their own realm. Guests are to be entertained but not allowed to monopolize or overthrow the camp."

Before departing, Brigid made one last purchase: The "wondrous" Psyche Complexion, only fifty cents a jar, assured a "beautiful complexion, a woman's chief charm." The almost magical powers within the bottle would cause all around to remark at the user's improved complexion. Enlightened and uplifted, it was with a heavy heart that Brigid set off for home, lost to deep thought and reflection, if a little weary at the prospect of questions about her trip from Ben and having to deceive him further.

Ben was waiting for Brigid at the station, which surprised her; she had not expected him to meet her. Feigning exhaustion and a headache, she hastily took her leave as Ben inquired after the other ladies and how he had hoped he might have the opportunity to meet some of them. Brigid, riddled with fear and anxiety, pulled Ben by the arm, calling out to the first carriage driver she saw. Ben was annoyed with her and told her that they would take the tram, a carriage was an unnecessary cost. Brigid firmly told Ben that she was unwell and would be unable to sustain herself on a tram. Sitting in the carriage in silence, Ben clearly read out their address, highlighting that they were local to the area in case the cab driver tried to trick them and take the long way home. Brigid went to her bed, distraught at the deceit she had created and for having to fool Ben. She told herself that in time, she would discuss everything with him, but not before sufficiently educating herself on all matters of the spirit. Her dream was that Ben would join her and together they would delight in the spirit world.

CHAPTER 18

Much and all as he tried, James no longer felt the call of the land which had once soothed his soul. He had lost his sense of place. He had no love for the summer mornings, the cattle that waited for him to stir them from their slumber, the scent of the hay in the fields, nor the mist blowing in from the shore. James could see in Thomas the great love he'd once carried for the place.

James told himself that Thomas could breathe new life into the place. He deserved to carry on the Kelly name, and James asked himself how he could deny Thomas what should be his. It was not Father's wish, nor what Thomas had ever questioned. This life of privilege, this life of assured comfort, this life that needed a family, needed new life that James knew he had no desire to give to it. He could not fool those whom he loved more than life itself. He was no longer for this village.

James had asked his father to come into the parlor, as he needed to speak with him in private.

Agnes, helpful as always, said, "What in the name of God is he thinking? Is he as mad as his sister? More likely he left a girl behind him in that wretched place. I told you he should never have gone. It was the boy that you should have sent on that wild goose chase."

This was not what Patrick needed to hear. He had been dealt a final blow in what had already been a tragic year. Patrick listened to what James had to say without uttering a question. He had some sense of James's unease, thinking it was a wanting of more space, maybe a place of his own to take a wife and start a family, growing from boyhood to man.

Patrick had no words to chastise, to question, or to comfort James, for he, too, had known the weight of the Kelly name, the weight of having plenty when others were wanting came with its own crosses to bear. "You'll be off soon, so will you be needing a few bob for your travels?" was all that Patrick could say.

James went in search of Thomas, wanting to speak with him before the word spread, and found him lying on a haystack in the midday sun, his hat covering his eyes. Not wanting to startle him, James gently pulled on his arm. Thomas jumped up, "What did you do that for? You put the heart across me."

James apologized and said, "I was needing to talk with you, Thomas. I have told Father of my decision to leave. I am going back."

Flustered, Thomas replied, "What, what are you talking about? What in the hell has gotten into you? You can't do this to Father, not after Kate. He needs you here. The place needs you—it can't run without you, James. You just need more time to settle yourself. Or is there someone special you left over there? Go on, James, is there? Did you meet a Yankee, one of those rich ones like Lord Doyne? We could do with a few bob around here. Go on, James, you can tell me. I won't tell anyone. Is there a special someone?"

With tears in his eyes, James replied, "No, Thomas. It's not that. It's just me wanting for something this place can't give me. You'll be great here, Thomas. You deserve this place. There is only a life for one of us here—only a home for one family, a family that you can give to this place."

Thomas pushed James by the arm. "Don't be talking like that, James. Sure the place has always been yours; I never questioned it. They'll be saying I ran you out of it."

"Stop, Thomas. Don't be talking like that. This is my decision. I'll tell them all at mass, and I won't have a bad word said about you. Will you be sure to look after Father for me, and Kate? I will help out where I can. I will send home money, same as before—whatever I can Thomas, whatever I can. You have my word."

Biddy O'Connor was beside herself with excitement when she saw them at mass. "My oh my. James Kelly is up and leaving again. Has a girl I heard—a foreign one—and she had his baby. I'll be damned. Who would have ever thought that James would be the one to bring shame on the family. That Agnes would tell you nothing—not a word out of her. I heard it from Father Dempsey. He said Patrick had told him a long while ago that James was not settling, and don't we all know what keeps them distracted—a Yankee. And sure he would have forgotten about her by now, so it *must* be a baby that is bringing him back."

Molly was upset by the gossip going about the village. "Biddy O'Connor, you had better stop that talk out of you. Patrick doesn't deserve it, and I know you take great pleasure in upsetting Agnes, but not at the expense of the Kelly family."

Biddy huffed, pulling her coat around her. "I'm only telling what I heard and nothing more. Mind you, Agnes would want to keep her powder dry—she only has Thomas left to look after the place, and if she is not careful, she'll be out on her ear when he takes a wife. She never had any time for that boy and, mark my words, there'll be some change in her now. It'll be Thomas this and Thomas that, not a word about poor Kate. She wasn't happy until she had her sent off to the madhouse. Sure she would send the lord himself into it."

Patrick made sure to tell James, "You had better visit Kate before you leave. This will surely shake her, and she'll be needing time to say her goodbyes."

"I would not want for Kate to hear it from anyone but me. Biddy O'Connor and her gossip won't have made it to Wexford town yet." James was only too aware of how this would take its toll on Kate, knowing out of all of them that she would feel it the most. He had visited with her only the once since she had been released from the asylum, a brief visit to see if she was all right. She wasn't—she was still shaken and needed rest. She would be back to herself by now.

He left for the town the next morning, taking a ride with young Johnny Sutherland, who was going in to see a girl. Johnny was delighted with himself to have a captive audience, wanting to know all about the girl James had left behind. "Will you go away outta that James and tell us about her. I bet she has a fine pair of American legs on her. Is she a young one or did you go for a sophisticated type? Does she show off the legs at all? I bet she doesn't cover them up like the ones we have here. Plenty of money too. Sure, why else would you be giving up the place? Go on, tell me, is she a daddy's little girl and you're getting a big dowry to take her off their hands?"

The more James tried to deny it, the more they said he was as guilty as sin. The story was growing by the minute, and he would have a wife and family hidden away before long. All James could do was tell it as it was, in his own words. He could not be responsible for the stories they told themselves. It was this small-minded lack of stimulation that kept them going from day to day, for without their gossip and stories what else would they have? He would not be sorry to leave this behind for a life of anonymity.

Kate was delighted to see him. "James! Oh, James, what a wonderful surprise, and how I have missed you. We never did get to have a proper talk the last time. How could we, with Agnes hovering about. I could not bear for her to know any of my news. I was worried that I might have offended you or hurt your feelings. Have I, James? Have I hurt you? Please tell me that is not true. I do hope I did not cause you a lot of trouble to come all this way for a visit. Well, I for one, am glad. I will make us lunch, and we can take a stroll for the afternoon."

James shifted from one foot to the other. "Ah Kate, why would you think that? You could never hurt or offend me. You will always be my number one."

Kate was beaming. "Oh James, you are so kind and good to me always. I don't know what in the world I could ever do without you. If not for you I fear that I may never have regained my spirit. Just knowing you were on the other side of that great wall waiting for me gave me strength and courage. Now let's have some fun. You simply must meet Mary."

James was flustered. "Kate, it is you I have come to see. Let's say we go for a walk, just the two of us."

"Not at all, Mary will be beyond excited that we have a visitor," replied Kate.

Kate brought Mary into the room. "Mary, meet my dearest brother, James. Yes, this is he, he who has traveled halfway around the world. What fun we shall have, cause for a celebration. I must bake a cake, a special cake, James, just for you. Let me show you all that I have learned. Now Mary, you sit here with James," she said and skipped off to the kitchen singing away to herself, delighted with life.

James sat and listened as Mary talked and talked—she could talk for Ireland, that one. Exhausted with all her chatter, knowing Johnny would be wanting to make the return trip home before dark, and after some two hours of needless conversation, James stood up from the table. "Kate, I need to stretch my legs before I sit back in that cart. Maybe we could take a walk, just us two."

Kate took her coat and as they walked, she excitedly talked about Mary, telling James that she had quite the eye on him. "I can tell, she is acting all silly, far sillier than usual. She has an eye for the boys; it is all she talks of and I just know she will have my heart broken with talk of you. Wouldn't that be something, James, you and Mary?"

"Kate, stop that with all your talk. Don't be embarrassing me. Actually, that's why I came to see you, I won't be needing any friends anytime soon." Pausing to catch his breath, he said, "You see, Kate, I'm going back." Stopping, he took Kate by the arm.

Oblivious, Kate continued on. "Imagine that, James, you and Mary. Oh what fun we would have. She could visit with us in Moling. I will suggest a visit. Agnes would be delighted for you to have a friend to visit."

"Kate, are you listening to me? I am leaving. I am going back to America. I have my passage booked, and Father has given me his blessing."

Kate put her hands over her ears, shouting, "Stop it! Stop it right now. I don't want to hear this talk out of you. Why are you doing this to me? Don't you know that I am trying to recover, and I don't need you coming here upsetting me like this. I won't stand for it, James; not now, not ever." She pulled away and ran up the street.

James ran after her. "Kate, please, I don't want to hurt you. I have to do this, I can't live this life, it is not for me anymore. I have tried, I have tried everything to stop the want, but it is with me morning, noon, and night, haunting me in my dreams, calling to me, pulling me back. It is no good, Kate. I have to go."

Kate pushed James away from her and turned her back to him.

"Kate, please, please don't let us leave it like this. Please, Kate. I need you to understand that this is about me, only me. I have thought of nothing else but you since my return—you and father and Thomas. I am at my wit's end, and it's killing me, Kate. I cannot bear for us to part like this. Please give me your blessing."

Kate shut the door in James's face as Johnny pulled up alongside with the horse and cart, ready for the road.

CHAPTER 19

Mrs. O'Toole knew he would be back, long before he knew himself. She'd had enough of them through the place to know homesickness when she saw it, and James had never shown as much as a bit of it. He was one of the few that caught a hold of the dream that others were so afraid of because they missed their mammies, missed the cold and the damp of Ireland. Crying themselves to sleep, they wished their life away until the day they could return to Ireland, with most of them never seeing that day.

James was happy to be at the bottom of a ladder he wanted to climb, not with ambition, not with a dream, not looking for love. It was a wanting for anonymity, to be just another immigrant name on the list. His smiling face turned ever skyward, he explored every turn that took his fancy, a knowing glance for all and a little more for those who needed it. No matter their color or creed, he met everyone the same.

San Francisco was exploding, people arriving from everywhere, monied and penniless all there together. James loved this about the city. He loved how there were so many different people it did not allow for the small-minded class system of the old country. The people in the city he now called home were filled with a sense of excitement and encouragement, a wanting for each other to do well, a kindness at the core, genuine and warm-hearted, not with one eye on the pearly gates. They called it the American Way—they were proud of it, celebrated it, cherished it, goddamn, they lived it. It wasn't for everyone, but it was for James and for those he surrounded himself with.

James smiled as he heard Mrs. O'Toole singing in the parlor.

> *"When Irish eyes are smiling,*
> *Sure it's like a morn in Spring,*
> *In the lilt of Irish Laughter, you can hear the angel sing,*
> *When Irish hearts are happy,*
> *All the world seems bright and gay,*
> *And when Irish eyes are smiling sure, they steal your heart away"*

Every time they played that tune, he felt that the words had been written just for him. Over and over it played in his head, and in every one that had a bit of Irish in them. It was the sense of pride and joy, said Mrs. O'Toole. It captured every heart that was green, and those that were wanting to be. There are always those that are wanting. Mrs. O'Toole would tell James, "Isn't it great to be the real thing, James, and not a half of anything."

"That's for sure, Mrs. O'Toole. That is for sure."

Mrs. O'Toole was very proud of her involvement in the great 1915 Panama Pacific International Exposition. "Will you be going to the Expo when it opens, or will you give it a while to settle itself? I'll be there the first day, lest you forget I am on the 'Woman's Board.' Tact, cultivated taste, and courtesy, sure why wouldn't they want me?"

Mr. O'Toole interjected, "Will we ever hear the end of it? You would think she was running the place. If you are lucky, you'll be making the tea, love, and most likely sweeping the floors. Sure, you are a great little scubber."

"Richard, stop that now, you have a bee in your bonnet that you were not called to the great cause. You had your chances, any number of them, but no, you said you had enough to be doing with yourself. Father Hickey was blue in the face asking you to help out with the Catholic stand."

The O'Tooles loved to tell themselves that they were busy looking after James when in fact it was fast becoming the other way around as they aged and slowed down. You would never be done with a house, there was always something that needed doing and it was James who did most of it. James would turn his hand at anything from cleaning the chimney to trying his hand at the pipe works. The O'Tooles were not in need of the rental money anymore, as they had enough to see them out, but James knew they needed the comfort of his presence. They would not take any money from him, saying he more than paid for his keep with all the work he did for them. They knew he sent home what few bob he had to help his father, especially with all that talk of war and Ireland needing to send their men across the sea, when they were trying to fight their own war. Thank God for those that gave their time to raising funds to help the old country.

James thought of home almost every day. He guessed it was too much for him to expect them to be thinking of him. Father had only written once, and when Thomas did write, it was a couple of lines at best. It was Kate that broke his heart. She had not written to him since the day he left, and he had no news of her either. Dr. Murphy had given James his word that he would keep a watch over her and give him news of her. And Brigid never as much as mentioned Kate to him, not in any of her letters and not when he had visited on his return. Kate's little upset was not his news to tell, so he left well enough alone and never brought it up to Brigid.

James never knew if the money he sent back to Ireland was needed, but he sent it anyway. He didn't need much for himself, just what supplies he picked up for the repairs at the O'Tooles. It was his way of giving back. He was a grown man with little experience of managing his own money, having never taken a wage from the family business. He had only ever taken what he needed and no more. Agnes had looked after the household and father had managed the books, always saying he must show him the ropes one of the days that never came to pass.

James easily slipped back into his routine with the Vincentians, living it every day, in the true spirit of the word. He was not one for broadcasting his good deeds, simply placing himself quietly in service to others. His pockets he always kept full knowing there would be someone in need of a bite to eat. He would kneel to acknowledge every bowed head, smiling into their eyes, asking their name, and remembering it the next time. To these people he was a lifeline in a world which too easily forgot them. For many years after they would recall the gentle Irish soul who sought them out on Christmas Eve with a wrapped parcel. It never mattered that it was only a piece of fruit—to them it was the only gift they would receive.

James had been asked on many occasions to take on a senior role within the charity, but his reply never wavered. He was not in it for the glory. It was the very reason why he never considered a life of religious service, wanting only to be the best Christian that he could, with grace and anonymity.

CHAPTER 20

Ben had insisted that they sit at the back of the room—it was a wonder in itself that Brigid had managed to get him there. She had spent weeks of cajoling that fast became insisting as she begged and he relented. He could not bear another meal with some article or other placed before him. Sir Arthur Conan Doyle was to be the headline speaker at the Niagara Falls conference on Spiritualism. Brigid was going, and that was that. Ben had not the least bit of interest in hearing what this man had to say. In fact, he was concerned for the man's welfare and questioned his state of mind. Ben wished only to arrive and humor his wife before leaving at the earliest opportunity.

The ballroom at the Clifton hotel was full to capacity. There was not a sound to be heard as the audience sat transfixed as Mr. Doyle bellowed from the stage, speaking with conviction.

"I was amazed to find that a number of great men—men whose names were to the fore of science—thoroughly believed that spirit was independent of matter and could survive it. When I regarded Spiritualism as a vulgar delusion of the uneducated, I could afford to look down upon it; but when it was endorsed by men like Crookes, whom I knew to be the most rising British chemist; by Wallace, who was the rival of Darwin; and by Flammarion, the best known of astronomers, I could not afford to dismiss it. It was all very well to throw down the books of these men which contained their mature conclusions and careful investigation, and to say, 'Well, he has one weak spot in his brain,' but a man has to be very self-satisfied if the day does not come when he wonders if the weak spot is not in his own brain."

Ben was embarrassed for the man—an Englishman, a former neighbor!—speaking with such idiocy. Ben even considered for a moment that it was all a great hoax. If not for seeing it with his very eyes, he would not have believed a standing ovation possible the likes of which he saw at Doyle's closing remarks.

"There is that which comforts the mourner and binds up the brokenhearted; that which smooths the passage to the grave and robs death of its terrors; that which enlightens the atheist and cannot but reform the vicious; that which cheers and encourages the virtuous amid all the trials and vicissitudes of life; and that which demonstrates to man his duty and his destiny, leaving it no longer vague and uncertain."

And there stood his wife, his Brigid, leading the charge, first on her feet, first to congratulate this man, this stranger for whom she had no acquaintance nor knowledge of what he said. Good Lord, what on earth did she think she was doing?

It was a quiet and lonely walk home for Brigid, the euphoria of meeting the great man himself dissipating as soon as Ben had taken her by the arm and told her it was time for them to leave. He did not need to say a word, for the look on his face told of his sentiment. When they were in the privacy of their own home, Ben made it very clear that he was having none of it, not now, not ever. She needed to stop this foolishness, for she was threatening their very existence. Ben demanded she tell him what had gotten into her. What would become of them in this town where nothing escapes the few? As he lay awake that night in bed unable to sleep with worry, Ben decided he would speak with Father O'Brien and seek his counsel.

Father O'Brien was very understanding. "I am in no doubt that Brigid is an educated young lady, and I am equally in no doubt that this is the cause of her malady. All this education of our girls, putting ideas into their heads that has no place. The first place of an educated woman's usefulness is in the kitchen. This is the woman's grand domain, her rightful sovereignty, regardless of her education. They cannot handle the intensity of rigorous thought, which makes menfolk self-controlling, steady, deliberate, calculating. This is why men are calmed by education and women, well, excited. Heightening an already emotional weakness. As for the lower classes of women, why, they are more fertile; they don't have the want of modern civilization and the follies of fashion.

"I have seen that wanting in Brigid—always wanting something or other when maybe at this time her place should be in the home, focusing on bearing you a child. You need to be firm, Ben, and stand your ground. There is no court in the land that would not stand behind you. It is the basic right of any man to have his woman bear him a child. The good Lord removed the curse of barrenness in the Kingdom of Abimelech, and you need to pray to our Lord for his blessing. You will be given guidance and all he will ask of you is your patience. He will bless you in time with the grace of a child."

Ben was somewhat comforted. "Thank you, Father. I did not know where else to turn. It will not be easy to take Brigid away from her work with the ladies of the parish, though. You might offer your assistance with lightening her load. It would be a help with having her focus her time in the home."

"Of course, Ben. Why, I will speak with Mrs. Hosford this very evening, but surely the monthly meeting is not too onerous a task?" replied Father O'Brien.

Ben was quick to respond. "No, Father, but it is the ancillary days out and talks they attend and then taking the two days away from home to attend that retreat in Buffalo."

Father O'Brien paused, trying to think back to the updates Mrs. Hosford had provided to him of the progress of their committee, not quite sure he was aware of that many outings and certainly not overnight. He would speak with Mrs. Hosford.

⚜

Mrs. Hosford was waiting to speak with Brigid before the start of the next ladies' meeting. "Brigid, would you come here a moment? I shan't keep you long. I had Father O'Brien speak with me last eve, after a visit from Mr. McCarthy, who told Father O'Brien that he had some concerns about the time that you are spending on your good works with this church. He asked that I reduce your duties to allow for you to have more time in the home. I did not know quite what to say—is our monthly meeting too much for you? Father O'Brien mentioned some retreat in Buffalo that you attended for two days with the ladies of this parish. Now Brigid, you and I both know that would be most unusual. Why, I have never been to so vulgar a place as Buffalo. My lady friends of this parish and I would never countenance such time away from our place in the home. Goodness only knows what would bring someone to even consider such a thing. Am I to believe, Brigid, that you were telling an untruth, that you were implicating my good name and that of the other ladies of this community? Is there something you wish to tell me, or will I just have to assume it for myself?"

Brigid had been caught off guard. Her mind went completely blank, and she was thrown by Loretta's vicious tone, never imagining that she could speak so coldly and accusingly to her. She was her friend. Brigid had supported her wholeheartedly, giving of herself to every cause. Brigid spluttered that it was all a terrible misunderstanding and that she would speak with Ben the moment he came home from work and that she would speak with Father O'Brien too. Loretta had no wish to hear what Brigid had to say, blinded by her fury at being implicated, as she saw it, in such an undignified and dishonorable situation.

Trying desperately to think of what words she could use in reply, Brigid's mind could only consider what had brought Ben to speak with Father O'Brien in the first place. Had someone spoken to him of the trip? Had someone seen her in Lily Dale with Mrs. Taylor? Loretta would surely be making her own inquiries, as only she knew how, and it would not be long before it would filter back to the menfolk and to Ben. Who knew what conclusions would be drawn? Brigid knew it would not be pleasant.

It was not a conversation that Brigid ever wanted to endure as long as she lived. She had agonized over what words she would choose in telling of her trip to Lily Dale, but it was all in vain. Ben simply would not listen. Had she fatally struck out at a person it would surely have caused him less upset. He was beyond rage and was devastated at what he saw as her betrayal. The betrayal of his trust—taking her leave with nothing more than a damned humbug who preyed off the idiocy of others. What in the name of God had come over her to go against the teachings of the Church, to take time away from the home, time away from the marital bed, denying him the most basic of his rights.

Ben was incensed. "I have been patient. I have allowed you your folly. Surely it is you who does not want for a child of our own. You've no wish for confinement, so caught up are you in this fanciful madness of 'fasting girls' and their telling of tales. Is it you, Brigid? Have you denied me a child all these years? What else have you kept from me? What else is there to know about the woman I call my wife? What would your father have to say? Heaven only knows that they will hear of it and then what are we to do? What are we to say when they next ask if you are in the family way, or if we are still too busy enjoying ourselves? Here you are, living the high life, off gallivanting with every fool, and there am I, working every hour that God sends for us, Brigid, for us and for the family I hoped we would have."

Brigid had nowhere to turn and no one to turn to. She had brought it all on herself. It was only a matter of days before she was asked, or rather told, to retire her duties with the ladies of the church. There was little for her to try and justify or explain; silence was the only avenue. Ben had warned her, should she open her mouth it would simply make matters worse, for what exactly had she to say? Tell of her fraternizing with the humbugs, traveling and spending a night in lodgings with one of them? Ben was perplexed, not knowing quite how to manage her. He had forbidden her from going about unaccompanied—no walks, no days out, no visits to museums. All the things which she loved, all the pleasures that had reassured her that she had made the right decision leaving her home. All so cruelly taken from her, taken by her beloved to protect her, to preserve her faith and her good name—his name.

The four walls became Brigid's constant, with the ticking of the clock that never traveled fast enough her only companion. Ben had asked that all correspondence be left unopened for his review. What money Brigid had left from her father was handed over for Ben to manage—another deceit, in his eyes. Had he not provided enough for her as it was? Had he not given her everything she had ever asked for?

There was to be no more invitations to "at home" days for Brigid, no more luncheon parties, no more theater parties, winter parties, white parties. Sunday mass was no longer a fixture of their social week, for when they did attend there were no smiling faces to welcome them into the pew. They were relegated to the back of the church, their "friends" bowing their heads as they passed.

Father O'Brien had prepared an entire sermon on the evil spiritualists that were invading society. "These fools are preying on innocents, preying on the feebleminded, preying on those in this very congregation. Immoral, senseless day dreamers, who will fill the nervous asylums of this country. Be in no doubt that Catholics are forbidden to take part in any of it. It has taken on ridiculous and disgusting forms—obscene behavior. They cannot be attributed to God. Their author must only be Satan, the archenemy of God. Pagans are those who believe that thirteen is an unlucky number, who think it would bring bad luck to spill salt at the table or to break the mirror, to marry in May or to begin work of a Friday. Be in no doubt that no member of this congregation will be welcomed to this church should they persist in following such a path. Amen."

The humiliation too great to endure, they slipped away during communion, the way cleared for them to pass as if inflicted with a contagious disease. They walked silently to a chorus of tuts and clicking tongues.

CHAPTER 21

March 1, 1915
Dearest Brigid,

Please tell Ben that the Western country is alive with every wonder. How I wish you could see it for yourselves. I know Ben has no love for a life in a city, but there are many fine towns in these parts, with opportunity almost everywhere.

Has word of the great Panama Pacific International Exposition reached you? My, what a wonder it is, bringing people from almost everywhere. Father would have plenty to say about the waste of the land given over to "amusement," some six hundred acres, the finest of land right by the water's edge. I am settled and happy living with the O'Tooles. I want for nothing. I enclose a booklet on the exposition from my last visit there. It will run for the year.

Your loving brother, James.

Ben ate his dinner in silence, reeling from their social exile. James's letter lay on the table beside him. The life they'd settled into in Niagara was no more. It did not take long for what began with the ladies of the church to soon travel the entire community. Ben had been relieved of his supervision duties at the factory and "asked" to go back to the night shift operating the machines without even an attempt at an explanation. When society turned, it turned fast and hard. Ben had known this would be the outcome. He had known it from the very first moment when Brigid had stopped to speak with

Annie Edson Taylor. Innocent infatuation never stood a chance with evil trickery. He knew Brigid was a good, kind person, and she had never anticipated or intended for any of this to befall them. He feared now for the toll this would take on her health. Ebullient, flourishing, confident Brigid was now withdrawn and listless. She hid herself away, unable to face the stares and whispered tones. There was nothing he could do or say, for even time would not heal this wound in this unforgiving society.

"I've written to James," Ben told Brigid quietly. "We'll be leaving here and joining him in San Francisco. We'll make a fresh start there."

Brigid stayed silent.

There were no sad faces to wave Ben and Brigid goodbye—no tears, no hearts broken, only harsh lessons learned. Gathering up what funds they had, they booked their passage West. They decided it was best for Brigid to use her middle name, Delia, so great was their excommunication.

Sending a telegram to James telling of their planned arrival, they told him they would be staying at the Palace Hotel and hoped he would be available to meet with them upon their arrival.

James was put out by the words, *available to meet with them*. What in the name of God was wrong with them—where else would he be? Hadn't he wished for this day? James smiled as he thought, *What of the decidedly "un-American carnival of secular humanism" that Ben had called the West? What of his worry about me among the warring tribes and "libertine" lifestyle out here?*

It must have been awfully hard for Brigid saying her goodbyes, as the very society she swore she would never be part of had fast become her world. When all is said and done the Catholic Church opened more doors than it closed, a passport into a way of life. But Brigid and Ben would want for nothing here, only an open mind and a willingness to work. Ben will want his privacy and a place of their own, it would be enough for James to know they were close by.

Mrs. O'Toole hosted a dinner in their honor, "Brigid—or is it Delia I am to call you? You will have to forgive me, as I am quite sure I will mix it up. You sit here by Mrs. Collins. She has promised not to have you working too hard at St. Mary's, and Ben, you sit here by Mr. Collins. There is not a man in this city he does not know."

James was proud of the O'Tooles and their kindness, wanting to do all they could to help Brigid and Ben settle into the city. He was embarrassed about the "Delia" nonsense; she would always be Brigid to him.

Mrs. Collins took her job at the church very seriously, keen to impart the good works of herself and the ladies at St Mary's, a grand Cathedral, no less. "Which church did you say you belonged to in Niagara? And what experience do you bring with you? No doubt we could learn a thing or two from your own good works."

Brigid's stomach was churning, her dyspepsia kicking off. She shifted in her seat. She didn't want to be rude but needed to put a stop to any inquiries. "Mrs. Collins, I have preferred to busy myself with the home. Ben is my priority, and it does not allow time for much else. We like to keep to ourselves. I am sure you can understand."

Mrs. Collins sat back, pushing her chair from the table, wiping her hands on her napkin. "My dear, forgive me. I had assumed that was why I was asked along. I do apologize if I have misunderstood. I am sure you will find plenty to keep you occupied in the home. How many of you are in the family?"

Ben, overhearing the conversation interjected, "The good Lord has not yet blessed us with a family of our own, Mrs. Collins. I thank you for your consideration."

Mrs. Collins smiled. "My dear, the Lord works in mysterious ways. Maybe it was to allow for you to see the light and come live in the West country. No sooner will you be settled than you will find that you are with child. Divine providence orders all things in life for our good."

Ben and Mr. Collins were soon slapping each other's backs. Both men of Irish roots, they had much in common. The men were deep in conversation on the progress of the city, the splendors of the Panama Pacific Expo, and how they were truly witnessing the greatest progress of their time. Ben was enthused about their future—a fresh start with much to look forward to. He didn't want to admit it but found himself thinking that maybe, just maybe he should have listened to James sooner. He heard his mother's words, "If ifs and ands were pots and pans, there would be no need for tinkers."

Brigid was not feeling quite the same enthusiasm. She struggled increasingly with headaches, and the dyspepsia was now a constant. Confining herself to bed, she was told that rest, complete rest, was the only cure. The travel had been far from restful, the train journey hideous. Brigid hid her discomfort from Ben, as he had enough on his mind. She just needed to keep up her strength for these first few days, and when they were settled, she would have all the time in the world for rest.

True to his word, Mr. Collins secured Ben a job. The next morning Ben dropped by the Rialto building on Montgomery and Mission, as the highway company was looking for laborers for the building of the Shute Highway. Ben was offered a foreman position on the spot—his experience in Niagara as a supervisor stood to him, and his genial manner found him favor with the men. The only caveat was that the work would take him out of the city. That was music to his ears, as he had no interest in the fast-paced city life and wanted Brigid as far away from it as possible to recover her spirit in what he called a "home away from home."

It was not hard for them both to fall in love with the golden fields and cooling fog of the Petaluma valley—dairy, eggs, and hay, its fortune. They had viewed a number of properties available for rent, but Brigid knew she was home the moment she set foot in the garden of a grand house on Bodega Avenue. Holding hands as they walked up the wooden steps to the door, they admired the pretty porch wrapped around one side, two rocking chairs inviting rest. They were greeted by their new landlord, Emily, who showed them around the ground floor. Brigid squeezed Ben's hand as they walked through the front door into the large hallway, rich mahogany woodwork giving an air of grandiosity. Two large reception rooms were to the left of the hallway, a large bay window in the front room with a cute picture window to the side allowed for the sun to shine through. A spacious double bedroom, kitchen, bathroom, and a pantry completed the space. It reminded Brigid of Molly's house next door at home in Moling—a proper home.

The landlords, Tom and his sister Emily, lived upstairs. They had inherited the home from their aunt, whom they had cared for into old age. They ran a small chicken business and a flower and vegetable garden that served the local community. Tom and Emily were equally as excited to see this young Irish couple join them in their home, the perfect tenants to share it with. Ben was taken with the work they had done to provide a modest living, and was intrigued as he walked the property, listening to Tom tell of his vegetable garden and chicken coup. Emily linked Brigid by the arm as they strolled through the flower garden, selecting her favorites to display. That very first evening, Ben and Brigid sat in their rocking chairs on the porch, looking out at the fields, waving to the passersby. They held hands and smiled. For the first time since leaving Moling they felt settled and were filled with a sense of excitement for their future.

>*November 5, 1915*
>*Dearest Molly,*
>
>>You will hardly believe how life has changed. You will note our new address—we have moved to the west! James had written endlessly of the opportunities, and Ben made the decision for our future. It all happened quickly and has been filled with excitement.
>>
>>Ben had indicated to the aluminum company for some time now that he was looking for more opportunity, so there

was little surprise when he told of our plans. We packed our bags and here we are. The train journey was long and arduous. However, we survived, and it has all been worth it.

James met us from the train, familiar as he is with the city. He brought us to our hotel, where we stayed for the first week. His landlady held a dinner to welcome us, and it was not long before Ben had secured employment. We have no wish to live in the big city, finding the most beautiful home right here in a lovely town called Petaluma. Oh, Molly, how I wish you could see my view just now. Looking out over the fields and farms, I imagine we are in your back kitchen looking out to the land.

The weather here is far more agreeable. We will no longer have those severe winters. I don't think I could have survived another freezing of the falls. They call this the "egg" capital of the world, supplying some ten million eggs to San Francisco. They even have an Egg Day Parade to celebrate all things egg! Oh, Molly, what fun!

Father would surely not believe his eyes were he to see the wagons at the creamery unloading their pails or the hay, most of which supplies the horse-drawn traffic in the city—some five thousand tons per month. He would be amazed at how things are done here. The only thing missing in my life now is you. How I wish you were here with me to share in my excitement. Please do tell of your news from home when next you write. For now, I busy myself with taking care of our new home and helping Ben to settle into his new employment.

Your fond cousin Brigid.

With all sense of remorse lifted, Brigid was consumed with an overriding sense of contentment. She had no want of the company of others, and the experience of Niagara now behind them, Brigid had given Ben her word that her sole focus would be on him and their home and the children they would surely be blessed with.

CHAPTER 22

Biddy O'Connor was in for her morning paper. "What news have ye of the Yankees? Have they produced any offspring for you yet? Goodness knows what the attractions of the New World does to a person, busying themselves with all that glitz and glamour. It is no place for any young man, or woman for that matter. You must be beside yourself with the worry, Agnes, as to what they are getting up to. Do you regret the day she up and left with that Ben fella? The McCarthys are no Kellys, that's for sure. A bit of gypsy about them, I'd wager. If you went back far enough, I am sure you would find a wagon on the side of the road."

Agnes was incensed. "Biddy O'Connor, I never heard the likes in all my life. If Father Dempsey heard you now, he would never again absolve you of your sins."

"Oh now, Agnes, you have to admit the Kellys are not quite the family you thought you were marrying into," said Biddy with a satisfied smile.

"We all have our crosses to bear, Biddy. Your day will come," replied Agnes, bringing an end to the conversation.

Patrick could hear the chatter in the shop and left Agnes to it. She was more than able to hold her own against Biddy O'Connor, and he did not want to be listening to her talk anyway. Thomas was doing a steady line with Margaret Kelleher. They had become engaged and were to be married in the spring. Agnes was happy with the match. A fine, big strap of a girl, there would not be any doubt about her reproducing. It would be the only hope they would have about the place, as they were not getting any younger, and the work was taking its toll.

Thank God for Thomas; he was like the savior himself. If they didn't have Thomas, sure where would they be? As for Brigid, she never could settle herself, moving on again, off to the West Coast, as if the East was not far enough. Patrick knew that he'd not see her again in this lifetime.

Patrick was lost in his thoughts as he headed off out to the fields, asking himself why in the name of God they'd ever had to leave. He would carry the loss of James and Brigid until his dying day. They had wanted for nothing. There was more than enough here to secure a good life for all four of his children. Patrick put his head in his hands at the thought of how James had turned his back on his rightful place as head of the family. With tears in his eyes, he asked the Lord for the strength to get on with his day.

Patrick was only ever to have these thoughts in the privacy of his own mind. He would never as much as utter a word of it to anyone, not even to Father Dempsey at confession. Was it a sin for him to feel this way, to hold this inward resentment, letting it fester deep inside of him all these years? Patrick kept his head held high when he knew all about him looked on him with pity. At least Biddy Doyle voiced it; the others gossiped behind his back in the parlor of Sutherlands.

⚜

Margaret Kelleher was delighted with herself. She had bagged the prize catch in Thomas Kelly. She had done all in her power to land him, more than aware of her own humble origins but with a knowledge that she was destined for greater things. Margaret was clever. She knew Agnes was the decision-maker in the Kelly household and made sure to bring a variety of homemade baked goods and fresh flowers from her garden on every visit. Agnes was suitably impressed; in fact they got along famously.

Thomas was relieved to know that there would be no trouble from that quarter, and felt an ease that Agnes would take Margaret under her wing and show her the ropes. Margaret was a quick learner and more than keen to get started. She and Thomas wasted no time in saying their vows. Patrick paid for the wedding breakfast, a grand affair altogether in the Talbot. Kate was missed, but she was minding the bakery shop in Wexford town that day and wished them well.

In Margaret moved to the Kelly home and business, the newlyweds, Patrick, and Agnes all living happily for now under the one roof. That was the end of any talk of Kate returning home, no matter what Father had to say about it. Margaret was the woman of the house now, and she would not want her sister-in-law living with them. Kate had not given much thought to her future, as she focused only on the day before her. Occupied with the bakery and mass, it was her world, and it afforded her some semblance of control. Routine, the strict schedule she kept for herself, cleanliness, and her prayers. When Father did manage a visit, all he cared about was her sleep, "Are you getting your eight hours, Kate? Do you take rest on your day off? Do you wake during the night?" Sleep, sleep, sleep; it was all that any of them ever cared about.

Kate no longer visited Moling and did not feel they missed her. They treated her differently anyway. The only one who ever left her alone was Thomas, and only because all he cared about was the shop and the farm. Agnes barely looked at her, never mind spoke to her. More often than not, with lips pursed as she passed, she'd turn her head the other way. Kate knew she was damaged goods, feared, treated with curiosity, to be handled with care. A hush would settle over the shop as she entered, whatever topic of conversation soon forgotten. There were no more potential suitors for Sunday lunches, no more marriage prospects in the offing, no talk of a future. Most pretended that nothing had changed, when everything had. They feared her, and she feared herself.

Mary, the one friend she had, was unable to withstand the test of shared lodging. They bickered constantly and found it impossible to find common ground. For all Mary's glamour, behind it she was nothing more than a brazen hussy. Kate, assuming a motherly role at the start, was happy to run around after her, but it soon lost its appeal. No longer able to stand her crude ways, the final straw was the day Kate reached for her good Sunday coat to find that Mary had been wearing it without her consent, leaving a used sanitary rag in the pocket. Enough was enough—Mary had to go. The stress of it all left Kate in an awful way, as Mary's eviction had resulted in Mary flinging Kate's things about the place, threatening all sorts of curses to befall Kate.

For Mary, leaving the accommodation meant leaving her role at the bakery—not a good outcome for her, and she was going to make sure Kate knew all about it. Kate locked herself in her room not knowing what Mary would do, and there she stayed until she heard Mary slam the door behind her. The proprietor, a single elderly bachelor who had no wish to be getting in the middle of the two women, had let them work it out between them. It was an easy decision that it might be best for Kate to live alone. Kate was the boss as far as he was concerned, and she could call the shots as to who stayed. A great worker, she ran the place like clockwork. He had tried many a time to chat with her and find out about her life and her family, but she had little to say. There was nothing wrong with that; all too many of them had too much to say, and that's what got them into trouble. A grand, tidy girl, the place had never looked so good—and cleanliness was next to godliness in his eyes.

⚜

Margaret Kelly wasted no time getting in the family way. The news was received with delight and relief. Patrick went about with his head held high, and Agnes was just short of putting up a notice in the shop. All was well in the Kelly household; the war years so far had been good for business with the increase in cattle and dairy prices. Thomas was the hero of the day, as it had all happened on his watch. There was money for a new Ford, and they could go for a spin of a Sunday, taking it out on trips to the seaside and even as far as Dublin. Their firstborn was a girl, good and strong with a fine head of hair. Margaret was back up on her feet in no time, and Agnes loved to have the little one in the pram beside her in the shop, showing her off to all that crossed the threshold.

Biddy O'Connor was the first in to give her commiserations. "You must be awful disappointed, Agnes. Sure, what use is a girl to you? Haven't you enough of them about the place and not a child between them. It's in the breeding. All of mine produced a fine strapping boy for themselves as their firstborn, every one of them. It gives us great peace of mind to know that the place will be looked after and in good hands, if you know what I mean."

"Indeed, and I don't know what you mean, Biddy O'Connor. Sure, we are not like that at all. We love all God's creatures," said Agnes through gritted teeth.

Patrick found himself slowing down and was not able to do as much as he once had. The doctor told him he would need to lighten his load, which was easier said than done for any man who had a business to run. There was always something to be done about the place. Agnes insisted that Thomas take over the mornings and told Patrick to lie in bed to give himself more energy to start his day. The business was in good hands, but Patrick was far from ready to hang up his boots. His own father had died on the very land he cherished, and there was no better way for a man to go. Life had never looked better. The Kellys had settled into a harmonious and profitable way of life.

CHAPTER 23

Petaluma offered Ben and Brigid the peace and relative quiet of rural life with all the wonders of a new world. Brigid began her day sitting out on the porch, watching as the sun illuminated the fog before Ben joined her with his cup of tea, enjoying the stillness in the peace of their surroundings. Brigid would ask Ben his plans for the day, knowing that whatever the job, he would be on the ground with his men around him, working as hard as any of them. It was easy to see how he had earned their respect, never asking them to do any job he would not do himself and always taking pride in his own work and how his workers were contributing to the advancement of the place.

As the flocks of chickens cackled, Brigid prayed to the good Lord that he would bless them with a family of their own. Those first moments of every day held the wonder of an anticipative mother. Did she feel any different today? Was that a rounding of her abdomen? Was she more tired than usual? Maybe today she was growing a new life inside of her, the first of the children they so desperately wished for. They were keenly aware that the clock had been ticking and with it all hope of a large family. Accepting of this, they talked of how modern it was to have fewer offspring. It was all that Brigid could think of and all that she knew everyone she met thought of, too, as they inquired about her family and how many children they had.

Brigid limited her trips to town, as she found these conversations a constant reminder of that which she dreamed of most. When she was forced to reply that it was just the two of them, there were no words of advice or encouragement, only a sudden change to talk of the weather.

How she wished there was someone to confide in, someone to give her the advice she so desperately sought. If only for a mother of her own, who would take her into her confidence and guide her in matters of a successful confinement. Molly, the one person whom she knew she could confide in, couldn't know of such torment with three kiddies of her own. Molly couldn't know what it felt like for Brigid, having to read her news of the children in every letter she received. Brigid was irritated by how everyone in Moling seemed to think her life without children was of their choosing. Did they think they were living the high life, too busy with new experiences to have the want of a child?

Brigid had sought medical opinion in the early days in Niagara, only to have the doctor pat her on her head, telling her nothing was amiss when she knew that all was going wrong. Every waking moment for her was consumed with willing a new life to grow inside of her, willing it with every ounce of her being. The frenzy of the fear at times took over all rationality. On those days Brigid prayed to those that had gone before, begging them to take the pain away, to relieve her of the cross which she had to carry, and when it all became too much, she rested her body, for her mind knew not what else to do.

James felt a sense of responsibility for Ben and Brigid's happiness and a genuine desire to see them prosper. Mrs. O'Toole had been put out by what she saw as Brigid's lack of respect at her introduction to Mrs. Collins. She could not understand why Brigid did not want to discuss her work with the ladies of the church in Niagara when it was all her letters had told of during her time there. James had no answer for her, as he had wondered the very same. That and all this "Delia" business was confusing for him too. But James respected Brigid's decisions and her need for privacy. She knew her own mind, and James was not one to question.

It did not stop Mrs. O'Toole from wanting to hear of their

progress. James's response never wavered, "Not much of late," was all he ever said. Brigid's letters covered the same ground—Ben's work and the weather. Mrs. O'Toole found it strange that after all these years there had been no talk of a confinement. What exactly was Brigid waiting for? When did she think the time would be right? It was not for James to comment, for what would he know?

Father's letters were filled with pride, felt in every word. The birth of Thomas's daughter, a granddaughter, had come into a house in need of some joy, and the business was surely prospering if they had money for a Ford. Agnes was not one to allow for luxuries. There was never any talk of Kate, not a word. James had not heard from her since the day she had closed the door on him; her pained face flooded with tears haunted him. All he could do for her now was pray for her happiness, pray that he would hear word of her settling down and having a family of her own—isn't that what any girl would want? Of course, there was never any mention of her "incident." With the luck of God, it was all behind her. It was up to each of them to get on with their own lives and make the most of the path laid out before them. James never looked back, so assured was he of his decision to leave.

James did not have to think twice when the invite arrived to visit Ben and Brigid in Petaluma. He followed their instructions and took the train from Sausalito. As he journeyed through the countryside, it was easy to see why Ben had chosen this place for their home. James arrived in a bustling town with people all going about their day. Ben met him from the train, and they walked along the main street, where there was a store for everything. Ben was beaming with pride as he greeted everyone with a nod or a wave, leaving James in no doubt that Ben had found his sense of place in Petaluma. James was familiar with this feeling and knew that there was no need for words. Walking past the chicken shacks, he was comforted by the familiarity of the smells as Ben told of how he loved what he called the little comforts of home.

Brigid, sitting on the porch, jumped up as soon as they came through the gate. "James, I am so glad you came! It really is wonderful to have you visit with us. It is younger-looking you're getting."

"Ah Brigid, you are too kind. It is just the fine weather giving me a bit of color," James replied.

"How was your journey? Did you enjoy the views? Please say you will stay awhile. It is so lovely to have a visitor, and there is so much we want you to see," said Brigid, taking his arm.

"I have the two days off. It was hard enough to get them together. They like to give the Saturdays to the men with families. I never mind—I'm happy to take what I'm given. I have more than enough time for myself anyway. What would I be doing with myself, only strolling the streets," said James.

"Oh James, we are so happy to have you, even if it is only for the two days. We must make the most of every moment and be sure that you leave knowing how happy we are here," said Brigid as she led him into the parlor.

All the talk at dinner was of the president's proclamation as James read the newspaper article about it.

> *America is stepping forward to do her part in making the world safe for democracy. In every city and town, in the most remote valley, hamlet, and at the wildest mountain crossroads, ten million sons of liberty are inscribing their names on the honor roll of the ages that the free governments for which their fathers died may not perish from the earth. White or black, married or single, sick or well, alien or native born—even enemy subjects of the kaiser—all men between the ages of twenty-one and thirty-one are expected to present themselves on 5th June from 7 a.m. to 9 p.m. for registration.*

James was twenty-nine years of age and Ben, thirty-two. They knew it would only be a matter of time before the age limits were extended and Ben, too, would be required to register. The war that had ravaged through Europe for three years had all felt rather remote up until now. The letters from home kept them informed of the restrictions. Molly wrote of the newspaper advertisements looking for the Irishmen to enlist, giving out that they were trying to make it all look like a big party, not ever a mention of the certain casualties. "IF YOU ARE AN IRISHMAN YOUR PLACE IS WITH YOUR CHUMS UNDER THE FLAGS."

James told them that he would not hesitate to be there on the fifth of June. He would be proud to support this country. Ben agreed with him and said that he, too, would do his duty when his time came. The time never did come for either of them. They had both been first in line to enlist and were proud of their draft registration cards, but neither of them were called to active duty.

Sitting on the porch in the evening sun, full to the brim after a feast of roast chicken and the Kelly trifle, James felt as if he was going to burst. "What news have ye of home?" he asked.

Brigid loved chatting to James. "Not much of late. Just the odd letter from Molly. She is busy with the children—she has time for little else, if you ask me. Thomas is not one for writing letters, and Agnes only writes when she has something to give out about. Father did write some months back to say that Lord Doyne had called on him and took him out for a motor. They have had a strong friendship over the years, strange as it is. Do you remember the early years after mother passed and Lord Doyne would send over the carriage to take us up to the hall? He never had any airs or graces. After a while you would forget he was a lord at all but for the accent. Father would never say, but he was proud of their friendship. We never saw much of their children. I guess it wouldn't do for them to be mixing with the locals. Father said Lord Doyne missed them when they went off to school in England. I guess there was not much excitement about Wells House for them. It was a good thing he married Lady Harriet or else the place would have gone to rack and ruin."

Happy to let Brigid chat away, James asked "What was Lady Harriet like, Brigid? What did you make of her at all."

"Hard to know really. I was always so afraid to put a foot out of place. Agnes had me so scared out of my wits about the do's and don'ts of the place that I spent more time worrying than I did enjoying. She was kind and friendly for a lady. She always made time for me and believed in my dream of a new life here. I think she grew fond of my visits—she often said they reminded her of home. I could have listened to her all day, talking of her life back in New York, growing up as an only child in a world filled with more money than sense. Of course, she did not see it that way, but I had never heard the likes of the trips she took with her mother to Europe to buy dresses and spend time with Lord this and Lady that. I think it broke her father's heart when she left. She missed him too. He died soon after. One day she told me that some said it was of a broken heart. I didn't know what to say to her—she had such tears in her eyes—so I jumped up and said I had better be getting home, as it was late. I always regretted that. I'm sure she thought it strange of me. Did you know that she called to the shop in Moling after we left to hear how we were getting on? Agnes was giving out, saying that if I had stayed, I would have been her lady's maid, but it was far from being a maid to anyone that I wanted from life," said Brigid.

"That was kind of her to call to Moling. What did you say in your letter to her?" asked James. "She must have been happy to hear your news of her home country."

"No, I never wrote any letter to her. She has more to be doing with herself than thinking about me. What would I have to tell that would be of interest to her anyway? No, that door is closed. Maybe Agnes wanted Kate to go up there after I left. I never asked, and they never said. I often wonder if Kate has had enough of the baking and will want to move back to Moling, though I'm not sure that she would be welcome with Margaret and the baby," said Brigid.

James sat back into the rocking chair and closed his eyes, listening to the song that played from the upstairs window;

Hello, Frisco, hello
Hello, Frisco, hello
Don't keep me waiting, it's aggravating
Why can't you hurry, Central, you're so slow
Hello, now can you hear
You know I love you dear
Your voice is like music to my ear
When I close my eyes, you seem so near
Frisco, I called you up to say "Hello"

Changing the subject, James asked, "Do you like the music, Brigid?"

"I don't have much choice, with Emily always playing some tune or other from upstairs. She does ask if it bothers us, but it's the American way. Let's go for a bicycle, James. It is such fun and the perfect way for me to show you the place. Or are you too old fashioned and tremble at the revolution of bicycling women? Ben bought them for us when we arrived. He thought it would be good for me to get out and about, and I get great enjoyment out of how it causes quite the stir to see me whizz past. Some of the older ladies would much prefer to see women stationary, with only the men allowed to be mobile. I have heard them say that female intrusion into the outdoor world of athleticism threatens the world order," laughed Brigid as she jumped onto her bike. "Let's get a move on, James, before dark."

James could only assume from this that there was no news of Brigid being in the family way, knowing Mrs. O'Toole would be all questions on his return.

CHAPTER 24

Agnes knocked on the bedroom door. "Thomas, Thomas! Get the doctor. It's your father—he is not well at all. He was up half the night with the coughing and can barely catch a breath. He was out in the fields till all hours last night with those bloody cattle. I am sick and tired telling him to take it easy, but sure no one ever listens to me."

"Leave him be, Agnes. I'll go and get the doctor now," said Thomas as he dressed himself.

Thomas told Margaret to go back to bed with the child as he left the house and walked across the lane in the early morning half-light. Molly, an early riser, opened the door immediately.

"Thomas, what is it? What has you up at this hour? What's wrong, you put the heart across me," said Molly, startled.

"I'm sorry, Molly. I know it's early, but Agnes was insisting I get the doctor. It's Father. He's been up half the night with the coughing, and she said she didn't get a wink of sleep. You know how she is."

"Of course, Thomas. I will call him straight away. Isn't that what he's here for? Don't be worrying; your father will be as right as rain in no time."

Patrick had known he was slowing down, but these last few weeks had been different. He could not get the heat into him as he sat by the fire or even when he wore extra clothes. He just could not shift the chill in his bones. Then he had started to cough. It had progressively worsened, with phlegm coming up from his lungs. All the while, he told himself it was nothing a good night's sleep wouldn't cure—until last night, when he could not catch a wink of it.

The talk in the towns was of the mysterious malady that was infecting the country with the return of the troops, the "Flanders Grippe." They'd been told to look out for fever, headache, sore throat, and black skin. The national papers were filled with stories of an invasion of disease. By all accounts it was worse in the South of the country. There was hardly a household in Clonakilty that did not have at least one person afflicted with this flu, and there was no post being delivered in Carrigaline, as the local postman was confined to his room with the disease. Policemen were laid up in Tipperary, and doctors the length and breadth of the country were on foot night and day. Everyone had gone mad, of course, with all the differing remedies. Washing the inside of the nose with soap and water, washing the floors with Americus disinfectant, flushing toilets, for those that had such luxuries, with carbolic. A few towns even sprayed the streets with Jeyes fluid.

There was to be no shaking of anyone's hand. Meetings were canceled and markets, fairs, and election rallies were all called off. Theaters were closed, dances canceled, and even the hurling final between Tipperary and Wexford was postponed. The archbishop called people to "earnest prayer" to deliver them from danger.

"Clean your teeth regularly, chew onions, eat plenty of porridge, and keep to the side of the road if someone in a house has it." Traveling salesmen made the most of the increase in sales and had all the potions. Gallaher's High Toast Snuff would prevent it, Genaspirin thoroughly repulsed it, Milton Mouthwash claimed "You cannot catch it," while Thompson's Influenza was like magic.

Moling had felt isolated from the pandemic and the news had not quite taken hold. Not one of them had thought of the flu, assuming it was just a bit of a cold that Patrick had caught. As soon as the doctor saw Patrick struggling to catch his breath, he knew there was little he could do for him now. Only time would tell if he would be strong enough to overcome it.

His thoughts were with Kate and how now was not the time for him to have that talk with Patrick.

Agnes had insisted they take Patrick to St. David's Well, which was said to have the cure. The doctor gave the go ahead, for he knew it would give some comfort for what might lie ahead. Patrick had become weaker by the hour, barely able to stand. They took him in the Ford. Agnes asked Thomas to hold Patrick as he walked down the steps to the water, and she and Margaret would say the prayer at the statue of St. David himself.

Father Dempsey was called to the house that night, and together they prayed to the Blessed Virgin to obtain the love of Jesus and three offerings to the most Holy Trinity to obtain the grace of a happy death. In the early hours of an October morning in 1918, in what was to be the second and most virulent wave of the pandemic in Ireland, Patrick silently slipped away into the arms of his beloved Ellen, who had been waiting for him.

The days ahead were a time in Dr. Murphy's career that would weigh heavily on his mind, for it was a time when he had to put his role as a medical doctor to the fore of all else. Mandatory protocol from the authorities stipulated that the Kelly homestead was prohibited and had to be fumigated for fear of contamination from the corpse. Agnes stopped the clock at the time of death, and the doctor opened the window to allow the spirit to leave the home, covering all the mirrors to hide the physical body from the soul.

Isolating Patrick's body and protecting himself with the required gown, mask, and gloves, he set to work on preparing the body for interment. These protocols held no consideration nor respect for the celebration of a life lived and much loved. There was to be no laying out of the body by loved ones in his Sunday best, no time taken to honor the tradition of the wake for all to come and see Patrick and offer their sympathies. No shaking of hands, no talk of what a smart man he was, what a great friend, father, husband. No time to stand by his coffin or touch his hands clasped in prayer, wound with his rosary beads. No gathering around the sandwiches and cake, no drinking the tea, no bottles of whiskey opened as the night wore on for the chosen few watching over Patrick. No telling of stories, no songs sung.

Patrick was taken to the church in the horse and cart that had so loyally taken him all over the county. Father Dempsey stood at the altar as Thomas and Agnes sat on either side of his coffin. Never before had the church witnessed such a lonesome farewell. No organ was played, no hymns were sung, no eulogy read. Father Dempsey offered the condolences of the parish, bowing his head as he once again said how sorry he was for their loss.

As Thomas and Agnes walked from the church, the square was lined with friends from near and far who had come to pay their respects to Patrick Kelly. Paddy Donovan, with his tin whistle, struck up the air to "Boolavogue" and with heads bowed, the gathered crowd sang the lyrics written in memory of the great Father Murphy.

> *At Boolavogue, as the sun was setting*
> *O'er the bright May meadows of Shelmalier,*
> *A rebel band set the heather blazing*
> *And brought the neighbors from far and near.*
> *Then Father Murphy, from old Kilcormack,*
> *Spurred up the rock with a warning cry;*
> *"Arm, arm," he cried, "For I've come to lead you,*
> *For Ireland's freedom we'll fight or die!"*
>
> *He led us on against the coming soldiers,*
> *And the cowardly yeomen we put to flight.*
> *'Twas at the Harrow the boys of Wexford,*
> *Showed Bookey's regiment how men could fight.*
> *Look out for hirelings, King George of England,*
> *Search every kingdom where breathes a slave.*
> *For Father Murphy of County Wexford*
> *Sweeps o'er the land like a mighty wave.*
>
> *We took Camolin and Enniscorthy,*

And Wexford storming drove out our foes;
'Twas at Slieve Coilte our pikes were reeking
With the crimson blood of the beaten Yeos.
At Tubberneery and Ballyellis
Full many a Hessian lay in his gore;
Oh, Father Murphy, had aid come over
The Green Flag floated from shore to shore!

At Vinegar Hill, o'er the River Slaney,
Our heroes vainly stood back to back,
And the Yeos of Tullow took Father Murphy
And burned his body upon the rack.
God grant you glory, brave Father Murphy
And open heaven to all your men;
The cause that called you may call tomorrow
In another fight for the Green again.

Thomas stood tall with pride, his head held high, knowing his father, the gentleman that he was, would never have expected nor believed the sight in the square in front of the home and business he had so loved. There was not a foe among them, for all were friends to Patrick and the Kelly family.

CHAPTER 25

Molly was distraught, for Brigid, for James, and for poor Kate—not one of them by Thomas's side as he bade farewell to their father, all alone in his grief. Molly shook with the tears as her body processed their grief. She cried for all four of the Kelly children that day, for the loss of both the parents they had cherished. There was nothing she could do for any of them now, only be there for Thomas in the days and months ahead in whatever way he may need her. And what of dear Kate? What in the name of God were they to do? Her father had told her that he had been called to the hospital the day before Patrick's passing to sign the required forms for Kate to be readmitted to the asylum in Enniscorthy, returning late that evening with the intention of speaking with Patrick. That was before Thomas's knock came to the door. It was a conversation he would no longer need to have, for there was nothing he could do for Kate now.

Dr. Drapes had been informed about the young lady who had been taken in during the night by the Royal Irish Constabulary officer in the town. She was said to have been roaming the streets, scantily clad and causing quite the disturbance, nothing and no one to identify her. She was unresponsive upon questioning. Dr. Drapes was called to the observation room before his rounds, and as he entered, he sensed that the young lady was familiar to him. But he was unable to get any sense out of her in her agitated state as she paced the room, oblivious to his presence. Chattering away to herself with her attention wandering, she jumped inconsequentially from one subject to another.

Throughout the day Dr. Drapes was preoccupied with this young lady who, while clearly unwell, appeared clean and well kept. Asking to be kept informed, he was advised that she was becoming more and more excitable and agitated, showing no signs of taking rest or instruction. That evening as Dr. Drapes looked back over the records it struck him that she was possibly the young girl who was known to his friend Lord Charles Doyne and had been a patient some seven years prior. Dr. Drapes thought it unusual that she had managed without care until now, as isolated episodes were rare.

With no other avenue open to him, he sent word to Lord Doyne, not wanting to unnecessarily alarm the next of kin.

> *October 14, 1918*
> *Dear Lord Doyne,*
>
> *I regret to inform you that I have a patient who has been brought to the asylum from the town whom I believe may be known to your good self. I am unable to ascertain identity and would be very grateful if you could check with the Kelly family as to the whereabouts of their daughter, Kate. If indeed this is Miss Kelly, I would be very grateful if you could arrange to make contact with the family and have them sign the required forms for her care. It is a matter of utmost urgency.*
>
> *Yours, Dr. Thomas Drapes*

Dr. Murphy was asked to call to Wells House, as Lord Doyne wished to speak with him. Utmost immediacy was advised.

On arrival to the house, the doctor was directed to the library, where Lord Doyne exchanged pleasantries about the weather, before discussing the reason for the meeting. Lord Doyne arranged for the estate car to be prepared, insisting on joining the doctor on his journey as he wanted to lend his support to the Kelly family. Arriving to the asylum as evening was drawing to a close, they were brought to the room where Kate had been moved for her own safety. The nurses had asked them not to enter for fear of overexciting her. Peering through the observation window, Dr. Murphy saw Kate lying in the corner of the room. He wanted only to open the door and take her in his arms, giving her what comfort he could, but he knew he had to obey orders. He confirmed that this was Katherine Kelly, fondly known as Kate, age twenty-seven years, single.

Kate was no longer in need of Dr. Murphy or anyone else's comfort. She had crossed the fragile line of insanity. Without any sense of awareness, her mind had turned against her. The force of frenzied thoughts had taken over and despite having fought so desperately and bravely to cling to reality, she lost the battle through no fault of her own. Kate had recently become convinced that she was being watched and that "they" were coming to take her away. She had locked herself into her room. There had been no one to look out for her, no one to be concerned for her, and despite her deepest fears, no one to watch over her. Her employer, assuming it was women's troubles and not wanting to ask, had left her be. Kate had fought the thoughts, fought to retain control of her mind that plagued her with nightmares when she closed her eyes. She became fearful of all and any noise, was tortured by a constant thirst, a wildly palpitating heart, and a deeply aching body. As the days passed to weeks, she slipped beyond any point of return.

Then one morning she awoke to the darkness having lifted, giving her a long wished-for sense of clarity. She felt all was going to be okay. The day was glorious and wearing her best dress, she took off down the town. Her first stop was mass, where she sat in the front row, saying her prayers at the top of her voice, as she needed to make sure God could hear her. The priest was none too pleased with her constant commentary as to how he was conducting the mass; he had missed a bit and then he had rushed the communion, so she asked him to do it again and a little slower this time.

Kate ran to catch the priest as he left the altar, barging her way into the sacristy to find she was not welcome. She knocked wildly on the door that had been closed in her face, until the sacristan told her to leave. Agitatedly she banged her way out of the church, the noise echoing as she slammed the door behind her.

Feeling as light as a feather, Kate skipped her way down the street, swinging her bag behind her, making plans as to all that she would do that day. A new dress. Oh, and yes, a hat and some shoes and a good winter coat. "I shall visit with Mary, see how she is," she told herself. "Why, we were the best of friends. Yes, I will call on Mary in her new job at the Talbot."

The sales assistant in the drapery was delighted to see Kate on a slow Tuesday morning buying the place out. Hat, shoes, dress, a new winter coat—there was no stopping this young lady, who knew exactly what she wanted.

"Put it on my account, please," she told the sales assistant.

"But my dear, we don't have an account for you," the woman explained.

"Then I'd like to open one, please."

"Oh my dear, that will take time, we usually require a recommendation for credit."

Kate, flustered, could not understand why she could not take the items with her there and then. Admiring herself in the mirror, she told the assistant to dispose of her old clothes.

Not falling for that, the sales assistant advised, "I will make sure to keep all of your purchases aside for you. When might you return?"

Kate was having none of it. "I want to take them with me now. I must have them. My father is a businessman. There shall not be any issue with my having an account or a reference. Do you not know who I am? I need them now."

The sales assistant grew impatient. "My dear, run along with you now and when your father is good enough to come here with you, we will be more than happy to settle your account. You can take the items with you then and only then. Take off that coat like a good girl, and I'll show you to the door."

Grabbing the hat, the sales assistant peeled the coat off Kate's back as she pulled her by the arm and shoved her out the door. Kate tried to put her foot in the way, but the assistant knew better and gave it a kick as she locked the door behind her.

Kate knocked on the door and banged on the window, agitated that the lady was not assisting her, shouting at her to give her the items. The shop assistant closed the blinds, turning the sign on the door to *closed*; it was time for her lunch anyway.

Dejected, Kate decided not to let the rude saleswoman ruin her day. Next stop, the Talbot to see Mary. She was told by the girl at the reception counter that a meeting with Mary might not be able to be arranged, as she was working in the kitchen.

"Well, can you tell her that her good friend Kate Kelly would like to see her? I have missed her terribly. We had the best of times. I think she had an eye on my brother, James, yes, *my* brother James. Just as well that did not work out, as he has gone and left us." Kate started to laugh, louder and louder until the girl at the desk nervously asked her if everything was okay.

Kate called out Mary's name in the reception area. "Mary, Mary! It's Kate. Come and let's have some fun together. We could go shopping or maybe to a dance, find ourselves some fellas."

Hearing the commotion, the manager came out from his office. Kate ran to him, "Please, I simply must speak with Mary. Run along now and get her for me, and you can tell her it's a surprise."

The manager called Mary from the kitchen, telling her there was a young lady in reception causing a fuss. Taking off her apron and wiping her hands, Mary went out to see who it was. Kate threw her arms around her and hugged her tightly. "It's me, Kate. Your best friend in the whole world. Where have you been, and why don't you come to see me anymore? Let's say the two of us go and have some fun for ourselves. You always loved the fun, Mary. Come on, what do you say? You and me, together again, just like old times."

Kate twirled herself about the floor, singing and dancing, pulling Mary with her.

Mary was mortified. What in the name of God did she think she was at, making an unholy show of herself? Mary pulled herself away and told Kate she was not welcome there and that she had no intention of going anywhere with her. Mary apologized to the manager and said that she had no wish to engage with this woman and that she would be going back to her duties. Turning on her heel, she hurried to the kitchen.

Kate shouted after her, "Mary, Mary come back! I want to see you. I need to see you. I have made plans for us." The manager told Kate to leave as he led her out the back door for fear a customer would see the commotion. Kate, unable to understand why Mary was being so cruel, begged and pleaded with her to come back as the lock of the door clicked behind her. Sitting outside in the back lane against the wall, Kate cried, calling Mary's name.

Kate had returned to her flat above the bakery as she tried to fight the intrusion into her mind, feeling the world was against her as it spiraled out of control. She lost all sense of routine, time, and fear. It was with the luck of God that the RIC officer followed up on the complaints about the young girl wandering the streets, going from euphoria to misery and back again by the minute. He had found Kate sitting on the pavement outside her lodgings, with only her nightshirt and a flimsy housecoat to protect her from the cold autumnal night. Kate was there only in body, for she had lost all connection to reality.

The officer, an older man, met her with compassion, thinking there but for the grace of God go any of us, seeing her as a daughter, a sister, a friend, as the person that she was and not what her world represented.

It fell to Dr. Murphy to inform Thomas of Kate's admittance to the lunatic asylum. They'd had more than enough on their minds the last few days, and he knew there was little they could have done for her. Anyway, she was safe now. There was no knowing how long she had been this way.

Thomas could not help but think how they had left Kate to fend for herself over the years, telling themselves it was all because of Agnes, who was always wanting to know what they were going to do with a girl who "can't make her own way." As far as Agnes had been concerned, Kate had no social advantages to offer, and though pretty, she was not fascinating, had no "go" in her, and was nothing but a burden to her father.

With no James to take care of everything, it fell to Thomas as the head of the family. He took himself off out to the fields to catch his breath, knowing he had to face this alone. Dr. Murphy had told him that they feared Kate may have infectious endocarditis, exacerbated by brain trouble and violent fevers. Thomas had read between the lines and knew she had been off her head. He was forever haunted by her last episode, the pitiful sight of her being forcibly removed from their home ingrained in his memory.

The asylum had placed two day and night nurses in attendance as Kate in her overexcited state had struggled so desperately. The immediate danger was her heart, weak from the strain, for she had not slept for many days and nights and had taken little by way of nourishment. As Thomas sat by her bedside, he told her to leave her dreams alone, that they were not real, willing her to sleep. Kate, recognizing him, kissed his cheek, laying her head on his shoulder and settling into a quiet rest.

Nine days after her admittance, Kate suffered a final convulsive fit. Making one last agitated struggle, she held out her hand calling to her mother as she sank slowly into hours of shallow breathing, until she stopped, the exact moment, no one knew. When Thomas came to see her in the coffin, her eyes were slightly open, looking into the beyond, her lips parted, just bordering on a smile. Thomas remembered the daisies that she had played with as a child, her smile as she made the chains for her dolls as she sat in the fields. Peaceful and beautiful, she would now remain with all who loved her, a memory of purity and of the goodness that she was. The death certificate noted her cause of death as "Acute Mania."

Thomas, wanting to protect Kate's memory, arranged for her to be laid to rest in the asylum graveyard, the graveyard for the bodies of those that had no one to take them home. It was a lonesome goodbye as she was lowered into an unmarked grave in a makeshift wooden box. Not a priest was in sight; they were too busy to be praying over the loss of a lunatic, too busy with the upstanding members of the community who feathered their parish purse, all fighting for a spot on the altar.

CHAPTER 26

November 1, 1918
Dear James,
It is with great sadness that I am writing to tell of Father and Kate passing away within days of each other. There was nothing more that could be done for them. They are at peace now. Due to the restrictions, we held a quiet service.
Will you please let Brigid know as soon as you receive this letter.
Your brother, Thomas.

James opened the letter and read the words over and over, as if each time expecting it to say something different. He had thought of this day, assuming he would hear of his father starting to falter, slowing down, or perhaps suffering from his heart trouble but not of his having died and been buried. The day he left home he thought he had prepared himself, but nothing could have prepared him for the news of Kate, twenty-seven years of age with her life before her. The sadness of it all so overwhelmed him that he took to his bed for the very first time in his adult life. Mrs. O'Toole, sensing something was wrong when he did not get up for work the next morning, knocked on his door. He told her he was unwell and was resting.

James did not know what to tell her, for he did not know himself what the cause of death was for either. Their father's death would be easier to accept but not Kate. If he could not make any sense of it, how could he expect others to? He would have to gather himself and find the strength to visit with Brigid—this was news that could only be told in person.

Mrs. O'Toole was worried about him and came again to his room that evening with soup and freshly baked brown bread. James struggled to find the words as he showed her Thomas's letter. Mrs. O'Toole put her arms around him, unable to hold back the tears as she comforted him in her arms. He had no words, and Mrs. O'Toole knew that there were no words, so she did not ask any questions. God only knew what had taken his poor sister from this world with her life before her, and within days of the passing of their father. What did some people ever do to deserve such affliction? There were times in life that no man could ever understand, and no prayer or words of comfort would make it any easier on those left behind.

James made his arrangements to call on Brigid in Petaluma. His freight supervisor was understanding and allowed him to take a couple of days leave. The next morning at breakfast with the O'Tooles, James saw the headlines of the *San Francisco Examiner*, "50,000 cases foreseen by Dr. Hutchinson." It was all that was being reported on. Picking up the paper, he read through the articles.

> *San Francisco holds its Church Services in Open Air to Avoid Contagion, Influenza is not abating, Ward off Influenza by Wearing a Mask on the Street, Epidemic Reaches Height Outside of San Francisco. Earlier that year 522 men at Fort Kansas were admitted to the camp hospital suffering the same severe influenza. It had started out with fever, sore throat, and chills, then the virus ravaged its victims' lungs, and within hours most would succumb to respiratory failure. It was causing havoc across the country and Europe. Mask wearing had become expected outside of the home and those in non-compliance risked being labeled a "Slacker."*

Dobell's solution was being given out by all the pharmacies free of charge.

> *Just bring your own bottle, any size up to a pint, see that it is perfectly clean, and if you can't find a good cork, they will supply one. The health authorities do not recommend Dobell's solution as a cure—it serves only as a preventative. It is used as a throat gargle and a wash for the mouth and nostrils. If you suspect that you have Spanish Influenza, see your doctor at once. In the meantime, don't worry, and keep yourself in the best possible physical condition.*

They managed a smile as Mrs. O'Toole read an article that caught her eye.

> *This is no laughing matter. We've kidded about the "Flu Fence" and the "Gas Mask" but this time girls, you needn't pucker up your nose and giggle. You've taken to the hobble skirt, barber-pole stockings, knee-length dress, and backless gown without a blush—you needn't shy at the mask. If Lady Duff Gordon had designed it and Mrs. Vernon Castle had introduced it, you'd all be running around in them, but just because a fad has come in that has a reason for being, you hesitate about appearing in public with it on. Take it from me it's just as becoming as a thousand other freak fashions we have fallen for. If you are a real San Franciscan—Prove it by wearing a mask!*

It had never entered James's mind that the cause of their deaths could have been down to the deadly influenza, as he'd assumed that it was a poor man's disease. But of course, it all made sense now. Father was elderly and vulnerable to the ravages of the deadly disease, and poor Kate must have been one of the unlucky ones who just did not have the strength to fight it. James was somewhat happy that he would have an explanation for Brigid later that day.

Brigid got the fright of her life when she saw James at the door. "James, you put the heart across me, I thought I had seen a ghost. Are you unwell? What is it that has you here?"

"No, no, Brigid. I'm fine, I'm fine. I am sorry for surprising you like this. I didn't have the time to let you know I was coming. I only got the letter yesterday, a letter from home. Let's go inside and make ourselves a cup of tea. You put the kettle on, and I'll read it to you," said James, gently taking her arm.

Brigid collapsed when she heard the news. The kettle boiled and boiled until the whistling cut through their tears. James told her how sorry he was to be the bearer and that when he got the letter, he knew he had to come and tell her himself. Never a family for showing their emotions James gently touched her arm, telling her that he was not the better of the news himself. Brigid cried until her heart hurt and there were no more tears left inside of her, the two of them united in their grief. Not knowing why or what had happened to them, they only knew that they were lost to them forever. They took some comfort that Father and Kate were in their mother's care.

"What now, James? What are we to do? Thomas will need your help back home. Ben and I could travel with you. Oh James, what are we to do?"

They did what any good Catholic would do—they went to mass, lit a candle, and prayed for their dear departed souls. Ben had come in from work to the news. He could see they were distraught and not thinking straight, and he tried his best to help them make some sense of it all. Ben told them both that Thomas was the head of the Kelly home and business now and was more than capable of running the place, as he had done for some years now without any of their help. Agnes had Margaret and their granddaughter to keep her company in the months ahead. They would only be getting in the way. Ben reminded them that this was something that every person who left the shores for a new life had to face at some point in their lives—hearing of the death of a loved one back home and having to accept that all they could offer was their prayers. It was a harsh reality that they could not be there to support the loved ones left behind, but they must be accepting of their fate.

Brigid was irritated by what she saw as Ben's lack of understanding, telling him, what would he know about grief when it had yet to knock on his door? How could he understand the depth of pain and the ache of the heart that never healed? Brigid asked Ben to leave her and James be, let them be alone in their grief and let them decide what was best for them at this time. Ben knew she was grieving, and he allowed her this. She had loved her father dearly. He also knew that she would be feeling the loss of a sister she had never quite understood, which would carry its own implications in death. James was embarrassed to witness them having words in front of him and simply nodded to Ben as much as to say he understood.

Brigid could not stop crying as she asked James over and over what could have happened to Kate and their father, what more he knew, what he was keeping from her. James showed Brigid the letter and told her that all he knew was what was in those few lines and no more. Brigid could not bear to look at the letter; seeing Thomas's handwriting on the envelope was enough to trigger the dyspepsia in the pit of her stomach. She never wanted to see his handwriting again.

James said to Brigid that he could only assume that they had died of the deadly Spanish Influenza that was in all the papers. It made sense. Brigid did not respond, as she did not know enough about it. James asked Brigid if it might be all right for him to take some rest. He had not slept properly since he had received the letter; knowing he was to be the bearer of bad news had weighed heavy on him. James did not want to leave Brigid alone yet also did not want to be there when Ben returned. He asked her if it would be all right for him to stay the night and that he would travel back early the next morning. Brigid said there would always be a bed in their home for him; he would never have to ask.

Brigid tidied the kitchen as she waited for Ben, falling into his arms when he came through the door. Together they sat on the porch until the early hours as Ben listened to Brigid reminiscing about her father and Kate. He let her talk, and he let her cry. She was right, he did not know about grief. But he did know that she was suffering and that she needed him by her side. Brigid had closed her eyes and fallen asleep in the rocking chair as Ben took her in his arms and carried her to their bed, hoping to get a few hours rest before he was to start his working day. Looking in on James, Ben was happy to see that he too was sleeping.

Sleep did not come for Ben as he lay wide-eyed in the bed, sensing this would take its toll on his beloved Brigid. Of course she was upset by such tragic news, but there was something else that niggled away at him, and he could not shake the unease.

They all rose early the next morning and ate breakfast together with not a word between them. Ben said his goodbyes as he headed off to work, thanking James for traveling to tell them the news in person. Brigid asked James if he would stay a while and maybe they could take a walk together, telling him about the awful dream she'd had the previous night and how she still was not the better of it. "I could see their coffins side by side, with neither of us there to say our goodbyes, and Mother looking on with a terrible sadness that the family had broken up."

James did not know what Brigid wanted him to say, for it was not far from the truth. Only Thomas was in the home that had once been filled with them all. James knew it would be hard for Brigid; she did not have much to distract her. He had his work at the railyard and with the Vincentians along with the O'Tooles, who always needed him for something or other. Trying to be helpful, James suggested to Brigid that she might consider getting involved in the community or the church. There were plenty of people worse off who could do with her help. Brigid snapped back, "No, I don't have any time for that carry on. I have more than enough to keep me busy in the home." It was a closed door and was not open for discussion. James was certain that too much time alone was not good for anyone. With that, Brigid took her coat and hat and walked out of the house. James followed after her, and they walked in silence past the small farmhouses with the smell and sound of poultry James had found a comfort on his first visit there. Brigid took them to St. Vincent's Catholic Church, where she suggested they go in and light another candle. Walking up the path, James smiled at the children playing on the grass, feeling for Brigid and how she had longed for a child of her own. Listening to the sound of the children's laughter brought James back to the days when they had played so happily together as children, finding solace in the haystacks. They'd used them for jumping on, running through, playing hide and seek in, or simply just to lie on top, hidden from sight, comforted by the warmth the hay held from the sun. The prickly sensation on their bare legs and the damp musty smell they held from the rain. Those haystacks held many a dream.

Brigid hesitated at the steps, so James gently took her by the arm and guided her through the heavy doors, thinking it was purposeful to have to push so hard to enter a church door, a sort of acknowledgment of the two worlds. There was not a sinner in sight as they were guided by the flickering of the candles, inhaling the comfort of the incense that medicated their troubled souls. This was James's favorite time to be in a place of worship, when it was quiet. Who could not appreciate the escapism, the comfort of the silence, being alone with his thoughts and answerable to no one. Seeking out the shrine of Our Lady, they both lit candles in memory of their mother, who'd had a great devotion. Heads bent in prayer, together they asked Our Lady to take Kate and Father into her care. Brigid walked alone to the front pew, where on bended knee she bowed her head and begged for the Lord's forgiveness.

James knew she was suffering and asked our Lord to listen to her prayers, wanting nothing more than for Brigid to be blessed with a family of her own, knowing only then would she find true happiness. He thought of Kate and how she had struggled, thoughts that he'd kept to himself. He'd never told Brigid of Kate's time at the asylum. But Kate was gone now, at peace with their mother and father who loved her and would take her into their care. That door was closed and best left well enough alone.

CHAPTER 27

Brigid could not shake the tiredness. She was barely able to prepare their food, never mind attend to the housework. Ben had asked her to go and see a doctor, as there was no sign of it lifting. Brigid knew there was little a doctor could do for her. It was grief, and she was accepting of this and had no wish to be told to rest, to be kind to herself, to lower her expectations at this time.

Ben, feeling helpless, if a little frustrated, insisted that she must see a doctor. Unable to listen to Ben's questions every evening as to what she had done during her day, Brigid agreed that she would call by the surgery. They had not yet visited any doctor in the town, so Brigid asked Emily if she could recommend one. Emily advised of a new surgery that had opened at the end of the avenue, and the reports were positive on the young new doctor who had come into town. Brigid called to the surgery later that morning and was greeted by an elegant young lady with a sweet, gentle voice sitting at a desk. Brigid explained to the lady that her husband had asked her to attend a doctor for his advice, as he was concerned about how she was dealing with recent grief. Brigid was a little self-conscious standing in the reception and was uncomfortable with going into too much detail, whispering to the kind lady that "it had been a tragic loss." The lady at the desk, sweet and considerate, offered her condolences, advising Brigid that she had come to the right place. Dr. Theodore Payne would see her straight away. Brigid had not expected to see the doctor there and then, anticipating a future appointment, but realized it would be helpful if she did not have to return.

Dr. Payne was younger than Brigid had expected, which she found disconcerting, skeptical of his experience. Directing her to take a seat, he asked her to tell him the purpose of her visit. Brigid spoke of how she'd recently lost her father and sister and that it had been a rather difficult time for her. Her husband was concerned by her increasing physical infirmity, as he saw it, with her lacking in energy and not feeling quite herself. Brigid told the doctor that she felt there was little that could help her situation and that only time would bring about an improvement. Dr. Payne allowed Brigid to finish before offering his sympathies, asking Brigid if she would lie on the bench.

Brigid hesitated, as she had not expected an examination since she did not have any obvious physical symptoms. Not wanting to appear rude, she made her way to the bench. Dr. Payne listened to her breathing, took her pulse, felt her head, and then her abdomen. Taking his time, he made sure to have a good feel, touching her tender breasts, first one and then both. Brigid was uncomfortable as he lingered, asking if she wore tight-fitting clothes. Brigid advised that as she was spending her days at home, she tended toward light day dresses for comfort. Dr. Payne told Brigid to fix her clothes and to take a seat at his desk when she was ready. Brigid sat in front of the doctor as he set down his pen and asked her when she had last menstruated.

Brigid was silent before hesitating a reply. "It was some weeks back. I cannot quite recall. With all that has happened, it has been a very difficult time for me, and I was not taking notice of these things."

Dr. Payne asked Brigid if she had a regular cycle.

"Yes, very regular, twenty-eight days, to be precise."

Dr. Payne continued. "Can you recall if you menstruated in the last four weeks?"

Brigid's mouth dropped open as she realized she had absolutely no recollection of experiencing menstruation, possibly for quite some time.

Beaming, Dr. Payne stood up to shake Brigid's hand. "Well, Mrs. McCarthy, I am delighted to inform you that you are with child."

Not knowing what to say, she asked him if he was sure.

Chuckling, Dr. Payne replied, "My goodness, Mrs. McCarthy, I think I should know a lady who is with child when I see one."

"I am sorry, Doctor. Forgive me if I appeared rude, but you see it has been a wish of mine for many years. We have been married quite the while, and I had given up all hope. I have been so consumed with my grief I had not given it a thought. Why yes, it does make such sense. Oh, I feel quite the fool. Thank you, Doctor, thank you. More than you will ever know, this is the most welcome of news," said Brigid as she stood to leave, leaning on the edge of the bench to steady herself.

"You are most welcome, Mrs. McCarthy, most welcome indeed. We are delighted to have you here as a patient and please know that we are here to help you with any of your medical requirements and that of your good husband," said Dr. Payne.

As Ben walked from the train that evening, he was startled to see Brigid walking toward him, knowing she had not left the house for weeks. Squinting in the evening sunlight as Brigid ran toward him, his heart sank, assuming it was bad news from her visit with the doctor.

Brigid, unable to contain her joy as the smile spread across her face, fell into Ben's arms. "Oh Ben! I have the most wonderful news. I am with child. I am having a baby, our baby, Ben."

Ben held her away from him, looking at her face. "What, what are you talking about, Brigid? Why do you say this? Did you go to the doctor today? What did he say?"

Brigid gushed, "Yes, yes, the doctor has confirmed it. I felt quite the fool for not ever thinking for one moment that this could have been the cause of my malady. Oh Ben, isn't this just the most wonderful of news? I just know that Father and Kate have answered our prayers. I could not sit still all day as I waited until it was time to meet you from the train. Oh Ben, dearest Ben, let's celebrate! Let's say we go to the Tivoli for our dinner and talk of all the plans we have to make. I must write of my news to home. I must tell Molly—she will be so excited for us, and she will surely be able to give me all the advice I need."

Ben, a steadying influence as always, told Brigid to settle herself, to not to get too excited and tire herself out. He asked what exactly the doctor had said.

Brigid smiled at his sensible approach. "He said to take good care of myself, eat well, get plenty of rest, and be sure to check in with him if I have any concerns. He could not quite make out when the baby is to arrive, but from his examination, he thinks I am most likely already some three months along."

Ben took Brigid in his arms, consumed with emotion like never before. If this was what it felt like to know that you are going to be a father, why, he was the happiest man alive. Always calm and in control, Ben wanted to shout their news from the rooftops.

They celebrated with a meal at the Tivoli and were hardly able to eat their food for talk of their plans. Ben told Brigid to slow it all down a little. He knew she was excited, but she would need to save her energy for what lay ahead. Their only priority now was this new life that she was bringing into the world, and everything else could take second place. Brigid loved seeing Ben so happy and, wanting to cherish this time, decided she would keep their news to themselves for now. It was their time to enjoy, just the two of them.

Brigid opened the wardrobe, carefully lifting the box hidden from view. Laying out the baby clothes and blankets she had kept through the years in anticipation, she was unable to stop the tears as she thought of her mother and Kate who, for differing reasons, did not get to raise a child to adulthood. She would be the only girl in her family to do so, which made her all the more determined that she would make it her life's work to love and care for this life inside of her. No more talk of grief—only joy and happiness as she prepared herself and their home for this baby.

All the while Ben agonized that they had not acquired a home of their own. Brigid assured him that it gave her great comfort to know that Tom and Emily were upstairs should she need any assistance. Emily would be a wonderful companion to her and their new baby.

Ben had his heart set on becoming a business owner, not wanting to settle into a home until he had first secured them a future. He was always looking out for opportunities and could see a good solid future in the grocery business—all he needed was the right place to present itself. Brigid was proud of Ben and of his desire to build a good life for them and now for their new baby.

⚜

One month to the day that they were told of the pregnancy, Brigid took ill. It started with an uneasiness in her loins and thighs, then a pain in the small of her back, followed by vomiting and shivering from chills. Soon after came the discharge of blood accompanied with severe pains in her abdomen. At the sight of the blood, Brigid screamed for Emily, who ran down from upstairs to be with her. Brigid knew by the look on Emily's face that she too was frightened by the blood on the floor and the bedclothes. "Emily, what am I to do, what in the name of God am I to do? I don't know what came over me. I had a sudden sharp pain, so intense it caused me to vomit. Oh Emily, please stay with me, please Emily."

Emily knew that Brigid needed a doctor and she told Brigid to stay in the bed and that she would get help. As soon as Dr. Payne opened the door to the bedroom, he saw the blood on the floor. Brigid, curled into a ball on the bed, turned toward him, riddled with fear. "Mrs. McCarthy, I need to understand what might have brought about this change in your health. Have you taken any medicines or have you been involved with lifting or straining your body?"

Brigid shook her head.

Dr. Payne continued, "Have you allowed yourself to experience violent cold temperatures, had any reason for sudden mental excitement, taken late suppers or overexerted yourself in any way with fashionable amusements?"

Brigid wanted to ask him what in the hell he thought she had been doing. She gave him a look of disgust.

"You will have to pardon me, but I do need to understand if you have partaken in excessive sexual intercourse?"

Brigid feared if she was to open her mouth it would only be to scream such profanities at this man that he would surely never darken her door again. She could not bring herself to respond, never mind to answer even one of his painful, senseless questions. She screamed inside her head. Did he not know that to be a mother was all she had ever dreamed of as a wife and as a woman? Brigid closed her eyes, hoping the stupidity of the doctor's questions would be apparent to him and he would leave.

Brigid did not need the doctor to tell her what she already knew—her baby was gone, no longer growing inside of her. It was dead and was being flushed from her body, from the warmth of her womb and with it, the love she had cradled it with and all hope of her being a mother. There was nothing he or anyone could do for her now.

The doctor continued to prattle on. "A simple application of cold water, externally applied, will produce relief. Cold cloths applied to the lower portions of the abdomen, along with perfect quiet, is most essential. You must stay in bed and ingest a teaspoonful of paregoric every two hours, drink freely of lemonade or other cooling drinks, and for nourishment subsist chiefly on broth, toast, or fresh fruits. Now, Mrs. McCarthy, I must ask you to lie on your back while I administer Dr. Hall's whirling spray. This will act as a cleanser and will provide immediate relief, stimulating both health and spirits. It has been known to cure barrenness and all diseases of the womb. After all, without cleanliness, the body is defiled and repulsive. The vagina must be cleansed with the same faithfulness as any other part of your body." Brigid no longer cared what he did, her baby was gone, lost to a void as black as the blood pooled on the floor.

Emily let the doctor out, and as he was leaving, he asked after Mr. McCarthy. "You might ask that he call by the surgery at his earliest opportunity." Emily looked in on Brigid, who appeared to be sleeping, so she sat on the porch and waited for Ben, wanting to make sure she spoke with him before he entered the house. There was also a part of her that had not wanted to sit by Brigid's bedside listening to her guttural sobs at the loss of something she herself had never desired.

Ben called to the surgery that evening. He was devastated by the news. Brigid was inconsolable.

Dr. Payne had been expecting him. "Mr. McCarthy, miscarriage is a very serious difficulty—the health and constitution of your wife may be permanently impaired. Of course, I have only recently become acquainted with your wife and therefore cannot comment as to her general constitution. Was this a welcome child? Your wife is not a young lady, and has not yet become a mother. Was she known to romp through the fields as a child, skip the rope, horse-ride, perform light house duties maybe? These are all very important for the development of the vital organs, and thus the laying of a substantial physical foundation so becoming of a good wife and mother. You see, Mr. McCarthy, a still, demure, and sedentary girl is really not worth having. Your good lady wife is small in stature, which is objectionable in a woman as it often pertains to having too much activity for their strength and consequently, feeble constitutions. The first and specific objective of marriage is the rearing of a family. 'Be fruitful and multiply and replenish the earth,' was, after all, God's first word to Adam. A young lady who does not wish to assume the responsibilities of a true wife, and with that become a mother, really should not consider getting married in the first instance. Take it from me, Mr. McCarthy, we have far too many ladies of the modern sort, who are quite open to admitting that they do not ever wish to be burdened, as they see it, with an appendage. Far better that such ladies enter some sort of honorable occupation and die an old maid by choice than abuse the most sacred function of her nature."

Ben took in every word of the learned man before him.

"Now, where were we? Yes, I see Mr. McCarthy you are concerned for your wife. However, it is important that we discuss if this loss was avoidable. Have you any understanding as to what may have prevented this pregnancy from taking hold? You do know that it is an offense and the most serious of crimes, the law has no mercy for the offenders that violate the sacred law of human life. From the very moment of conception, a new life commences, a new individual exists, another child is added to this world of ours. The mother who deliberately sets about to destroy this life, either by want of care, taking tinctures, or using instruments, commits as great a crime and is just as guilty as if she strangled her newborn infant. Its blood is upon her head. The crime she commits is murder, child murder!"

Ben was speechless and was struggling in utter disbelief at what he was hearing, not daring to question or disrespect the role of the doctor. He feebly replied, "Having this baby was Brigid's greatest wish since the very first day of our union, and I never knew her to be any different."

Dr. Payne appeared satisfied with the response. "Right so, Mr. McCarthy. It will be very important that your wife adopts every measure possible to strengthen and build up her system—most definitely no heavy lifting or work of any kind. Your wife will need to take frequent sitz-baths, eat plain foods such as oatmeal and graham bread, absolutely no rich foods, gravies, late suppers, or highly seasoned foods. And yes, I must ask you to consider sleeping apart for the next few months to allow your wife adequate time to recover. Displaying self-control at this time is a form of courage, a primary essence of man's character."

Without hesitation Ben replied, "Of course, Doctor. I will do whatever it takes to restore the health of my wife. I wish only to see her recover. She has suffered a great number of burdens in recent times, and I am very concerned as to how this latest upset will affect her."

"It is very possible, Mr. McCarthy, that your wife will experience melancholy and possibly hysteria brought on by the upset of this loss to her system. Don't be alarmed by any of this; it is perfectly expected, and if you follow my advice, she will recover her spirit. You will, however, have to beware of idleness. It is not normal for a lady to be without a family of her own, and this can lead to indolent leisure.

There is a lot of poisonous literature out there only too ready to prey on the unoccupied mind," lectured Dr. Payne.

Ben thanked the doctor and bade his farewell. Walking home he was consumed by what the doctor had said. He had never heard such talk in all his days yet he was acutely aware that he had little experience with doctors. It would be for the best that he did not mention any of this to Brigid. He had no need to mention his visit at all—there was nothing to report, and he was none the wiser anyway.

CHAPTER 28

Of all the blows Brigid had experienced in her life, this was by far the cruelest. To have had that glimpse of motherhood before her, then to have it so brutally taken from her darkened her soul to its core. She wanted only to be left alone and had no wish for Ben to return to their bed, finding comfort in sabotaging their marital relations. She shut her eyes from the world to wallow in the destructive thoughts her mind fed her. She was defective. She had deserved this and had brought it all on herself. She should have stayed in Moling, led a quieter life without distraction. This must be the Lord's way of making her pay for leaving her family, thinking only of herself and her dreams.

Her dearly departed father had never tried to stop her, and she knew her singular focus to leave their village and Ireland behind her—up and marrying the first man that showed any interest in traveling with her—had broken his heart. She had spared no thoughts for how it must have hurt them to know that she was so desperate to get away. She was going to be sophisticated, glamorous, and live in a place that would appreciate her. Turning her head when they told her "Far away fields are not always greener," she'd planned to show them and come back and take the eyes out of their heads.

Who was the fool now?

Ben was walking around her on eggshells. Why couldn't he just be annoyed with her and get it over with, tell her she was damaged goods? The doctor had as good as said so.

Ben left her be, left her to take her penance. Sleeping alone night after night did not stop his flicker of hope that maybe the next night she would not close the bedroom door behind her. They had less and less to say to each other as the days passed, and what he did say seemed only to irritate her. She was lost to a world he could not reach. That was just how it was and how it stayed until slowly he saw seeds of change.

After many weeks, Brigid began to have a lift of sorts in her spirits. They started taking their evening stroll together again, and Brigid began to help Emily in the garden. There would be no talk of all that had gone before. Ben returned to their marital bed, and Brigid expressed her intention to try for another baby. She was feeling quite recovered. Gone was the melancholy, replaced with a renewed hope and determination, and knowing that she had successfully conceived once, she saw no reason why it would not happen again. Life settled down for them in Petaluma, and they went about their lives with a renewed vigor in achieving a successful confinement.

Emily tentatively gave Brigid her copy of the *Ladies' Guide in Health and Disease* that her own mother had once passed onto her in the hope that she would settle down and have a family of her own. It had seen little use. Emily was proud she had stood her ground, happily living an independent and sedentary life with her brother. Smiling, she flicked through the pages that her mother had once marked.

> *The ideal old maid is one who is scrupulously neat in appearance, by most people considered very nice, possibly somewhat prudish in her notions of modesty and unwillingness to place any confidence in the opposite sex, but a very useful sort of person in cases of illness, a ready worker, and on the whole, quite an indispensable member of society.*

She really did not care what they called it. If she was an old maid, then so be it. She had no desire to put the other advice offered by the book to the test, most of which horrified her. Brigid may as well get some use out of it, as it was only gathering dust on her shelf.

Brigid was thrilled and beyond grateful to Emily for thinking of her, spending the entirety of the next day immersed in the chapters. Words she had never before heard spoken of were written as plain as day. She read the chapter on the "Effects of Solitary Vice in Girls" over and over, but even then could not quite understand what was being referred to.

> *This soul and body destroying habit, where a young girl quite often receives her first instruction from a "hoary-headed" fiend in human shape. The victim of this evil habit is certain to suffer sooner or later the penalty which nature invariably inflicts upon those who transgress her law. From month to month, we have seen the roses leave their cheeks, the luster departs from their eyes, the elasticity from their step, the glow of health and purity from their faces. The girl who begins the habit will scarcely escape great suffering from some form of sexual disorder.*

According to the guide, every ailment that could possibly befall a girl originated from this evil act, and the book listed signs for mothers to watch out for in their daughters.

> *Sudden decline in health, marked change in disposition, loss of memory, unnatural boldness, a forward or loose manner, languor and lassitude, unnatural appetite, leucorrhea, ulcerations, biting fingernails, the expression of the eyes, palpitations of the heart, hysteria, nervousness.*

Brigid focused her attention on the "Anatomy and Physiology of Reproduction," trying to understand how a child was formed. "The budding process is where one little bud attaches to another little bud, which goes on to develop into a perfect human being." The referencing throughout the book to the reproduction of the lower animals and plants was all very confusing, proving too difficult for

Brigid to distinguish who exactly was being impregnated. But there was some comfort knowing that it could only happen when uniting with a similar bud from a human of the opposite sex.

Of course, it would never do for Ben to see her reading this, as he might be offended by the forthright manner in which it was presented. No doubt he would question her choice of reading material. For Brigid, it provided an understanding of her body and, in particular, the vagina. She needed no convincing that if she lay in bed with her legs raised it would help the spermatozoa travel directly to her tubes where her little buds were waiting for Ben's little buds, and that rest after sexual congress would favor conception. With no time to waste and not wanting to take any chances, Brigid sought Ben out every night for two weeks, willing to take her chances with some of the book's warnings. "The set of organs which after marriage are brought into legitimate activity, highly sensitive and being subjected to excitements of an unusual character, are exceedingly liable to take on inflammation." Surely that passage did not relate to her, for it was far from unbridled lust that was her motivation.

Ben had his own preoccupation—finding a business and a home of their own. Being a renter was alien to him, and he dreamed of the day when he could write to his family and tell of his success. It would be the ultimate achievement having a business and a home of his own, and he knew it would be talked of with great pride.

Brigid was venturing back into the community, her scars from Niagara fading. Ben loved seeing her back to her old self, full of energy and their plans for the future. He even allowed her to go and have an "egg shampoo" with Fanny Tassi in the salon on Main Street in preparation for the Egg Day parade festivities. It was all the rage, and all the other wives were having it done. If it was good enough for them it was good enough for his Brigid.

Bert Gibbs, master advertiser, had been hired by the chamber of commerce to promote Petaluma and his very first action was to bill it as the "Egg Capital of the World," with the August Egg Day Fair becoming the highlight of the summer calendar. Ben teased Brigid about auditioning to be a "farmerette," a local beauty who posed in dungarees, checkered shirt, straw hat, and knee socks, bringing a bit of glamour to the occasion, all vying for the prized title of Miss Petaluma. There'd be singing, dancing, eating, and as much socializing as one had the energy for, all in the name of the egg!

Ben and Brigid, not wanting to appear rude, saved their commentary for when they were home, falling into bed exhausted and exhilarated, laughing their hearts out at how the people back home would never believe the things they'd seen at the festival. They would mock and scorn what they would see as the ridiculousness of spending all that money on promoting an egg. They loved this place, and they loved the American way—the "can do" attitude prevailed almost everywhere. It was the land of the great and the free.

Over time, Ben felt Petaluma was losing its uniqueness with all the ranchers that were flocking to town. On Sundays they would take the "chicken and cow" train line through the San Geronimo valley, stopping off at the various townlands to see what was on offer outside of the bright lights of Petaluma. Known for its dairy farming, Ben felt this would be more to their liking as a place to lay down their roots.

There was a lot of talk of progress in these communities and a greater influx of people wanting to settle there. Armed with their newspaper cutouts of the Marin County real estate section, they set off.

> *A real Sunday outing, in a glorious country—spend Sunday at Woodacre and Forest Knolls, just a step from the city; swimming, tennis, fishing, hiking trails through virgin redwood forests: bungalows ready to move into $15 per month; call for tickets; have luncheon at Woodacre Lodge.*

Passing through the White's Hill line to Woodacre, they pulled into the station. Most of this land had once been owned by a wealthy family and had been bought by the Lagunitas Development Company, who had big plans for it. A wooden arch with the name *Woodacre* made from the majestic redwood trees, greeted them. There was talk of manicured public parks on every block, not one but two train stations at either end of the town, and a fancy recreational area in the middle. Ben had seen a reel showcasing a swimming pool with dancers dressed as mermaids. With all the daily advertising in the city newspapers, Ben felt that Woodacre would become more and more suburban, which made him nervous; that was exactly what he was trying to escape.

Traveling onwards to San Geronimo, they stopped to talk to a young gentleman by the name of Simms. He told of how his grandfather had been an early settler to that area and a very successful one by all accounts, holding some eight hundred acres. The first schoolhouse for the entire valley had been built here in 1875, and Mr. Simms appeared very proud of this fact. His grandfather, being a founding member of the community, had been a dairyman, stagecoach driver, and had run a shingle mill. It was difficult to get away from Mr. Simms, so enthused was he about promoting the area. He showed Ben and Brigid another great wooden arch displaying the name *San Geronimo*. Ben wondered if he was on a commission and assumed it would be going the same route as Woodacre, with more great plans to cater to the influx of new residents. Brigid was weary of Ben's dismissal of these pretty communities, but kept her thoughts to herself, respecting that this was Ben's dream and she would support it, just as he had always supported her. Calling to a mercantile called the Little Store, they chatted with the Mildreds, who told of how they too had tired of the pace of city life and had been overwhelmed with the influx of people and industry following the great expo. Mr. Mildred was full of enthusiasm for the Forest Knolls Improvement Club, which organized dances and festivals, and even had its own clubhouse.

As Ben's eyes glazed over, Brigid wondered if he would ever find what he was looking for. He loved the people he was meeting, but there was a part of him that hankered for the idyllic picturesque setting of home. He seemed to be trying to find something that would equal the villages they had left behind.

As the train slowed at the Lagunitas stop, a handsome grocery store came into view. They smiled at each other. The stop was a hive of activity, and without as much as a word between them, they headed straight for the store directly behind the depot. Ben, not realizing his haste, walked on ahead.

Achile Bonati was sitting on his stool behind the long mahogany counter in the warm summer afternoon, "Look for the Silver Lining" playing in the background on the radio. Ben was full of admiration for the handsome store as Mr. Bonati, beaming with pride, offered to show them around. The building was perfectly proportioned, with two entrances opening to the front and a decorative tiled canopy overhead. The roof with its fancy scalloped edge lent a grand air to the place. One side was in use as a general store and the other side was occupied by the Pedoni Lumber Company, which paid a handsome rent for the use of the space. Ben took Brigid's hand and gave it a little squeeze. She lowered her head, for she knew he could see the longing in her eyes—a longing for Moling, where their shop was the heart and soul of the village, not only for the provisions it provided but for the connection it gave to the community.

Ben was impressed with the constant flow of customers, all headed for Camp Taylor. The store got all the passing trade. There was no sales pitch needed, no push to get them to go and see the real estate office. Just the friendliest of welcomes was all it took.

Mr. Bonati was busy serving his customers, so Ben and Brigid strolled across the street to St. Cecilia's church, taking the opportunity to light a candle in a new church. Pushing open the magnificent redwood doors, they entered the sanctuary, which was glowing from the light of the glorious stained-glass windows glistening in the late afternoon sun. Taking a moment to adjust their focus, they luxuriated in the smell of the wood marinating with the incense in the heat.

The silence and the peace provided comfort to all those that ventured inside. Brigid lit a candle as they both kneeled before Our Lady to pray the Hail Mary. They were lost in their deepest thoughts and prayers, an intimate moment with God. Ben asked for divine inspiration in helping to secure their future as Brigid prayed for the blessing of a successful confinement. They pleaded with all those that had passed before them to keep them in their prayers and to give them a little help from the other side.

CHAPTER 29

Ben did not want to be answerable to any man for his livelihood and sought out every opportunity that he heard rumored of. Time and again returning disappointed, he was unable to voice exactly what stopped him from making the commitment, but he believed that good things come to those who wait.

Brigid had obsessed over the book Emily had given her and was in such a state over it all that Ben took a hold of the guide himself to see what could have upset her so. One passage read: "It should be mentioned that arrest of development is the leading cause of those hideous creatures to which women sometimes give birth, known as monsters."

Brigid had fixated on "the seed," and how it was so "exceedingly delicate," and worried that an imperfect seed sown in poor ground would mean a sickly harvest. It was becoming a cause for concern not only with Ben but Emily too, who had to listen to her when Ben was at work. Ben sent her off to see Dr. Payne to assure her that all was perfectly well. Mrs. Payne welcomed her into the surgery, offering her a cup of tea whilst she waited. Brigid, feeling very delicate and increasingly anxious, having not slept the night before, was overwhelmed by her kindness and could not hold back her tears.

Mrs. Payne exclaimed, "Oh, my goodness! Why, there is no need for such tears. Now, now, Mrs. McCarthy, it is not good to engage in such sorrow. Whatever it is, I am sure the doctor will put your mind at ease."

Self-conscious and embarrassed, Brigid apologized and explained how she was very tired, that was all. She was terribly sorry to bother her and had no need to stay, she would take her leave. Mrs. Payne was having none of it, "Not at all. I won't hear tell of it. You are here now, and you simply must see the doctor."

Sitting in front of the doctor with a quizzical look on his face, Brigid thought how silly it all sounded. Without even attempting to hide his dismay, he patted her hand and told her to put the books away, that reading was not good for her brain. "Now Mrs. McCarthy, while you are here, you might as well step up onto the bench, and let's take a look at you and see what might be causing this upset to your system."

Brigid lay down on the bench, self-consciously pulling her skirt around her ankles and her coat around her body. The doctor put his hand on her forehead, before making his way to her breasts, smiling away to himself, humming to dim the silence as he felt one breast, then both, using his left hand, then his right and then both of his hands. Brigid was rigid. No man had ever touched her that way other than her husband. She moved herself on the bench until the doctor sensed her discomfort and moved the examination along.

Dr. Payne smiled as Brigid left the surgery, telling his wife that they could expect to be seeing a lot more of Mrs. McCarthy now that she was once again with child. He shook his head in exasperation at her silliness. Quite how she had not noticed the expansion of her waistline was beyond his educated thinking. That poor husband had some challenge on his hands, albeit an attractive lady. A baby would soon put a stop to her gallop.

Brigid had a sense of knowing about her, some called it a gift. Sometimes thinking about having the thoughts made her fearful, a fear that she would somehow encourage it along, give it an energy that would make her thoughts reality. Unable to shake the sense that hung over her, she hid away in her room, holding her head in her hands, begging for it to stop, pleading with her mind. Brigid was unable to see her baby anymore, there was no comfort in the knowledge that it was growing inside of her. When it all went black, Ben held her in his arms, willing her to eat, to take some air, to have a talk with Emily, who desperately wanted to help. There was nothing anyone could do. She knew she was sabotaging this confinement, and she could not stop herself.

When the blood came, she let it flow, for she had already grieved the loss. Dark reddish-purple clots oozed out of her, the pieces of her that would no longer make a baby. She let it flow, the blood, the urine, the feces, the badness coming out. There was no getting through to Brigid as she curled herself into a ball. Holding her legs tightly, she cried a river as Ben helplessly watched over her.

Dr. Payne confirmed the loss, all the while telling Ben that there was no need for overreaction to nature's way of discarding imperfection. "The body is, after all, a mechanism of nature. It would have been helpful to have the bubbly lots to examine. I don't suppose you kept any of it?"

Ben did as the doctor advised, trying to get Brigid back up on her feet and to not encourage any of this feeling sorry for herself. He listened to Dr. Payne when he told him to be firm and not to take any fevered nonsense. Ben put his trust in the doctor.

Their lives were flung into disarray. The house was in constant darkness, with little air penetrating Brigid's desire to suffocate all emotion. Ben was banished to the spare bedroom, shut away from his wife and her world. He loved Brigid, and it pained him to see her suffer like this. The ups and downs of their married life were taking their toll. There were days when Brigid would appear as if she had not slept, troubled, agitated, pallid, flushed, looking at him with an unpleasant expression on her face. When he would try to speak, she would react with an unaccustomed irritability of temper, at times so consumed with an evil she believed had befallen him, shouting that it was he who had caused the loss of their baby.

And then Brigid told Ben that he was becoming too fond of Emily. Ben's patience was wearing thin, and it became increasingly difficult to hide his frustrations. Life was passing him by with little to show for it; they had no home of their own nor a family to fill it.

Confiding in Dr. Payne, Ben was met with absolute understanding and a sense of unfairness as to how he was not being looked after in his marriage. The doctor reminded him of his wife's duty and that her behavior was quite simply unacceptable. "The weakness of woman is all modern. Too much time has been given over to educating their brains. They just cannot handle the intensity of rigorous thought without tipping the energy balance. Education in menfolk makes for self-controlling, steady, why even deliberate and calculating thinking, but I'm afraid it has quite the contrary effect on the female brain. Men are calmed and women are excited by education and become the bundle of nerves that they are."

There was no one to advise Brigid.

Dr. Payne reminded Ben that he simply must be firm and let his wife know that he would not, could not, stand for her behavior a moment longer. They were not getting any younger, and maybe it was time for them to give up on this idea of starting a family. Ben admitted he'd had this very thought himself but was too afraid to ever voice it. He told the doctor of his plans to be a business owner and how Brigid's want of a baby was his greatest challenge to this. They would never move forward in their lives as long as she was fixated on conceiving.

Dr. Payne applauded Ben's admission, telling him about the studies that clearly indicated "brain workers" lived longer than "muscle workers," and it would be good for him to consider a different path in life. Ben had allowed his own dreams to take second place for long enough. It was time for him to take control and be firm with Brigid, tell her that they could not keep their life on hold while chasing the notion of having a child.

Full of courage and buoyed by the doctor's advice, Ben left the surgery with absolute clarity and conviction. Prepared for the conversation that needed to be had, he arrived home to an empty house. Brigid had not moved from her room in days, so he called out to Emily upstairs, assuming maybe Brigid had ventured a visit. Emily had not seen nor heard anyone all day. Together they came down the stairs, calling Brigid's name.

Quick as a flash, Brigid jumped out in front of them. "I knew it! I just knew I would catch you if I gave you half a chance. You disgust me, both of you!"

Emily turned away, not wanting to make this any more difficult for Ben than it already was. She had known there was something amiss with Brigid of late, as she had rebuffed her companionship at every turn. Ben forcibly took Brigid by the arm into their bedroom. Closing the door, he told her he'd had enough of her carrying on and would no longer stand for any of it. Brigid fell onto the bed crying and wailing, telling him she loved him and could not face losing him too. Ben lay by her side as she wailed about how sorry she was and that she could not face a loss again.

Ben realized that now was not the time to have the conversation he'd been planning. But in time, Brigid would see the sense in it herself and accept that she could not risk the loss of another baby. Brigid slept that evening with little obvious disturbance. Ben was relieved, knowing that a good rest would be all that was required on her road to recovery. Leaving for work the next morning, he was unable to avoid Emily working in her garden. Ben made an attempt to apologize for Brigid's behavior, mentioning her distress of late and that she had become quite confused and not at all herself. Emily lowered her head and went on with her work, horrified and in shock that Brigid would ever think such a thought. Ben excused himself and said he had better be going. Emily prided herself on being considerate of all women, however she could not bring herself to understand why Brigid would accuse her of being a "fallen woman," so loathsome to her moral sense. Never one for theatre going, novel reading, dancing, or fashionable parties, not to mention partaking in any form of flirtation, it was inconceivable. Emily was proud of her womanly modesty, mostly bashful in the company of men but for those she knew personally. Never in all her years had been accused of such abhorrent behavior. It could only be Brigid herself that was guilty of such evil thoughts that could transgress into such evil acts. A mind accustomed to thinking of sin comes to look upon it as desirable, and not by one fatal plunge, but rather in little departures.

❦

Dr. Payne could not get Ben McCarthy out of his thoughts. That poor husband, suffering at the behest of a frenzied woman. It was abominable to think that any man would be subject to a life never knowing what he was to face on his return from a hard day's work. That husband was far too understanding and forgiving for his own good and was not helping matters. He seemed keen to take the advice and tackle the situation once and for all. And surely Mrs. McCarthy would settle herself, if she knows what's good for her.

Ben was struggling. What in the name of God had come over Brigid? Emily could not so much as look his way. He had been horrified by the vile accusatory comments that had come out of his wife's mouth. Ben began to stay on at the sites, last to leave in the evening, in no hurry to return to a place that no longer felt like a home. Walking the avenue with his head bent, the weight of the world on his shoulders, he was unable to make eye contact with any of his neighbors for fear they had heard.

CHAPTER 30

February 15, 1920
My Dear Brigid,

Forgive me for not writing sooner. There is always something or other to be done about the place, and what with the children and the surgery, I find my days are not my own. I often wonder what life must be like for you with no encumbrance, all that time for just the two of you. What have you been up to at all? Please do write and tell of your news, and don't drop us out of your life altogether now that your connections to the place are nearly gone. Please tell me you will always call Moling home.

What news have you of James? I am sure he has found himself a nice girl and maybe is thinking of settling down. You could build a new Kelly network over there between you!

Mother takes up a lot of my time now. Of course the girls are a great help, but most of the work is left to me. Give my love to Ben and write of your news. Don't be worrying about upsetting me, I want to hear it all—the lovely restaurants, the fashions, the people you meet from the different countries. Anything would be more exciting than the goings on in Moling.

Your fond cousin Molly.

Months had passed and Brigid had shown no improvement. Ben sat in front of Dr. Payne listening intently.

"Nervousness can be a physical, not a mental state. Its phenomena do not always come from emotional excess but from nervous debility and irritability. You see, my good man, all this talk of wanting to be with child is not good for your lady wife. It must be said that feeble parents generally have feeble children. Like begets like. Disease and debility are thus propagated from one generation to another and the great American race becomes woefully deteriorated. It is mostly a female affliction. Men are subject to it, though not so frequently. You really must make Mrs. McCarthy see sense. In the meantime, I suggest some healthy and pleasant employment should be urged. Avoid excessive fatigue at all cost and mental worry. If required, the use of stimulants and opiates will help. However, plenty of good food and fresh air will do far more than any drug."

Ben considered himself a lenient man, but Brigid's constant state of melancholy was proving tiresome in their marriage. Without the support and confidence of Dr. Payne he did not know how he would have navigated these times. He was a man of sound advice, a trusted and upstanding member of society, why, Ben even considered him a friend. There was never going to be a right time to discuss with Brigid the doctor's recommendation, and Ben decided it would be best left to him to take charge and make the decisions.

It had all been arranged. Brigid was to be admitted under the care of Dr. Albert Sydney Bell at the Franklin Hospital, pleasantly located in a scenic park with large sun-filled rooms and the best of cuisine. Brigid was admitted and prepared for surgery. With all going well, she would be home in her own bed in under one week, and Ben had arranged to take those first few days off from work to be with her and make sure that she took the rest which was advised. A fresh start was awaiting them, and Ben felt a huge weight had been lifted from his shoulders.

Brigid never hesitated to put her trust in Ben. Feeling utterly dejected, she was very grateful to have him take care of her and consult with the doctors on her behalf. She was willing to do whatever was advised by the experts to help achieve her dream of motherhood. There was nothing for her to do now, only to rest and allow her body to recover.

Achile Bonati had not forgotten the young Irish couple, immigrants, like himself, trying to make their way in this world. And he knew an honest man when he met one. Ben had opened the envelope to a simple few words scrawled across the page: *Keen to discuss the store, come visit this Sunday. Yours, Achile Bonati, Lagunitas Grocery Store.* Father Ryan from St. Cecilias had been very taken by them too. Brigid had spoken to him of their village in Ireland and how her own family shop was the center of their community, also across the street from their parish church. The similarities were striking, and Father Ryan said it was no coincidence that they had been so taken with Lagunitas.

Ben held the note in his pocket, taking it out to look at it as he willed the train journey to go faster. His mind was imagining all sorts of scenarios. Excitement interspersed with doubt, allowing his thoughts to run amok. What exactly did "discuss" mean? Did he want someone to rent it, or maybe a manager to run the place? Ben was only interested in a straight sale, nothing less—his own business to do with as he saw fit. Traveling alone to let Brigid recover, he had taken the very first train to Lagunitas that Sunday morning. He rehearsed over and over what he had to say, as he had his price and could not go a dollar over it. He was aware of the stories of the swindlers who were robbing the Irish blind of their life savings, although he wasn't one for paying too much creed to the stories from the building sites of all the "great" men who spent their free time on the bar stool telling anyone that was fool enough to listen of the great fortunes they had made and lost.

So busy was the store that Sunday morning that it was a while before Mr. Bonati saw Ben standing by the door. Welcoming him inside, he asked after his good lady wife. Ben mentioned that she was taking a rest at home.

Mr. Bonati replied, "Nothing serious I hope?" with a nod and a wink.

"No, thank God," said Ben.

"How about you stay for dinner? My wife sure would love to meet the great Irish guy I have told her about. We can talk some business first, man-to-man, if you know what I mean. You see, my girl finds it all too lonely out here in Lagunitas. She misses her mama and what with a baby on the way, she says there is no way she is going to be stuck indoors while I am in the store morning, noon, and night. She needs her mama, and if we don't move soon, she will take herself back home. I can't have that, and I'm figurin' I just gotta move now before she takes matters into her own hands. A Mr. Warn has approached me. He's selling out himself, over in San Ansalemo, a great big business in the Baeur building on Red Hill Road—pool hall, barber shop and cigar stand. Would ya believe his biggest seller in the pool hall are those Red Spot candies? He says the boys sure like 'em. I told my girl that she won't be seeing a lot of me there either, but she says she doesn't care 'cause she will have her mama by her side. He said it's mine for the taking, but I gotta wrap it up fast. That's when I got to thinking, hell, you said you have nothing to hold you back, said you were ready to move. So, what do you say, can we do a deal?" Mr. Bonati had barely drawn a breath.

Ben replied, "Whoa, whoa, steady on! That sure is a lot to think about. Are you saying the place is for sale? I figured I'd come out here and find out what you had to say, talk with you man-to-man as you say. You've caught me by surprise. I guess if we can agree to a fair deal, I just might be your man."

Ben talked only of Marin County from that moment on and of the surrounding areas that were growing. He had no doubt in his mind that the new residents would all be in need of local services, and he was going to meet those needs as the proud new owner of the Lagunitas Grocery Store.

The brochures and advertisements in the newspapers were all selling a lifestyle—aimed at the monied San Franciscans. Marin County was billed as "the playground" of California. So easily reached, only twenty miles from San Francisco. These advertisements called on motorists who had become tired of being always on the go, with no definite place to serve as "outing headquarters." In Marin County, fishing, boating, and deer were all plentiful. *Marin County—real country with all the attractions of town.*

CHAPTER 31

Ben thanked his lucky stars for the kinship of the great Irish connectors. There was nothing like the introductions and the helping hands, never pulling up the ladder behind them. He would miss the men but not the work. It was only ever a means to an end and now that end had arrived. Time for them to move to their new home and life, to the peace and tranquility that Lagunitas would offer. A bright, fresh new start, a future for just the two of them. Ben had made his peace with it.

They packed up and left Bodega Avenue with no one home to see them off. After her surgery Brigid had begun to recover, looking forward to a fresh start in Marin County where she and Ben could build their family and their business. Brigid, not remembering all that had transpired during her dark days, had called to Emily almost daily, leaving little notes and baked goods, all of which were ignored. Emily had felt betrayed having so warmly and graciously taken Brigid into her confidence and her home, only to have that reciprocated with Brigid's vile accusations. She could not bring herself to forgive Brigid.

Brigid's new start brought with it the hope of new life, but first and foremost, this was Ben's time to shine. It did not stop her from her thoughts—frantic thoughts of needing to have their baby soon, as time was not standing still.

Ben stood ten feet tall behind that counter, greeting customers, suppliers, locals, and any who came to meet the new proprietor. Community was at the heart of every interaction. The Pedonis and their lumber business kept the place alive with their laughter and singing. The days were always sunny, prosperous, and above all for Ben, peaceful. He had found his home in God's Country.

Across the street at St. Cecilia's was where Brigid found her solace. The Lord himself held her in his arms, soothing her, giving her respite from herself. Pushing open the church door, the sound of the felt on the floor comforted her as she adjusted her eyes to the darkness, breathing in the comforting smell of the incense, tingling all over as the stillness enveloped her. She crept quietly, alone into the pew, seeing the dust in the sunlight spreading colored beams through the darkness. Lucid moments of fear overwhelmed her as she closed her eyes, allowing the tears to come. Time stood still. She knew deep in her soul that all was not as it should be.

Back home in Moling, Agnes was proud as punch. "Isn't that something! My Brigid has got herself set up in business, and not just any business in any town—supporting a county she is, the whole county of Marin. Did you hear me, Biddy? Did you hear the great news of the Kelly legacy finding its way to the furthest parts of Yankeeland?"

Biddy was preoccupied. "There was some talk of it at mass. It must be that Ben fella finally found himself something to do. What a relief that must be to his parents. It's not normal, all that moving about. Sure, how could you get anywhere if you keep moving from Billy to Jack? A bit of an aul shop or something, selling a few vegetables is all I heard. I guess they need to put food on the table, even though there's only the two of them. But it's not like they have a lot of mouths to feed. Is there any sign of them procreating at all, or are they still having too good of a time to bother with it? It wouldn't be for me, nor would it be for any of mine. Blessed I am, surrounded by my devoted children, each and every one of them with a family of their own, and big ones at that—coming out of the woodwork they are. I'm right blessed."

Agnes, fired up, was quick off the mark. "Well now, Biddy, we believed in letting them live their own lives—no point in holding on to the old ways forever. The more intelligent of the young are progressive, you see, all about seeking out a better life for themselves, fortunes and all that. It will be great when they come home and show us the fruits of their success. As for the money they send home, sure, we don't know what to be doing with it. Piling up in the bank it is. We won't have a need for half of it in our lifetimes. Oh, there's the postal delivery now. I'd better be going. Good day to you, Biddy."

Brigid was surprised by a postcard from James, as they weren't the type to be sending each other cards. She admired the pretty little postcard with a picture of a beautiful young lady surrounded by flowers. A poem was printed on the side.

> *A HAPPY BIRTHDAY TO MY DEAR SISTER*
> *A message for your birthday,*
> *A greeting fond and true.*
> *Speed out in glad remembrance now*
> *My sister dear, to you;*
> *So many gifts and blessings*
> *I'd choose to be your share,*
> *And many years to follow this,*
> *All brightness everywhere.*

James had written on the reverse. *From a loving brother to his loving sister Brigid.*

It was his way of letting her know he was thinking of her—no news of his life and no questions of hers. With the passing of time there was less and less to be said; knowing they were settled and that Ben was a good husband was all he needed to know. That is what Father had sent him over for in the first place all those years ago, to ensure that she was safe. Or was it? They never questioned why Father had sent him and any reasons he had were now buried with him in the grave, a deep, dark Irish secret.

Like clockwork, every morning as soon as Ben closed the door behind him, Brigid undressed, checking herself in the mirror for any signs of change. Did her skin look a little patchy? Was her middle rounding? Did she feel nauseous, faint, weak? Morning, noon, and night, she checked and double-checked.

Later, Ben locked up the store and strolled over the little bridge that crossed the creek, exhausted and exhilarated from a hard day's work. Ben was finding his rhythm for the store. Walking around the back of their little yellow clapboard house, he could see Brigid lying on the bed with the curtains open to the cool evening breeze. It was early for her to be sleeping. Not wanting to startle her, he quietly let himself in. The kitchen table was bare, the hallway floor littered with clothes, and as he walked closer, he could see baby clothes strewn about—cardigans, dresses, and booties knitted in the softest of wool. Brigid came out of the bedroom and, seeing him holding the clothes, threw her arms around him as Ben reached out to comfort her, "Shh now. It's all right. Everything is all right."

Beaming, Brigid looked at him quizzically. "I have the most wonderful news. I am with child. I am having a baby, Ben." She twirled about the floor, singing and cradling her arms as if holding a child, looking with love and devotion at a face that was not there.

Brigid was euphoric.

Ben was incredulous.

Ben gently told her to rest herself and that they would visit with the doctor in the morning. Brigid was clear that she had no need for doctors—she had her book from Emily.

Sleep did not come for either of them that night. Brigid was too excited, she said, with too much to do. There was much to be arranged for the baby. She was moving furniture, making room for a nursery. She cleaned the floors and washed the walls; everything had to be sparkling clean for the baby. Ben tried to reason with her, begging her to rest, pleading with her to listen to him, but all the while she became more agitated by his advances, telling him to leave her be, to go on to bed and she would join him when her work was done.

Ben had drifted off in the chair and awoke to Brigid moving the furniture out onto the lawn, saying it needed to be aired and purified before a baby could be brought into the house.

Ben was worn out. "Please, Brigid. Please take some rest. It's not good for you or me to be without rest."

Brigid was agitated. "That bloody store. Is that all that you care about? Is that all that you will ever want in your life? Is there no place for me, for our baby?"

"Brigid, stop that! What are you saying? Why are you speaking like this? You know how hard I have worked for us to have this life, how hard we have both worked for this day."

There was no stopping Brigid now. "No, Ben, how hard *you* have worked. I never wanted any of it. I only ever wanted for us to have a baby of our own. But no, you won't even allow me that."

"Please, Brigid, listen to me. Take some rest. I will help you clear up this mess. We have a few hours before the store opens, and we can rest ourselves and you can lie on after I leave. You will see sense with rest. You will be okay after a good sleep. Come with me now, Brigid. Please."

Brigid raised her voice. "Stay away from me! Don't touch me or I will scream!"

"Brigid, stop! Why are you behaving like this? What has come over you?"

Brigid looked up to the ceiling reciting, "Hail Mary, full of grace. The Lord is with thee. Blessed art thou amongst women—"

"Brigid!" Ben hissed. "Keep it down! You are shouting, and it is the middle of the night. You will surely wake our neighbors."

Brigid peeled off her clothes and ran into the yard in her undergarments, rosary beads swinging from her neck, begging the Lord to save her, begging for his protection for her and for the child inside her.

Ben fell to his knees, pleading with her to come back inside. Brigid was oblivious and continued until she eventually exhausted herself. Ben picked her up and laid her on the bed. She clung to him, crying and begging him to protect her and to save her and their baby. She wouldn't let him move from her side, eventually dozing off into a fitful sleep. It took all his might to slip himself off the bed. He was riddled with fear that she would stir.

Seeing a shadow pass the window, Ben hurried to the door, quietly stepping outside to speak with Mr. Pedoni, who was calling to see if everything was all right, as the store had not been opened.

"Mr. Pedoni, I am so sorry for this trouble. You see, Mrs. McCarthy is not feeling herself and has been unwell during the night. I lost all track of time. Would you be so kind as to open up for me this morning, and maybe that fine young son of yours would watch over the store until I can sort everything out here?"

Mr. Pedoni was immediately understanding. "That'll be no problem at all. I'm sorry if I disturbed you. I sure hope Mrs. McCarthy is doing okay. Father Ryan passed me this morning and said he thought there might be something amiss, so I said I would stop by and see if I could be of any assistance. He said he heard a commotion during the night."

Ben needed to protect Brigid. "Yes, yes. It's all fine now, just fine. Mrs. McCarthy was not quite herself, but she is resting now, and all is well. Thank you for your concern, and you can tell Father that there is nothing to worry about here. Actually, well maybe there is something you could do for me, Mr. Pedoni. Would you be so good as to take me over to Petaluma? There is an urgent message I need to attend to, and it would be a great help if you could take me there in your truck."

Ben arrived at the surgery, asking to see Dr. Payne. Dr. Payne sat and listened to what Ben had to say, shaking his head. How could Brigid think herself pregnant? "Slow down Mr. McCarthy. Slow down and start again. What exactly were the events of last eve?"

Ben spoke of how Brigid was consumed with the belief that she was with child, which had sent her mad in herself. She'd gone from fits of laughter to tears, overexciting herself, swinging from euphoria to melancholia. Ben was frightened and felt helpless watching this change come over his wife. He wasn't sure he knew who this person was anymore.

Dr. Payne took notes, asking if she was experiencing any tenderness along her spine or any disturbances of digestion. "It quite simply is not possible that this lady could be with child," he said, shaking his head. Looking through her file, he found the report from her recent hospital admission and showed the letter to Ben. There it was in black and white.

Ben rubbed his hands through his hair, choked with emotion as the years of worry over Brigid's behavior overwhelmed him. He told the doctor that he did not think he could continue to manage his wife's outbursts. He had always been there for her, but he just did not see how it could continue. He had a business now that needed him. He had invested their life's savings into it for their future—it had to be his priority.

Dr. Payne was in no doubt as to how difficult this was for Ben, watching him as he tried to control his emotions and struggled to find his words. This man had carried his cross with devotion, and the situation was long overdue for intervention. It was time for this man to get on with his life. It was his duty to take control and help Ben. And he knew just the place. St. Agnews, over in Santa Clara, could help Brigid. He had never been there himself, but he knew of patients who had. She would have to be taken there, as she was not going to get better on her own. He had no doubt that she was quite past that point.

Dr. Payne was clear in his reasoning. "Be assured, Mr. McCarthy, that progress—indeed, unprecedented in its rapidity—has been made in the medical treatment of functional diseases of the nervous system. This last quarter of a century has seen progress like never before, not only in the use and administration of medicines but also in the scientific study of diet, exercise, sleep, rest, and even in the application of such agencies as electricity and water, both cold and hot. Individualization is the key, as no two cases should be treated alike. Your wife will be given the latest and the best of care available to her, and all in a surrounding which has been purpose-built for the promotion and cultivation of the spirit of the patient. For now, your wife is up against opposing winds and fretting currents, and in time she will enter the harbor of calmness and peace."

Ben closed the door of the surgery behind him a broken man. He had failed in his duty to his wife. How had he let it get to this point? Why had he not seen the signs and stopped it sooner? If only he had encouraged her to rest more, watched over her diet, taken her out with him in the evenings to get fresh air.

Mr. Pedoni jumped from his truck, nervously inquiring as to what kind of meeting Ben had just had. Ben could not look the man in the eye. But he knew he would need his neighbor's help with getting Brigid to Santa Clara, so, in a barely audible voice, he took Mr. Pedoni into his confidence. Paulo Pedoni steered Ben to the nearest saloon to steady him for what might lie ahead. Ben was never a man for taking a drink, but that whiskey gave him the courage to talk and the strength to face his duty. Mr. Pedoni sat and listened, touching Ben on the arm when he grew overwhelmed at times and could not speak.

Ben knew that Brigid needed more help than he could give her. He thought of his vows of "in sickness and in health" and how in God's name was he meant to have her locked up with lunatics.

Mr. Pedoni spoke of his mother. She too, had suffered with the nerves, and had spent time herself at St. Agnews. "So fine a place it is, she didn't want to leave. She spent much of her life there, now isn't that something."

Ben was not listening, as he wondered how he was going to get Brigid to Santa Clara. What could he possibly tell her that would not involve further upset to her nervous system? It was not going to be an easy journey for either of them. But, he told himself, it would only be a temporary upset. The doctor had said she would be back to herself in no time after plenty of rest and supervision. Ben held the doctor's referral letter in his hand. He had been assured that they would be attended to immediately, as this was an urgent admission.

> *January 28, 1922*
> *Agnews Insane Asylum, Santa Clara*
>
> *Please admit this highly nervous lady of Irish origin whose husband, a businessman in the county of Marin, can no longer care for her at home.*
>
> *It is my educated opinion that this patient is experiencing the symptoms of nervous diathesis. You will note from her appearance that she is of a fine organization, liable to varied and recurring attacks of diseases of the nervous system, and appears to have had a comparative immunity from ordinary febrile and inflammatory diseases. I have no awareness as to the patient's susceptibility to stimulants and narcotics and am not aware if she has been prescribed prior to presenting as a patient at this surgery. The patient has a history of sensitivity of the digestion and female-related complaints.*
>
> *I enclose all relevant medical information from my files. On review you will note the husband's acute sense of alarm when the patient most recently announced her successful confinement, believing herself to be with child. It is on this basis that I am recommending this patient for urgent assessment and admission to your facility.*
>
> *Yours sincerely,*
> *Dr. Theodore Payne, Petaluma, California.*

CHAPTER 32

There was no need for Ben to worry about how he was going to get Brigid to Santa Clara, for when he returned, he was met by Father Ryan, who was waiting for him at the store. "Now Ben, don't be alarmed. Brigid is in safe hands—we saw to it while you were away. Officer Cordell came right over as soon as we sent for him. Brigid had calmed a little, and he took her in the patrol car, said he would meet you at the station."

Ben was furious. "The station? What station? Brigid will not know what to do without me, she will be scared out of her wits. When did this happen? How long has she been gone? I must get to her immediately. Excuse me, Father, but I really must go. I apologize for any upset this may have caused."

Father Ryan said, "I'll get my hat and go with you, Ben."

Ben was having none of it. "No, Father, not at all. You have done enough for one day. Mr. Pedoni has offered his services with his truck. You take your ease, Father. We will leave right away."

Mr. Pedoni had the engine running as Ben jumped into the truck with a bag stuffed with the items he felt Brigid may need. When they arrived at the station, Officer Cordell was waiting for them at the door. "Mr. McCarthy, slow down there. Your wife is resting. We got the doctor to give her a little something to take the edge off it."

Ben was not deterred. "Officer, please, I need to see my wife. She will be looking for me. Now where is she?"

Officer Cordell tried to steady the situation. "I am not so sure your wife is aware of anyone right now; she'd gone and gotten herself into quite the state by the time we picked her up. Father Ryan tells us there was quite the commotion over at your house last night?"

"Officer, I had to leave my wife's side to visit with her doctor in Petaluma, needing his advice on a private matter. I have here a letter from him to have my wife admitted to a hospital in Santa Clara," advised Ben.

Officer Cordell leaned back on his chair. "I just said that myself. The only place for the poor lady now is Agnews. They take them all, and the sooner the better, if you ask me. No telling what she could do. Father Ryan is a good man, very kind to her he was, calming her the way he did. Don't know how we would have got her here without him."

Ben had enough of the small talk. "Thank you, officer, for your help today, but I do need to get my wife to Santa Clara."

Officer Cordell outlined the situation to Ben. "Mr. McCarthy, you won't want to be taking that journey. We will finish the report, and we will take her on over there. No need to be troubling yourself—ain't no place for any man."

Ben was insistent. "Officer, I will not have my wife go alone. I will take her there myself. She will be frightened and will not understand if I abandon her to your care."

Officer Cordell spoke clearly and loudly. "Mr. McCarthy, we have done this many a time. Take it from me, you need to understand what it is that I am telling you. It ain't no place for anyone other than those that need to be there, and there ain't no need for you to be there. Hand me over that letter, and we'll take care of everything."

Not wanting to fall afoul of the law and already concerned as to what report was being prepared on his wife, Ben stepped away. Mr. Pedoni moved to stand by his side, taking him by the shoulder and telling him he had better listen to the officer and let him do his job. Ben was willing to take that risk; he was not going to let them take his wife away without him. He asked Mr. Pedoni if he would drive him in the truck and they could follow behind.

As soon as Ben closed the door behind him, Officer Cordell said, "That poor husband—looks like he's a good one. How he ended up with a lunatic is anyone's guess. The bloody Irish, they're all mad. It's either the booze or the madness that gets them. Nothing but trouble, the lot of them."

Brigid was floating, clouds carrying her as she reached out to touch them. Behind the clouds a man was looking at her with a sad face. He was taking her by the arm to a car, a nice man taking her for a motor. Maybe they were going to the seaside. Brigid then doubled over, as she was reminded of the searing pain in her abdomen. Oh no, not the baby! She had to protect the baby. What were they doing to her? Her mouth was moving, but she could not hear her words. She tried to move her body but it was still. Sitting now in the back of a car, she could see the back of their heads. There were two of them wearing hats, funny hats. The car was moving very fast. Brigid opened her mouth to shout at them, but they continued to look ahead. Brigid was scared, frightened, and angry as she bent her head in prayer, asking the Lord to take care of her and her baby.

There was not a word said between Ben and Mr. Pedoni as they journeyed behind the patrol car, neither knowing what lay ahead. Ben was embarrassed, and Mr. Pedoni did not know what to say to a man who had to take his wife to this place. It had been different for him with his mother, as only his father had ever visited, and even then it was only on her birthday—not that it ever really mattered, for he said she was always "away with the fairies."

Ben asked Mr. Pedoni, "If you could maybe park up awhile, I'll go and settle her in."

"You take your time there, Mr. McCarthy. There ain't no hurry from me. I've got nothing to be getting back to—only the orders, and they can wait. Another day won't change anything. I'll have myself a little snooze in this fine afternoon sun."

Brigid smiled when she saw Ben. "Ben, my love, my dearest love. You are here. We haven't been to the seaside yet. I wanted to paddle.

Would you come with us? That would be just wonderful—you, me, and our baby."

Ben's heart was broken. "I'm here now. I'll make sure they take good care of you. They will help you to have a good rest for yourself. You will be back home in no time."

Brigid was confused. "We cannot go to the seaside? But why? Who are all these people? Tell them to get away from me. Don't let them touch me, Ben. I don't want to go with them; I want to go home with you. Tell them you are taking me home, that you will take care of me and our baby."

Two nurses took Brigid from the car, holding her firmly by the arms, directing her to the building while two more waited in the wings. She twisted her head around toward Ben. He stiffened as he saw the realization register on Brigid's face, and turned his back as she frantically began to call out his name. Brigid's screeches echoed through the corridor as the doors closed behind her.

A doctor came to Ben's side, telling him they would take over from here and it would be best for him to take his leave as soon as all paperwork was complete. They directed him to the admission building beneath the clock tower. Ben handed over the letters with his head bent, unable to look at the man behind the desk, who was just doing his job. The man kindly asked Ben to take a seat. Ben didn't want to stay a moment longer than he had to, feeling his skin crawl with unease. The admissions clerk looked through the referral letter and notes from Brigid's recent hospital stay and nodded. "I see. The cause for admittance is clear. Not an easy time for you and your family, Mr. McCarthy. Have you many in the family?"

Ben whispered, "No, just my wife and I."

The admission clerk probed further. "So, this has been a preoccupation of your wife? Has she had any other fixations?"

"No, she is reserved by nature. It is just all this want for a child that has gotten the better of her."

"Is there any family history of insanity?"

"Absolutely not. It is the bereavement of her father and her sister over the last few years, as both were taken suddenly. That and her want of a baby and the loss of two in the early days of confinement. I have tried everything to support her and to help her, but I can no longer give her the time that she needs. I cannot watch over her day and night, and I cannot let her ruin our future in our new home, our new business, and everything that we have worked toward."

Walking from the office having signed the required forms, Ben passed a young man standing by a palm tree. The man appeared to be talking but Ben could not hear what he was saying. As there was nobody else in the vicinity, Ben walked over to acknowledge the gentleman. Drawing closer, the man was now whispering as he put his arms around the trunk. "I'll see you here again tomorrow, same time, same place." Kissing the tree, he whispered, "I love you."

Ben turned and climbed into the truck.

CHAPTER 33

June 20, 1922
Molly,

You must help me. You must find a way. They have locked me up here, and I am all alone but for my baby, my baby that is growing inside of me and will die if you do not help me. I will die. Please listen to me, Molly. I know that you will not let this happen to me. I know that I can trust you and only you.

I hear them talk, saying I won't be going anywhere anytime soon, but they don't know that you will come and take me out of this place. They don't know that you will find a way to take me back to Ben, my Ben, who loves me and who will take good care of me, of me and our baby.

Please, Molly. Please hear me and find a way.
Brigid.

They had told Ben that they would write when there was an improvement, that it would be best if Brigid was left alone until then. No need for unnecessary distractions, visiting was not encouraged.

Only one letter came advising of her progress. Brigid had been admitted to the women's receiving building and was responding well, albeit slowly. Ben did not know what to say when he was asked how she was by neighbors and friends, not that many did. There was never any doubt that Father Ryan was a good kind man, if a little loose with his tongue. He liked to visit the houses and needed things to be talking about. Ben knew the talk. He'd heard the whispers of how Brigid suffered with her nerves and he left it be.

There had been no word from those at home and just one letter from James, and Ben decided it was best to spare them this news. What had he to tell? Brigid would be home soon and all would be right again. They could put it all behind them.

Ben knew the official envelope when he saw it in June of 1924—Brigid was coming home. The asylum wrote that they would be grateful if the necessary arrangements could be made for her collection. There was only one man for the job. He went next door to look for Mr. Pedoni.

As per the instructions, Ben arrived at the clock tower on Palm Drive. Jumping from the truck, he walked to the building where he had last seen Brigid being led away. There was no staff to be seen, and all the doors were locked. Ben pulled on a rope leading to a bell. After no response, he gave it a few more pulls before wondering what to do next. An elderly man appeared in an apron. Opening the door, he said, "I don't see too many wanting to get in here in a hurry. Are you all right there, sir?"

"I've had a letter asking me to come for my wife," replied Ben.

"Take a seat, and I'll get the nurse for you," the caretaker said, pointing to a nearby bench.

Instead, Ben stood against the wall in the light-filled hallway as a gentle breeze blew through mixing with unappetizing smells he supposed were from the dining hall. He focused his attention on the Spanish terracotta tiles beneath him until the sounds of approaching footsteps jolted him out of his stance. Nurses rushed past calling out, "She's at it again! She'll do herself harm. Get the room ready!" He could hear a distant wailing down the hallway, along with a sharp banging sound.

The banging stopped, but the screaming didn't.

"She bit me, goddammit," exclaimed a nurse.

"That's enough now, Maria. Stop that! You need to calm yourself down. A little stay in here will give you time to think about what you did. We can't have you harming the staff."

Another nurse brushed past Ben, heading into the room where Maria was. "Settle down everyone, the show is over. Maria got herself a little excited is all."

Ben was horrified, thinking of how hard this would be on Brigid, and thankful that hadn't happened to her. She wasn't capable of such outward aggression. A nurse approached Ben and asked if he was expecting someone.

"I have a letter to come and collect my wife—Mrs. Brigid McCarthy."

"Let me check with the ward," said the nurse, disappearing through a locked door.

Ben knew it was Brigid as soon as he heard the footsteps. He turned in the direction of the sound, and he saw her walking toward him. Jumping to his feet, he ran and swept her up into his arms, holding her close, whispering how happy he was to be taking her home. Brigid pulled away, straightening her skirt—a skirt he had never seen her wear before—as she shyly looked about her, waiting for direction from the nurse.

"Now Brigid, you'll be missed about the place. You have been a very good girl for us, no trouble at all. Take good care of yourself and you know where we are if you need us."

Taking Ben aside, the nurse handed him a package and told him it was private stuff, for his eyes only and that he could dispose of the contents as he wished. She then advised Ben to keep a close eye on his wife over the next while and to let them know if all was not well. She did not see any reason why Brigid would not be right as rain. She had been the best of them, responding to the warm packs and compresses, finding solace in the garden.

"And what of the baby?" whispered Ben.

Smiling, the nurse replied, "Oh no, sir. That is all forgotten now. As soon as we got the sleep right, it all sort of fell into place."

Ben thanked the nurse as they took their leave, not wanting to stay a moment longer than he had to. They climbed into the truck as Mr. Pedoni tipped his hat. "Good to have you back with us Mrs. McCarthy."

※

Brigid was quiet in herself as she returned to her life in Lagunitas. Ben felt it was like a light had gone out in her. There was no talk of her time in Agnews, and Ben would never probe for fear of upsetting her. The least said the better.

Brigid reminded herself that there was a lot to be said for routine.

※

May 10, 1925
Dearest Brigid,

Forgive me for not writing sooner. It seems an age since we were in correspondence. I'm sure your life is busy now that you have your own shop to run and all the excitement that goes with it.

What of James? How has life turned out for him? Is he still on his own or has he met someone special? No encumbrance for him either? My, you all must be having such fun over there, far too much excitement to have time for those back home.

We had Canon Hannon give his sermon over to what he calls the "willful sterility" of the human race, the one sin whose punishment is national death, the death of the Irish race. "A race is worthless if its women cease to breed freely!" There was the usual huffing and puffing about the place and sure, some of them are barely able to keep their heads above water for all they have borne.

The kiddies have grown up fast, I guess they would be

young ladies to you now. My days are quieter with Mother no longer with us, God rest her soul. Thomas and Margaret are keeping well, kept busy with the shop and the children, just the two for now but no doubt there will be more. Margaret is a good strong woman, there is not much she cannot do. I am sure it is lonely for Thomas with you all gone and not even a letter to keep him company of a night.

Give our love to Ben and to James if you see him. We think of you often.

Your cousin Molly.

Brigid was heartbroken reading Molly's words. It was hard for her to relate to all that was before, with little familiarity in her mind's eye. Molly's letter increased her acute sense of isolation, feeling alone in a world where she no longer held any sense of place. Brigid had become guarded with her trust, the very people whom she believed would be there for her had let her down and turned the other way. Ben had allowed her to be locked up, shut away and treated as if an imbecile, and Molly had left her there. All trust had been shattered and with it any hope of protection from being sent back to that place, the place where she was just a number in a bed in a ward, invisible as the person that she was.

There had been so many others just like her, all locked up for the sin of insanity, inherited, part of being Irish, they said.

Brigid was somewhat thankful for small mercies like laying her head down on her own pillow, in her own home. She was thankful for the quiet of the early morning, the sun always shining, the breeze always gently blowing, the sky always blue. Her morning ritual gave her the courage to face each new day as she slipped into St. Cecilia's to ask the Lord for his forgiveness.

She asked the Lord to take away the badness, praying with all her might that it would never take hold again. The Lord was someone to tell her deepest of fears to without judgment or fear of retribution.

Knowing the Lord was listening, feeling his comfort as the pain in her chest eased and her breath slowed, allowed her in those moments to be at peace. No thoughts of what was before or what might follow, just being present in that moment with the arms of her Lord around her. There was nothing he did not know.

⚓

Mrs. O'Toole loved her morning chats with James. "You must be proud of your Brigid and her Ben, finding themselves a business of their own, and all thanks to you, James. I hear no talk of her being with child. God love her, she must feel that she too has been useless in her day and generation."

James smiled. "Oh, now Mrs. O'Toole, they did it all themselves. Ben is a fine man, always had ambitions. He was chasing that dream from the very first day he set foot in this land, and I never doubted him. As for Brigid, I know she has the want of a child, but as for the Lord listening, I guess we will have to wait and see."

James was happy with his lot. He had no one to bother him, and he was happy for Brigid and how her life had turned out. She had never needed him. Ben and Brigid had achieved what they had come here for, and he wished them nothing but the best. James had done his fair share of watching over the years, especially all those that came and went, each and every one of them unable to settle in themselves, all chasing a dream—big talk without substance. Alcohol became their solace, the core of their existence. He'd listened to countless fools on the stools who got into brawls and never knew why, waking with wounds and an empty pocket. They often mocked him, believing he had no ambition for himself. "Be wary of a fella that doesn't take a drink; it's not normal," they said. It went in one ear and out the other, for James was at peace. He was the lucky one. He was the one with a sense of peace deep within, thankful and grateful to rise each day with food on his table and money in his pocket. He had only himself to worry about and sure, what would he have to be worrying him? Kate was never far from his thoughts. Dearest Kate. She never had the opportunity to exist in peace. Her tormented soul was not for this world.

James was a lifeline to many who crossed his path. It came naturally to him. It was not a vocation, not a hobby, not just passing his time, it was just how he lived. Having the greatest gift of all, peace, allowed for not having to think of himself, only of others.

The O'Tooles felt like the luckiest of all. Mrs. O'Toole had long since given up on her matchmaking, resigning herself to the fact that it was not his preference, and it was not for her to meddle. She was content in knowing she had tried and grateful he was still with them, taking care of their needs as they slowed. Honorable to the last, he'd leave his rent on the table long after they had told him not to, agreeing to disagree.

Mrs. O'Toole wondered when the letters slowed. "Have you any news of home, James? How is Brigid getting along up there in Lagunitas? Do you hear much from any of them?"

"I'm sure they are all grand," was James's usual reply.

Mr. O'Toole told her not to be worrying about that which she knows nothing of and to stay out of the man's business. Still, she would ask, "Anything in the post for James today?" ever hopeful.

Mr. O'Toole read in the morning paper of a prominent Philadelphian who had died and left several Catholic churches and institutions substantial bequests. "Such a comfort to the poor man in his dying days to know that the church will put it to good use, and not have some relatives he never knew in far flung places squandering it."

"I wonder, Richard, should we be thinking of the same for ourselves? It's not any younger we're getting," remarked Mrs. O'Toole.

"Whist now, Suzanne, will you stop that aul talk of dying? There is a lot of life left in us yet. We won't be going anywhere anytime soon. We have all the time in the world to be worrying about that," replied Mr. O'Toole, raising his eyebrow.

Mrs. O'Toole was not deterred. "I sincerely hope you are right.

I would give it all to James in a heartbeat if I thought it would make him happy, but I know it would only be upsetting him if we did that. He has no want for anything of ours. No, we will do what those before us have always done and let the Catholic church put it to good use. All the service they give and little to show for it in the way of comfort or a bit of luxury, only the knowledge of all the souls they have saved."

Thinking for a moment, Mr. O'Toole said, "What about the work he is doing with that Brother Barnabas, what is it he calls himself? A 'boyologist?' He's looking to set up a boyology course. James devotes himself to those boys. I could listen to him all night when he gets to talking about those poor boys who are exposed to the badness in the world through no fault of their own. They need leaders, and they don't want the preaching evangelical type. They want men that can mix with the boys, study them. What was it James said, was it eighty percent of the delinquent boys are Catholic? Those bloody reform schools are the greatest evil, throwing them in with the worst element in the country. With $9.80 the club can make an upstanding citizen out of a boy instead of some $500 to make a crook out of him. That fella Hart was on the money, education should begin as farming does, with a soil first, then with tools, and lastly with seed and intelligence blending all three."

"You're onto something there, Richard, wouldn't it be grand to have one of those clubs in our honor? Why would we wait until we are gone when we can help those poor unfortunates while we are living? Oh, Richard, that really would be something. Let's have a think about it and maybe we could see about doing something with that money we have put by for the rainy day that never did come."

CHAPTER 35

Molly sat in her parlor looking out at the square, lost to her thoughts. It occurred to her that Lady Doyne had not set foot in the place since her last visit to inquire about Brigid years before—no doubt she had given up wondering, like the rest of them. It was on the damp, gray maudlin days that Molly missed Brigid the most, taking her back to the days of their hideout in the loft. They'd giggled at just about anything, nestled away with only their foolishness. How she missed Brigid and her passions, her want of getting away from this place. And here was Molly, left in the big house with all the expectations that went with it. Having to be turned out in nothing but the best, making time for everyone whether she liked them or not. There was always someone with something to say, that was what she hated most—and it was what Brigid had hated too. Molly knew she was blessed with a fine husband and her girls, but she also knew she had been forever cursed with longing for another life. It would eat you up if you let it.

Brigid had the courage, and now she had the fancy life to go with it. Brigid had let her keep the magazines, saying that Molly could look at them if she was missing her. Molly could never bring herself to look at them, but neither could she get rid of them. They were stuffed into the drawer beneath her undergarments.

Molly's days held the same rhythm. She looked out at the square, just as her mother had done before her, wondering to herself what it was she expected to see, for nothing ever changed, only the flowers with the seasons. How she wished she had asked her mother through the years what she thought about in those moments. Did her mother have dreams? Had she too sought the sanctuary of the loft, escaping to a world that was not Moling? Did she have secrets with Brigid's mother? Surely as sisters they too had shared their dreams.

The sameness got to her. There were never any visitors to break her day, her week, her year. The only people who came to Moling were those with a purpose. Their village was off the beaten track. It was what Agnes loved most about the place—they never had to worry about undesirables lurking about. There was many a day that Molly would have welcomed an undesirable. The men had their games up at the alley. They had the pub and their trips to the market. The women had the church—the rotation list for the flowers, the cleaning, looking after Father Dempsey when he needed someone to take him about the place to replenish the parish purse. Needlework, knitting, and the children, that was their domain. A life of solitary confinement inside the realms of village life.

"Charles, you must think it rather strange that the Kelly girl never did correspond. The last time I inquired she had moved West. Goodness knows what those Indians have done to her. I think I shall take another trip to Moling. Why don't you come with me? You have not visited since Patrick Kelly passed. It would be rather encouraging to the son to have you pay a visit," said Lady Harriet.

Lord Doyne drawled, "Darling, darling, why do you worry yourself? That poor girl has gotten on with her life—goodness knows what excites her. Leave well enough alone, I say."

Lady Harriet called to Moling on a Friday wanting to escape the hustle of the house being prepared for their guests, a constant these days with the children residing in London. They often dropped off the children ahead of some tour or other. Good old Mama and Papa would watch over their care. Of course, the nannies came too, and the lady's maids, and if Arthur had anything to do with it, the butler. Charles welcomed the young blood about the place, assured of securing the bloodline long after his demise.

Lady Harriet arrived at Thomas's shop in Moling one afternoon. Of all the days it was the one when Agnes had asked Biddy to step in for her. Biddy's default was to assume a position of authority, as if it were she Lady Harriet had come to see.

"Milady, come to the parlor. Oh no, no, no. Heavens above, let me take the weight off your feet," she harped as she pushed Lady Harriet in through the door to the parlor

Lady Harriet brusquely replied, "Please, no fuss. It is the Kellys I have come to see. I have no wish to disturb them from their day."

Biddy was not to be deterred. "Not at all, not at all. They will be along soon. Let me offer some refreshments while you wait. I would be more than happy to make your acquaintance."

With the forcefulness of her nature, Biddy pulled her along into the parlor of the house, showing her to the settee. She told Lady Harriet to rest herself there while she waited. "You must be parched after your journey."

Running into the kitchen Biddy called out to Molly's daughter, who helped out at Thomas's shop. "Maggie, Maggie, would you ever drop whatever it is you are doing and put on the tea. And none of your dilly dallying! Three scoops, and find the cream and sugar, wherever Agnes hides it. Now run next door to your mother and get one of the good cakes, the ones that she keeps for Mrs. Waters. Jesus, Mary, and Holy St. Joseph, would you run, girl! As if your life depended on it!"

Maggie scampered next door. "Mother, mother! Biddy sent me. She needs a cake, one of the really, really, good ones."

"What in the name of God is wrong with you girl? Calm yourself down," said Molly.

"I can't, I can't. A fancy lady has landed herself in the shop, and Biddy has me in a tizzy," replied Maggie, breathless.

"And what is Biddy doing in the shop in the first place? What is she up to? You just can't trust that one at all. I'll soon put a stop to her gallop," said Molly.

Maggie told her, "Oh, no, this is for real. Look at the horse outside and the fella in the uniform with the shiny boots."

"That's the Doyne livery! Lord above, let me in there. It must be the Lady," Molly exclaimed, running next door.

"Now, Biddy that'll do, that'll do," Molly said as she rushed into the parlor. "I have called for Thomas to let him know he has a visitor; he will be along in no time."

Biddy was none too pleased with the interruption, as she'd been extolling the virtues of all her children and grandchildren to Lady Doyne. "Molly, there is no need to be troubling you. I have everything in hand. Now did you bring the refreshments?"

"Indeed, and I didn't, Biddy O'Connor. Now off you go with yourself, and I'll take over from here," Molly announced. Taking a good firm hold of Biddy's arm, leaving her with no choice but to lift herself from the settee, Molly showed her to the door as Biddy huffed and puffed, craning her neck to have a last look at Lady Harriet, telling her not to be a stranger.

Molly apologized to Lady Harriet. "I am terribly sorry about all of that, milady. Biddy cannot quite contain herself sometimes."

"I am well used to her sort. Now, this fine young lady tells me she is your daughter. She is very polite and well mannered. We look for such young ladies to chaperone our granddaughters on their travels on the continent. I would be more than happy for you to make their acquaintance. What would you think of that, my dear girl?" said Lady Harriet, smiling at young Maggie.

Molly could see the smile on Maggie's face and couldn't help but think, *If only it could have been me.*

CHAPTER 36

"Little one, do your parents know that you are here? Have you gone and run out again without them knowing? We can't have you getting yourself into trouble, now can we?" said Brigid, smiling at a young boy who was wandering the store.

The children of Lagunitas were drawn to her warmth and gentleness. Whether it was cuddling up with a picture book or comforting them when they tumbled down the hill, Brigid was always there for them with a heart ready to soothe. Ben would catch himself when his thoughts drifted to what might have been, knowing these times with the children filled a void in Brigid's life.

Brigid would forever associate her want of a baby with her admittance to the asylum. Nothing would ever ease the longing. It was always there waiting for her, a physical weight which she carried as an ache. She knew when it flared up that she had been overthinking.

Ben had lit a fire in the garden and cleared the house of all the baby paraphernalia that Brigid had stored over the years in anticipation. Everything was burned while she had been recovering from her nerves. Now and then, Brigid would unearth an odd item that he had missed, and she would destroy it herself, lest it trigger her darkness as it seeped through her body, down her chest, and into the pit of her stomach. First came fear and then panic as she would take a hold of her side, taking a sharp intake of breath with or without relief. Brigid never knew if this one time it would overwhelm her once and for all, never to lift. The thoughts creeped about, teasing, taunting, trying to take control. She was adept at keeping them at bay. Brigid smiled through her days, telling herself to act normal, cautiously concentrating on every motion, every smile, nod, and sigh, not quite knowing what normal was but knowing that no one seemed aware that she was not.

Fear would take a hold without any remedy, stifling Brigid's ability to rationalize the emotions that were overwhelming her. All she wanted was to be held and told everything would be okay, that she was sane of mind and always would be. There never was anyone to provide that reassurance, for no one knew what went on behind the facade.

Nothing in Brigid's life was ever the same, every moment tinged by a cursed lens. She had only herself to think of, alone by day and alone by night in this world inside her mind. No matter how close Ben lay beside her, it never eased her sense of isolation. The ache to be with child was not new, but amplifying the fear was. All the rationale in the world provided no consolation—it was not meant to be. A child was not for her. It was God's will. Brigid wondered how a woman knew when she was done, knew when to accept that it was not to be. Would the want in her ever go away, fade with the passing of time? Brigid found it impossible to imagine how it could when there were signs of new life almost everywhere, making her wonder in that moment if it was a sign just for her. Advertisements for nursery decorations, baby clothes, the latest baby apparatuses. Advertisements for the home always showed a mother and child—that is what normal was. Being childless was an obvious complaint, everyone assuming it was not that way was unable to hide their surprise when it was revealed. For what woman did not want to have children of her own?

> *August 1, 1925*
> *Dearest Molly,*
> *Thank you for your most recent letter. I am always pleased to receive word of home. It will always be home to us.*
> *Ben is getting along the finest with the store. I will try and enhance whatever updates you already have of the place, for*

I am sure the McCarthys have been only too happy to talk of Ben's good fortune.

Who would have thought that we would come all this way to run a shop? I am sure you smiled when first you heard of our news. I do not have much to do with the running of the place, for Ben takes care of everything and only likes for me to help out if he is busy with errands. I myself am busy in the home, making it comfortable and making sure Ben has fine food on his table. He is always looking for ways to expand his services and has made friends with just about everyone. Most are the same as ourselves, from across Europe, all in search of a new way of life. Lagunitas is a fine place, with the prettiest little church at the corner of our street. I go there most days now for the peace and to get in out of the heat.

We don't see much of James, for he is busy with his life in the city, and I am sure if there is any news he will be in touch. He knows he is always welcome.

Remember us fondly to all in Moling.

Your loving cousin, Brigid.

"Who is it to today? Another one to James?" Ben asked as he watched Brigid writing.

"No, just the one to Molly. I am sure she does not want to be hearing of the humdrum of our lives, expecting excitement," Brigid replied.

Ben loved to hear any talk of home. "It must be lonely for her there now with the girls nearly grown. Does she have much news of the place? Still the same characters going about no doubt."

Wistfully Brigid said, "Oh, don't you know, same old, same old. Nothing ever changes there. Isn't that what we miss most about the place, the sameness?"

"Ah, no, Brigid. We've been gone a long time now, and there is nothing there for us anymore. We have surely outgrown the place." Ben was confident in his reply.

Looking into the beyond, Brigid replied, "Sometimes I wonder, Ben. Sometimes I ask myself what is it all for? Why was I so desperate to get away?"

"No point in looking back, my love. We have a lot more than most, and I for one am grateful for our lot," said Ben, drawing the conversation to a close.

Grateful was not a word Brigid thought of too often. It reminded her of all that was wrong with her life as the dread crept in like clockwork. Brigid would have to move her body, walking away, putting one foot in front of the other, distracting herself in the kitchen as she swept out the floor, perfecting how to navigate it. She was not always able to stop the flood that overwhelmed her senses. In those moments she thought only of survival as the thoughts fought their way in while she feebly begged them to stop. They always won, for they had the power of habit.

⚜

Father Ryan startled her. "Brigid, is that you? Aren't you great for your devotion. There is not a day that I don't see you come through those doors. I knew when I first laid eyes on you that you were one of the devout."

"Good morning, Father. My mother would be proud to hear you say that. It was said she had a great devotion to Our Lady. They said it got her through many a day," replied Brigid.

"But I don't see you at confession, Brigid. Is there anything I can help you with?" Father Ryan kindly asked.

Smiling, Brigid replied, "No, Father. I was never one for confession. I tell Our Lord my transgressions, and he gives me great strength. There is no need to be worrying about me, Father. Sure, what sins would I have."

"We are all sinners, Brigid, born with Original Sin, lest we not forget," said Father Ryan, with a warm smile and a wink of his eye.

"Thank you for that, Father. I'll be sure to remember." Brigid smiled too, knowing it was his way of reminding her he was always there for his parishioners. Not that she felt particularly special in his eyes. She knew he gave the same comfort to all. They say he was fond of the drink, but she couldn't see what harm it did.

Father Ryan called out to her, "Brigid, before you go. I have been meaning to ask if you could spare me some of your time and help out on a committee. Miss Ruth and Miss Gelding are leading to resolve the 'Education of our Girls' and before you hesitate, I really must say that I do feel your opinion would be of benefit."

"Thank you for thinking of me, Father, but what would I have to contribute to such a discussion? I really do not feel in the least qualified on the subject matter," said Brigid.

Not taking no for an answer, Father Ryan replied, "It is your firm but fair approach that I see as the distinct advantage when it comes to the usual members of our committees. Sometimes they tend to lose the run of themselves, and the matter at hand gets quite lost."

"Well, Father, I am not one for committees. However, seeing as it is you that has asked, I will go along and see what I can do," sighed Brigid.

Delighted with himself, Father Ryan told Brigid, "That's a good girl. The time has come for the higher education of girls, and Catholics cannot afford to lag behind the movement."

Brigid recognized most of the faces before her at the committee meeting. Father Ryan had called for her on his way to the parish hall, and she could tell that some had their noses out of joint. It would be a long night.

Father Ryan opened the meeting. "Welcome everyone, and thank you for giving your time. We have among us the brightest minds in our community. Let me remind you all that we must hold the flower of Catholic manhood and womanhood to the cause of education. Lest we lose sight of the purpose of our meeting, it is to support the most pressing of subjects, that of educating our young girls."

Being the controversial topic that it was, many were on the edge of their seats, waiting to jump in. Mr. Jacobs, unable to contain himself, was first. "If I may, Father, I simply must lead with how all this talk about our women meeting men on equal terms is pure moonshine. Women are not and never will be content to meet any man on equal terms, always playing the role of queen to our king. Why, when I reach the streetcar on my way home from my office in the city, tired to death, I can scarcely secure a seat before a bevy of women, crying out for the privilege of equal rights, board the car and straight away we men must relinquish our seats to our 'equals' and hang onto a strap the rest of the way home. It is high time that we heard something about the rights of men! What's more, throwing girls in among a lot of young boys in our universities to take their thoughts away from their studies and to keep them focused on the fair sex, digging into the paternal exchequer to buy theater tickets and soda water and candy is carrying the joke a little too far."

Mrs. Harris was quick to respond. "Mr. Jacobs, I am not surprised it is you who is first out of the pen. If our young men in colleges are such imbeciles as you paint them, it is about time that they had chaperones appointed to protect the poor dears against the girls!"

"Now, now, Mrs. Harris, calm yourself. And as for Mr. Jacobs, well said. And if I may, I might add that just the other day a friend sent a girl to us, and when my wife took her to the kitchen and began to instruct her concerning her duties, the girl grew quite indignant and asked my wife if she really expected her to stand over a hot stove, letting her know in no uncertain terms that she was a high school graduate," piped up Mr. Miller.

"I see, gentlemen. Am I correct in assuming your points amount to this—that women must choose between being a sort of upper-servant for some man, to cook his meals for him, to make the beds and nurse the children, to look up to him most devoutly, and coddle him for a week at a time when she wants to get a new bonnet or a new dress, or she must get a college education and through it, independence and freedom to come and go as she pleases. How long do you suppose our young women will hesitate between these two alternatives?" replied Mrs. Harris.

"That is hardly fair, Mrs. Harris. All I have said is this: All women who do not intend to become sisters should fit themselves during their school days to discharge the duties of wives and mothers, because there is really no telling where the lightning will strike, you know," said Mr. Jacobs with a sense of triumph.

"My oh my. Here we have it. Man has had woman as his slave so long now that we must not blame him if he now finds it hard to give her freedom. The future woman will marry, and she will not be the sweet silent partner, devoted only to her husband. She will not consider the highest joy of life the cooking of a Sunday dinner for her husband's friends and relatives. The future woman is going to make more of her time, to fill it with effort along intelligent lines," declared Mrs. Tanzi.

Brigid was unable to get a word in edgeways and knew early on in the debate that it might be better for her to take on the role of observer. She agreed wholeheartedly on the subject matter at hand and thought how if it were Agnes, she would surely have a thing or two to add and would have taken over the meeting long ago. Here they were, thinking they were ahead of the curve in supporting women's rights when Agnes had been fighting the cause long before most of them were born. When all was said and done, Agnes had the best interest of the girls at heart. She was progressive without ever knowing it.

CHAPTER 37

Ben had not encouraged Brigid's attendance at the meeting. "It is probably not the best idea for you to be getting involved, Brigid, in any committees. We know what happened the last time," advised Ben.

"I have no intention of being involved. It is only that Father Ryan asked me himself and I felt compelled to go. He came to the door to walk with me—I do not know how else I could have refused. A lot of hot air anyway. I don't see them getting very far with that committee. Some strong voices. If you ask me, it will all end in tears. I will not be returning. I have absolutely no intention of putting myself in the firing line, but thank you for your concern." Brigid ended the conversation. There was nothing more to be said on the matter.

Brigid had a way of being firm, and Ben could see why Father Ryan had asked her. He liked to remind himself it was those traits that had first attracted him to her all those years ago—the righteousness for all the right reasons. Now life had quieted her somewhat. She kept more to herself these days. But she would always be the Brigid he'd fallen in love with, nothing would change that.

※

Brigid felt a happiness about her that she had not felt for the longest time as she sang away to herself in the kitchen, "I'm Sitting on Top of the World," over and over, twirling and smiling. She talked to the birds, the hens, even the pansies that she said were like little faces smiling up at her. Life had become so busy for Brigid that she was soon missing morning mass. There was far too much to be done at the store. She decided it needed a spring cleaning, even though it was autumn. And, as if the store was not enough for her, she decided it was time to help the Pedonis with a spring cleaning too—help they were none too pleased to receive.

Ben could sense the irritation rising in him and he hated having to check Brigid in front of others. "That's enough now, Brigid. We don't want to be getting in anyone's way, now do we?"

"Oh Ben, don't be interfering! I am helping the Pedonis. They are far too busy to have the time to keep the store in order. I can't have ours looking like a new pin and not do the same for our neighbors. They are delighted with my help," replied Brigid.

Brigid was staying up until all hours. She had taken on more tasks that she could manage and was tidying, dusting, airing, and washing all the while playing her music and singing away to herself.

Ben was weary. "Brigid love, it's late. Why don't we turn off that music and get some rest. Tomorrow is another day."

"I have all the time in the world for rest. You go on in to bed, and I will follow just as soon as I have the floor washed," said Brigid, humming away to a tune.

But Brigid didn't follow after. Ben awoke early the next morning to no Brigid in the bed and no sign of her having been there all night. He was confused but not yet alarmed. Checking through the house and the garden, Brigid was nowhere to be seen. Where in the world could she be at four o'clock in the morning? Ben dressed himself and left the house to the dawn sky at half-light. Walking to the corner, he was startled by a dog scurrying away from some trash bins. What was wrong with him? Why was he on edge? He looked over to the store standing in all its glory, glistening in the morning dew, before noticing a light on in the parochial house.

Trying not to let alarm get the better of him, he hastened his step back to their home, assuring himself that she had returned while he was out. Checking through the house again Ben noticed dishes in the sink, correspondence spread across the dining table, and copies of *Ladies Home Journal*, "the magazine women believed in" strewn about the floor. What in the name of God had she been up to while he was sleeping?

Ben told himself not to panic, that everything would be okay. Surely she had just popped out to get some air. That was all. Sleep had not come, so she had taken herself out to shake it off. She would be home any minute.

Father Ryan did not have many night callers. Brigid was pounding on his door. "Take your ease, Brigid. Calm yourself. Goodness knows what has you in such a state. Is it Ben? Has something happened to him?"

Brigid was frantic. "Father, Father, please let me come in. Please, Father. You must protect me, Father. I have no one else to turn to, no one I can trust. You understand me, don't you, Father? You will protect me, Father, please say you will. Please, Father?"

Father Ryan reassured Brigid in his soothing voice. "What is it, my child? Of course come in, come in. Tell me what it is I can do for you at this hour."

"Oh, Father, I am so frightened. Ben simply cannot know. I cannot tell him, for he will not understand, and he will make them take me away again. Please, Father, not this time," cried Brigid.

Confused, Father Ryan calmly asked "Tell him what exactly? What is it that troubles you my dear?"

"You simply cannot tell a soul, Father. You must promise me that you will not tell of my news. Oh, Father, I am with child!" exclaimed Brigid.

Father Ryan sat down to steady himself. "My heavens! Why Brigid, that is surely the most welcome of news. Are you sick in yourself? Are you feeling unwell? You must tell Ben; he is your husband and you cannot withhold such information from the father of this child."

"Please, Father, you must understand, I cannot face this alone.

Please, Father, pray with me. Ask for the Lord's protection over me and my baby."

"Yes, my child, let us pray." Together they knelt in front of Our Lady and said a decade of the Rosary, Brigid intently praying and holding tightly to her rosary beads. Father Ryan's thoughts were on the McCarthy marriage and the devout, expectant mother by his side. Yes, she was of a mature age, however our Lord does sometimes work in mysterious ways.

⚜

To distract himself Ben made a start on tidying up the place. As he picked up the copies of the *Ladies Home Journal*, cut out advertisements dropped to the floor. Looking at the images by his feet, he steadied himself on the arm of the chair.

> *If your child is thin and nervous or eats poorly, by all means try giving*
> **NEW IMPROVED OVALTINE**

Another clipping showcased Curity Layettecloth Nursery Pads.

Another was for Clapp's Cereal Food—new, for young babies.

As Ben read another clipping, this one a full-page article, he sank into the chair.

The Luckiest Babies in the World—These babies are beginning life in the safest of all places—a modern hospital. This year over 1,200,000 babies will be born in America's hospitals. As the percentage of hospital births has increased, the infant death rate has rapidly decreased.

With his head in his hands, Ben wept.

⚜

Father Ryan motioned himself out of the chair, careful not to disturb Brigid, who had fallen asleep. The poor dear needed her rest, had herself exhausted with the worry of it all. Taking his hat and coat, Father Ryan closed the door gently behind him. He was going to confront Ben McCarthy. There was nothing else for it—no man should instill such fear in his wife.

Knocking on the door, Father Ryan called out Ben's name. Ben opened the door immediately. "Father, is it Brigid? Have you seen her? I cannot find her anywhere. I am at my wits end worrying about her."

"Now, now, Ben. There is no need to worry yourself. Your wife is with me, taking shelter and rest," replied Father Ryan, a little more sternly than was usual.

Not noticing, Ben thanked him. "Oh, thank God for that, Father. I was beside myself with worry. I am so sorry that she has disturbed you. I am worried about her, Father, worried about what has come over her."

Having prepared himself, Father Ryan came straight out with it. "Well now, my son, I shall tell you what has come over her. The poor lady was in need of comfort. You know, Ben, it is not good for any woman in her condition to be getting herself upset."

"Excuse me, Father, in her condition?" replied Ben.

"Now, now, Mr. McCarthy. It is not for you to be worrying about what she did or didn't say. Let's just focus on what your wife needs at this time and for you to do your husbandly and, indeed, fatherly duty," said Father Ryan, taking Ben by the shoulder.

"Father, what has she told you? Brigid cannot be with child, Father. She does not know what she is talking about. Please understand that it is just not possible. She has allowed herself to become overrun and gotten herself into a state again. Please Father, I will need your help," pleaded Ben.

"Now Mr. McCarthy, as a man of the cloth, it is my duty to protect the mother with child. The dear girl has sat with me this very hour, and together we prayed to our Lord for guidance. What's more, she has confided in me that she has not felt able to share this news with you, and I think I can understand why." Coughing, Father Ryan turned to leave.

Ben stood in his way. "Father, please listen to me. I beg of you to understand. Brigid simply cannot, I stress, *cannot,* be with child. Take me to her, Father. I will speak with her. I will take her home and she can rest. All she needs is rest. A good sleep and she will see the sense of it all."

Father Ryan paused for a moment, then said, "I can see that you love Brigid very much. She's a lucky woman to have a husband so concerned for her well-being. I will advise her to return home. She'll be safe with you."

⚜

Ben was inconsolable, angry with himself. What if he had seen the signs earlier? What if he had encouraged her to rest? What if she had access to her medical records? What if he had not listened to Dr. Payne and his advice that it was best to keep it between themselves and not be bothering her with such matters? Wasn't he as her husband perfectly capable of deciding for her? Over and over, he tortured himself with the pain of having to watch the person he loved most in all the world suffer in such a dehumanizing way. Was it not enough that she was to live a life without children? Dear, kind, gentle Brigid suffering in silence on this journey she must travel alone.

Ben was sitting at the kitchen table with his head in his hands when Brigid walked through the door, Father Ryan following close behind her. Father Ryan stood awkwardly as Brigid threw herself into Ben's arms, crying and wailing that she was sorry and that everything was going to be all right now that they were having a baby. Father Ryan slipped out through the door as Ben wept holding onto his wife.

Ben knew in that moment what he must do, but the trickery went against everything he stood for. There was one place Brigid had begged him to never speak of, the place that haunted her dreams with visits from the other traumatized souls who had been looked upon as no more than imbeciles. It was the only place that could save her.

Ben devised a plan. "Take some rest my dear, and then let's say we take our truck for a motor. We'll get the Pedoni boy to watch over the store. It won't be busy of a Monday, and we can take this time for us, just the two of us."

"Ben, darling Ben. That sounds wonderful. Just the two of us? That will be so special, our very first motor in your new truck. Why, I will pack a lunch, and I must take a hat. Oh yes and a blanket in case it gets cold. What shall I wear? Do you think I will need my warm coat or a light shawl? We must take care now, Ben, for the Lord is with us this very day, watching over us. I will take my rosary beads, and we can stop off at the churches along the way. We might even take in a mass. Wouldn't that be special?" Brigid was delighted with the suggestion.

Trying to keep her calm, Ben agreed to everything. "Yes, dear, pack some nice comfortable things with you for the journey and maybe some of your toilet items."

"Oh Ben, how exciting. The good Lord above is by my side. Why, I can almost see him. Do you think he will mind if I have missed mass these past few days? Surely he will understand that I have been very busy. Let me run and check on the store before we leave. I must make sure that young Pedoni boy knows what he is doing up there."

Rain began to fall as Brigid started toward the store.

Ben called after her. "Brigid, there is no need to be running about the place. Haven't you done enough of that? It's beginning to rain, so we should get a move on. Can't you just settle yourself and we will start making our way."

Brigid stopped in the middle of the street, unbothered by the rain, which had begun to come down steadily. "Do *not* tell me what I can and cannot do. If I want to go, I shall."

"Brigid, darling, I have it all in hand. There is nothing for you to worry about. You are only causing yourself strain. Come now to the truck. You're getting soaked."

Brigid began to shout. "Stop it! I said, stop telling me what to do! I am capable of making my own decisions. Now get out of my way."

She skipped toward the store, singing away to herself, no protection from the rain lashing against the wind.

Ben grabbed a few items he thought she might need and hastily shoved them into a suitcase, then tossed it into the truck. Holding his coat over his head, he hurried toward the store but noticed Brigid had crossed the street and was standing in front of the church, trying to stop mass goers for a chat as they scampered into the church. Ben took her by the arm and steered her toward the store. She was soaked through, completely unaware, beaming with happiness.

Mr. Pedoni greeted them with his usual smile. "Not the best day for an excursion, Mr. McCarthy. Headed anywhere nice?"

"Just a drive. I wanted to give the motor a run out," replied Ben.

Mr. Pedoni could see Brigid was not dressed for the rain. "You'll surely want to be drying yourself off there, Mrs. McCarthy, you'll catch your death if you go out like that."

"Why, a bit of rain never harmed anyone, Mr. Pedoni. We have so much to do today—places to go and people to see."

Taking Brigid by her arm, Ben tried to distract her. "Yes, dear. Let's get a move on ourselves."

No sooner had he gotten her out of the store than Brigid changed her mind. "Ben, Ben, I must speak with Father Ryan. I will pop across to him now—catch him before he leaves for Nicasio."

Brigid ran back across the road and into the church.

Ben sighed, exchanging a weary look with Mr. Pedoni.

"I'm sorry, Mr. Mcarthy," Mr. Pedoni said. "You have my prayers."

Ben nodded, and silently walked across the street and into the church. Father Ryan was at the altar with his arms in the air, the holy chalice above his head as he started to say the Our Father. Brigid ran straight up to the altar as if it were her day to do the flowers. She whispered into Father Ryan's ear, and when he did not appear to take any heed of what she was saying, Brigid turned to the congregation. "I have the most wonderful of news. I am with child! Please everyone, join me in the celebration of this new life."

Ben held up his hands as he walked down the center aisle toward her. "Brigid, Brigid, stop that. Come with me now. So sorry, Father. Sorry, everyone. Please accept my apologies. We will take our leave."

Brigid started to cry. "No, no, don't do this to me. Please let me have this baby. Please Ben, don't do this to me." The congregation murmured to each other, shaking their heads and whispering.

Ben needed to get her out of there. "Now, Brigid, come with me. It will be all right, love. Let's get a move on, and we can talk all about it in the truck." Taking her hand, he calmly led her out of the church, his eyes focused straight ahead as the parishioners cast pitiful looks at his wife as they passed them. He led her to the truck, not saying a word, for he knew not what to say and nothing was registering anyway. Brigid, clinging to Ben, had calmed some and climbed in next to him.

No sooner were they on the road when Brigid wanted to stop off at a church. It was good luck to light a candle in a new church. When they came out, the rain had stopped and they continued on their drive.

Soon Brigid spied some children playing hopscotch by the side of the road and wanted to stop and say hello. She wanted to have a go for old time's sake. Ben followed behind, watching her every move. Brigid was oblivious.

The journey to St. Agnews took an entire afternoon with all the stopping and starting and Ben trying to keep everything calm. It helped that Brigid was not familiar with the surroundings on the journey as they neared Santa Clara. She sat contentedly looking out the window, enjoying the scenery and singing away to the tunes in her head. Turning onto Palm Drive, the clock tower came into view. The singing stopped. Ben put his foot heavier on the pedal up the palm and linden tree-lined avenue without looking Brigid's way.

They pulled in front of the main entrance to St. Agnews, and Ben stopped the truck. As if in slow motion she turned her head, opened her mouth, and began to wail. She desperately tried to open her door and run, but Ben held onto her, holding her tightly as she kicked and screamed. The nurses, familiar with these scenes, ran from the women's receiving building, trying to soothe Brigid but holding her firmly. They told Ben they would take it from there, and he should just run along into the office and complete the forms.

He knew the drill.

Ben dragged himself away. Peeling Brigid's fingers from his arm, he was sick to the pit of his stomach. With his head bent, he told the man at the admissions desk, "She has been a patient here before. But she needs help once more."

EPILOGUE

Visiting Boston in September 1993 was the last stop on my travels that had taken me away from Ireland for some two years. I was one of the few who chose to return after spending time in America. Traveling alone, I was reliant upon the hospitality of family and friends, which took me to Boston, where a Kelly cousin had settled.

I had vague memories from family folklore of the entrepreneurial Kelly relatives who had run a store and soda parlor beside the Golden Gate Bridge. Visiting Boston was my opportunity to find out more about this intriguing detail from my family's past. As the only Kelly relative in America at the time of James's passing in 1964, the cousin had been summoned to California to settle the estate. It was a deeply personal experience for her, having to clear out James's little yellow clapboard house, opening the drawers packed full of prized possessions and keepsakes, sorting them into bags, all with a plan to go through them at some later date. In those moments had she, too, been drawn into their story, innocently opening one of the sealed envelopes, reading Brigid's harrowing words intended for Molly? I know from her husband that something had deeply affected her, but I also know that she never destroyed any of the items that she had taken with her that day. Those bags sat for twenty-nine years in another container of history, even after that cousin's death, until that September morning when they were handed over to me, and I was told I could do as I wished with them, knowing I had stirred a dark memory.

I can still see the excited twenty-one-year-old sitting on the basement floor, delicately removing each item with a profound respect for the historical significance as I weaved my way through their lives. The magnificence of the artifacts, the elegant faces with strikingly similar Kelly family traits, the mementos from the first-class transatlantic passages all told of a luxurious existence. The glamour of the gilded age was laid out before my eyes. Maybe the stories of their success were true after all. I have no recollection of time passing that day, only that darkness fell as I continually went back and forth through the letters, such was the enormity of the secrets that were unfolding. Realizing the strikingly similar family traits were not only cosmetic, it was then that I knew why those bags had waited for me.

Leaving the brownstone with as much of the information as my backpack would allow, I vowed to find the truth. My youthful enthusiasm at having found these connections that explained recent events in my own family was met with forceful resistance—it was easier to remember the successful, affluent entrepreneurs. I was told to leave well enough alone and to stop asking questions. Assuming it was because I was young, and in those days the youth were to be seen and not heard, maybe I had missed the conversations. Not yet indoctrinated in the significance of the family secret, my naivety kept me searching.

The documents that had traveled back to Ireland with me were a prized possession I carefully took care of through numerous house moves as I married and had children. I never stopped asking questions. There were never any deep or meaningful conversations with my family or my relatives. No one wanted to discuss it. It was only with the onset of the internet that I slowly began to find answers.

It was common psychiatric hospital policy in the best interest of the patient to withhold all correspondence, which was then handed over to the patient's next of kin. This was not only true of St. Agnews but also of the asylum in Enniscorthy, where Kate had died. It was considered a courtesy to patients and their families, for patients often wrote insulting or disturbing letters to their families, and the families themselves wrote hurtful letters to patients, all of which it was felt was appropriate to protect the recipients from. Ben and then James were the keepers of Brigid's correspondence. Brigid's letters to Molly from St. Agnews were never posted, and Ben never shared them with Molly and never told her of Brigid's incarceration. The letters remained sealed for over seventy years. I found page after page of frantic, desperate letters with Brigid's writing scrawled across the pages, begging the one person she knew she could rely on, the one person she could trust, to come and take her out of the asylum.

It was devastating opening that first envelope, the first of many addressed to Molly, and it would be several years later before I could bring myself to review all of the contents, such was my heartache at Brigid's words. The early letters were filled with an assurance that they would be actioned, then an understanding that Molly could not get away from her responsibilities to her family, and finally an acceptance that maybe she had been wrong to assume their friendship would stand the test of time.

Molly's early letters to Brigid told of their great love for each other. Bundles of letters tied together in velvet ribbon detailed every moment in Molly's life, the celebrations, the sorrows, the secrets. As Molly's letters to Brigid became more sporadic, I frantically checked the bags to see if I had missed any, sorting them into chronological order as the love slipped away. The envelopes were no longer stuffed with pages of Molly's beautiful writing or contained photographs of the children as they grew, but were reduced to one page of perfunctory information. No longer signed "Your fond cousin," these were simply signed, "Molly."

Brigid was to spend most of her adult life in America institutionalized. St. Agnews, which was intended when first authorized to be an asylum for the chronic and hopelessly insane, was lavishly praised as a "place of exceptional plan and interesting design, an advanced and modern mental hospital, primarily for its minimum of patient restraints for the comfortable care of the chronically insane."

Brigid was to find her glitz and glamor after all. The picture cards of Marilyn Monroe I found scattered in the bags I realized were not simply an infatuation with the iconic Hollywood starlet. Gladys Pearl Baker, Marilyn's mother, and Brigid had spent many years together institutionalized in St. Agnews. They shared a commonality as women locked away from the world with only each other for company. Was Brigid in awe as Gladys talked about her days as a flapper in the roaring twenties, a red-headed beauty with twinkling green eyes? Did Gladys tell of her affair with her boss at RKO Studios, who fathered her third child, Norma Jean, who became Marilyn Monroe? Had Brigid lamented on her youthful desperation to live the life of her dreams in Yankeeland when maybe her life in Ireland was not so terrible after all?

Ben continued to run his beloved store alone, which did not allow for him to have the luxury of time off to make the 160-mile round trip to Santa Clara to visit Brigid. Life went on for Ben, and he would have thanked God for the small mercies and the community who never asked any questions. Brigid became withdrawn with the years, losing his trust. He had no choice and never stopped missing her. Brigid was never reunited with her husband in this life, for Ben died tragically in 1945 at the age of fifty-nine. His death notice read a "business man and postmaster at Lagunitas was found dead in the creek adjoining his property on the morning of March 27 by rural mail carrier Humphrey. Neighbors believe he may have suffered a stroke and fallen into the stream, death ensuing from drowning."

I found a letter referring to a trip James took out to the store to put his mind at ease, having not heard from Brigid in some time. I don't know how that meeting went, but I can imagine Ben struggled with his words, turning the sign on the door to *Closed* as he told of Brigid's "little problem." James knew what the nerves were capable of. I imagine his mind frantically remembered Kate and all he'd witnessed with her. But Brigid, she was the strong one, the one who was going to make something of her life. I have no doubt he thought of their father and his insistence that he travel with Brigid all those years ago, giving up his son for the love of his daughter. What had he known? Kate's death certificate noted her cause of death as "acute mania." Upon reviewing her hospital medical records, it had been noted under the family history section, *Paternal aunt insane, died in asylum*. Someone had known that this was not an isolated case. Did Patrick carry that fear, that his daughters would suffer the same way his sister apparently had?

Following Ben's death, James fulfilled his father's request to always be there for his sister, and ran the store until his own death in 1964. The customer record book was filled with the details of customers to whom he had given credit to over the years, never to be repaid. James continued his life of caring for those less fortunate until the end of his days, for all debts to the store died with him. I found no records that ever indicated that he visited Brigid. I suppose it would have just been too hard for him to see her like that, still being traumatized from his memories of Kate.

Brigid was released back into society for the last few years of her life, where she sat by her brother's side on a wooden rocking chair inside the front door of her beloved store. She was fondly remembered by those that knew her as a gentle old lady who showed great kindness to the local children, helping them to read and write, providing comfort and candy, watching as her brother James took care of the customers.

There were few formal documents in the bags, seeing the typed envelope addressed to Mr. Ben McCarthy, I knew it was important. It confirmed the successful sterilization of Mrs. Ben McCarthy. "Your wife will no longer be troubled with any concerns of reproduction," it read. The operation Brigid believed would help her conceive had ensured she would never have the family she'd longed for. Brigid's mental problems had labeled her as "genetically undesirable" in a time period where theories about eugenics were widely accepted. There were an estimated twenty thousand forced sterilizations in California alone, and that may be an underestimation.

She was the victim of a society that made the decision for her. I was heartbroken for Brigid and agonized over *what if*. If Brigid had known that she'd been sterilized, how would that have changed things? Would it have made her mental instability worse, or might she have come to accept it and been able to have a contented life? What if Ben had not taken that secret to his grave and had given Brigid the opportunity to understand his part in the decision and his concern for her? And, what if Brigid had never followed her dream of a life in Yankeeland?

I have agonized over the outcome of Brigid, Kate, and Molly's lives in particular. Kate stayed in Ireland, dying at age twenty-seven in an asylum. Brigid, who followed her dream to live in America, had her womanhood taken from her and ended up living most of her adult life locked up in an asylum. Molly, who stayed home in her village of birth, led a traditional life as wife and mother, all the while wondering what she was missing. These decisions, these hidden, unhealed outcomes, carried their own implications for the future generations.

Becoming a mother helped me to understand the unexplainable "want" of having a child connecting me with the emotions that Brigid may have experienced through the years. I tried to comprehend the depth of her personal journey without the supports that I had, such as modern medicine, the ability to openly discuss these issues, having had a child to ease the pain, and a husband who was allowed to understand. The church and society no longer stared women down with scorn and hypocrisy.

In writing this story, I know that I had to live these intervening years to have the depth of experience required to truly connect with the enormity of Brigid and Kate's experience. My words are lived, they are experiential in the ways of family trauma that is passed down through generations. The debate rages on if mental health is genetic, environmental, or a defect from birth. I believe it is all of those things, and I believe trauma is generational, carried through the lineage until it is healed.

Brigid passed away on August 23, 1958, and today is August 23, 2023, the sixty-fifth anniversary of her passing. Now I have finally honored Brigid and Kate and told their story and the story of thousands of women just like them.

My overriding wish is that Brigid and Kate's story will support those touched by mental health whether directly or indirectly. We cannot change the past, but we can influence the future generations affected in this way. My research has shown that not enough has changed in the treatment and societal view of mental health over the last one hundred years.

To this very day, patients in large city hospitals continue to be relegated to Victorian basements, overly reliant on medication and under reliant on community support or rehabilitation. Society still does not know quite what to do with those affected by varying degrees of mental health.

I have no doubt the secrets in this story came from a place of love, but surely truth is a far greater act of love. Information is power, and overcoming secrets offers liberation from the shackles of the past, allowing for progress and hope in humanity. Illness is part of being human—it is how we choose to manage it that will define us. We must embrace our differences, for it is our shadows that cause the greatest of our conflicts. Brigid and Kate were tragically human, but there is no shame in that—or at least there shouldn't be.

ACKNOWLEDGMENTS

I'd like to thank my husband Ferghal, always by my side, supporting my ambitions, and my three beautiful children, Jamie, Lauren and Juliette—my love for you is beyond words. Your kindness and love will carry through the generations. This book is for you; it couldn't be for anyone else.

Special thanks go to Katie Wylie, who read my first drafts, encouraging me with her passion for my words. To the Lagunitas community and the parishioners of St. Cecilia's church, who spread the word in advance of our arrival in 2018, you are forever in our hearts for your warm welcome. Thanks also to Geraldine and Joe Walsh and Rich and Suzanne O'Toole, who welcomed us into their magnificent homes and lives; all will remain life-long friends.

My friends have always been important in my life, and I am grateful to be surrounded by the very best. To each and every one of you who listened to me talk about this story for what must feel like a lifetime, thank you for always believing in me and supporting me. You know who you are.

It is with gratitude that I refer readers to the notes, which serve as a guide to the many documents I consulted in the course of my research.

Thank you to Greg Fields for his kindness and professional support and guidance, my editor Becky Hilliker, and all the team at Koehler Books.

I am forever indebted to John Tanzi for giving me the only photo of Brigid that we have ever known.

I owe special thanks to my mother, Alice, who showed me the

true meaning of love and how it really does conquer all.

And finally, to ten-year-old Annmarie—of course you were always going to write.

AUTHOR'S NOTE

In writing this book, my insatiable need to walk in the shoes of my characters led me down a path of discovery far deeper than I had imagined from my leisure reading of the period. My rich memories of childhood stories brought a depth to this story which comes from lived experiences.

The *Images of America* books published by Arcadia Publishing were a fantastic source in researching life in the early 1900s in Niagara Falls, Petaluma, and San Geronimo Valley. *The Humbugs of Niagara Falls Exposed* by David Young also helped paint a picture of Niagara Falls. The classic reprint series by Forgotten Books on *American Nervousness* by George M. Beard; *The Making and Unmaking of a Dullard* and *The Education of our Girls* by Edward Thomas Shields; *Ladies Guide in Health and Disease* by John Harvey Kellog; *The Fasting Girl* by Michelle Stacey; and *Manners for Women* by Mrs. Humphry provided insight into societal issues of the day. *In Search of Madness* by Professor Brendan Kelly provided a deep understanding from a psychiatrist's travels through the history of mental illness. *St. Senan's Hospital Enniscorthy* by Hugh Kelly gave me insight into life in St. Senan's and the historical records that were stored there.

Additional sources included: the Catholic Research Resources Alliance; the Library Guides at University of Missouri Libraries (which covered prices and wages by decade); the GG Archives (for steamship passage tickets and contracts); the RMS Lusitania Collection; FoundSF (for a San Francisco digital history archive); the Irish Association; UCR Center for Bibliographical Studies; Research

California Digital Newspaper Collection; Petaluma Historical Society; and the Project Gutenberg ebook of *Searchlights on Health: The Science of Eugenics*; *Eugenic Sterilization in California in the 1920s and 30s: The Human Betterment Foundation's Study on the Effects of Sterilization* by Meaghan Watters. I located the "Biennial Reports of the Californian State Commission in Lunacy" at the Hathi Trust (which were issued following the enactment of the California Insanity Law in 1897) along with the *Eugenics and Social Welfare Bulletins*. The Library of Congress Historic Building archives provided information on Agnews State Hospital.

Music sourced from the period connected me to the experiences I was writing about, each song bringing me into the world of my characters and connecting me to their dreams. You can find this playlist on Spotify at bit.ly/YankeelandonSpotify

Nothing could compare to the local knowledge I received from my visit with the wonderful community of Lagunitas, a community in the true spirit of the word.

www.ingramcontent.com/pod-product-compliance
Ingram Content Group UK Ltd.
Pitfield, Milton Keynes, MK11 3LW, UK
UKHW040111110325
456067UK00002B/57